Also by Ellis Sharp

Novels

The Dump
Unbelievable Things
Walthamstow Central
Intolerable Tongues
To Wetumpka
Lamees Najim
The Orwell Girl
Neglected Writer
What Vronsky Did Next
Twenty-Twenty
Alice in Venice
Full English
The Riddle

Short Fiction

The Aleppo Button
Lenin's Trousers
(with Mac Daly) *Engels on Video*
To Wanstonia
Driving My Baby Back Home
Aria Fritta
Quin Again and other stories
Dead Iraqis: Selected Short Stories

Non-Fiction

Sharply Critical

ELLIS SHARP

MONTH OF THE DROWNED DOG

Zoilus Press

A Zoilus Press paperback
First published in Great Britain by Zoilus Press in 2023

A CIP catalogue record for this book is available from the British Library.

ISBN 9781838489878

Cover design by The Ever-Shifting Subject

Typeset by Electrograd

ZOILUS PRESS
York, England

MONTH OF THE DROWNED DOG

Heavy matters, heavy matters. But look thee here, boy. Now bless thyself; thou met'st with things dying, I with things newborn.

The Winter's Tale

1

It must have happened around that time the writer was watching the Dirk Bogarde film. A Blu-ray disc. He couldn't shake off the Spanish subtitles. Afterwards the writer went to his atlas of Greater London and found the junction of Chepstow Rise and Chichester Road, Croydon. The internet told him that the house and the neighbouring ones had been demolished. In their place stood architecturally barren, cramped modern social housing. There would be no point in visiting the neighbourhood today. The wide empty streets were now cluttered by parked cars. The leaf-laden magic was entirely gone. Some film locations survived. Not this one.

2

Turble fond o' study on't roads, especially at night time, and with a girt voice bumming away fit to flyte aw the chilre to death a' most was how one local resident remembered William Wordsworth at the time he lived with his sister in the house now known as Dove Cottage.

3

That summer the writer read *From the Diary of a Snail*, *Anna Karenina* and *Transparent Things*. But fiction is so easily forgotten. What linger, as in a life, are certain highlights. The writer's Nabokov phase was long over. The content of most of those novels had emptied from his mind. His favourite Nabokov story was 'Spring in Fialta'. The ending made an impression. From time to time he re-read it, just to arrive at that last page. But the Nabokov sentence which stayed with him most of all was the final one of the story which appeared in *Soglyadatay* (Paris, 1938) and was later translated into English in *Playboy*, December 1971. He read it in *A Russian Beauty and Other Stories*, the Penguin edition. The brown cover featured a photograph by Jacques-Henri Lartigue. The story, 'A Dashing Fellow', is not a particularly striking tale. But he had never been able to get its last sentence out of his mind.

4

Out of the blue – a strangely resonant cliché – he remembered the girl on Twitter, whose lover had been knocked off his bike and killed. The cyclist had been on a public road, travelling across the London Olympic site during the construction work before the Games. The girl and her lover were in their twenties. They each Tweeted updates on their daily lives. He remembered looking at the dead cyclist's final stream of public messages. They were brief, jaunty, daily reports and then, abruptly, they stopped. He didn't see it coming, in every sense. She, bereft, Tweeted a quotation.

Because these wings are no longer wings to fly
But merely vans to beat the air

5

Craving commercial success, the writer had once written a novel attempting to emulate the style that *The Guardian* liked and promoted. The narrator is a young woman, a publicist for a London publishing house. Her name is Jane Tain. She is trying to solve the mystery of her father's death. In the course of achieving her goal she falls in love and finds the happiness which had eluded her father. The story ends on an uplifting note. The writer imagined seeing it in paperback, with a bright cheerful cover and a multiplicity of praise from the reviewers of the corporate press. It would be on display in airport bookshops. It would only be a matter of time before a delayed traveller saw it, one in particular. Seeing the author's name, scanning the blurb, the traveller would quickly buy it and begin reading. The novel was called *The Professor's Wife*.

The Professor's Wife.

A story can begin almost anywhere, and perhaps this one truly starts with Edward Blake's attempt to discourage me from flying to Wick.

'Jane, it's not necessary for you to go all that way,' he said. He reached forward and gave my hand a quick nervous squeeze. Blake was our family solicitor. He was a lean, wintry man with a pale, skull-like face and thinning white hair.

He seemed oddly anxious about my decision. He was nearing retirement, which meant he was almost forty years older than me. He was the expert, the man of experience, offering solemn advice to someone who was supposed to take it.

'Perhaps not, Edward. But I still intend going.'

I'm told I have a stubborn streak in my character. I don't like people telling me what I should and shouldn't do – not in my private life. I've also been told I'm mildly obsessive. When there's a problem I like to solve it, even if the effort involved far exceeds the importance of the solution. Alec, my ex, once told me I was 'not quite on the spectrum, but very nearly there'. He was hinting at obsessive-compulsive behaviour. In retrospect I reckon that was simply Alec slapping a label on me to justify his own behaviour and cut me down to size. I just never saw it at the time.

Blake held up his hands in a gesture of quiet despair.

'It really will be a complete waste of time,' he said.

We sat facing each other across his narrow walnut desk in a gloomy room at the back of a Holborn office block built long ago. The room was oppressive. I wanted to be out of that stuffy place. The meeting had gone on too long. The more he tried to dissuade me from attending the inquest in Wick, the more I was determined to go. My attention started to wander. That's another of my faults. When people start to bore me, I lose my grip on what they're saying. I might seem to be paying attention, but I'm not. I switch off and my mind wanders.

While Edward Blake continued his soft, authoritative

monologue – variations on the theme of why Jane should not and must not go to Wick – my mind wandered back to the moment when my father's body was first discovered.

7

Thursday afternoon now. A day since the writer discovered what has occurred. He listens to the 61-minute version of 'Thursday Afternoon' by Brian Eno. Later he remembers a book he has yet to read. *The Afternoon of a Writer*. Having read a recommendation on the internet he bought it a couple of years ago, second hand. The writer sits down and begins reading about a character known only as 'the writer'. His interest quickens. On this grey day, in this state of mind, he is in the mood for prose like this. It has honesty. Whereas *The Professor's Wife*, just like the fiction that clogs the corporate media, now seems dishonest. As artificial as polystyrene. Tidy plots, manicured 'characters', an ending that supplies a deliciously satisfying dessert and a board of well-cut cheese. *I devoured it in one go! Tasty! Deliciously entertaining! I gulped it down!* Confidence men (and women) serving up plates of shining grease; selling beautifully wrapped empty packages. The heavy perfume of praise rising from every corporate quarter. The author inevitably bobbing up on the 'Today' programme.

8

It was a local fisherman who saw it first, from the estuary. It was at first light, very early in the morning. The man knew that remote and lonely landscape well, and he noted the anomaly in the familiar scene. Reaching for a pair of binoculars, he focused his gaze at the blanched graveyard on the low headland to his left. His first, dark suspicion was confirmed. He put down his binoculars and took out his mobile phone. That morning, fortune smiled: he got a signal.

Some twenty minutes later a white car rolled down the bumpy track to the cemetery gate. The driver stopped beside the car that was already there. The roof and windows of this parked car were thickly coated with crystals of ice. It had evidently been there all night – a hard, bitterly cold October night.

The driver climbed out, shivering. When he exhaled his breath was like a surge of white smoke. He glanced round the frost-carpeted graveyard. This place was familiar to him, and he felt a sudden stab of melancholy. But then he recalled his purpose in being here. His gaze focused on the human shape lying beside a marble pedestal towards the middle of the cemetery. He hurried towards it, his footsteps crunching on the stiff, frozen grass. Seeing the fisherman, who was lingering close inshore, not far from the nearby road bridge, he waved, and received a wave back. Then Inspector Donald Boston approached the figure lying there, stiff and motionless.

Let me say at once that this is not a crime story, even though there is the riddle of an inconclusive and ambiguous death at its heart. You could call it instead a tale of hopelessness and undying love. But that would be to ignore a love that grew out of the cracks in the story of that hopelessness and its aftermath.

The body found lying in that graveyard in a remote part of Scotland was my father's. His name was Jon Tain. He was a distinguished geologist and a widower. I am his only child.

'Completely unnecessary, you see. That's what I have been informed. There is no ambiguity about it. None whatsoever. However, I am prepared to attend myself if you wish it. If you would like a professional record of the proceedings...' He straightened haughtily in his chair.

'It might not be necessary for me to be there, Edward, but I want to hear for myself everything that's said. Kind though it is for you to offer to represent the family at the inquest, I don't want a report from you or anyone else. Besides, I have to make a statement.'

I'd had a number of meetings with Edward Blake since my father's sudden enigmatic death, and now the date had drawn close for the inquest. For this I was grateful. It felt like the final part of a long and painful ordeal which had begun with the police at my door and then progressed in stages. After that abrupt breaking of terrible news had come the bitter agony of the funeral and then the piercing repetition of dark cloudy emotions at the memorial service. The inquest promised the sweetness of closure.

How wrong I was. The inquest was not the end but the beginning – and if I'd listened to Edward Blake's advice nothing that follows would ever have happened.

My solicitor sighed and looked tired. He liked deference in a client. Disagreement was disagreeable.

The distant, muffled sound of sirens on the Strand merged with the soft cooing of pigeons fidgeting on a nearby ledge. Heat rose in waves from an ancient ribbed radiator with the complexion of an over-ripe avocado.

'Let me repeat it, then. Just in case you have not entirely understood.' Blake put the veneer of a thin smile across his obvious discontent. 'I spoke to the Procurator Fiscal's office. They assured me a statement in writing from you is perfectly acceptable. And as I explained earlier, it's not called an inquest. In Scotland they call it a Fatal Accident Inquiry. In reality it all boils down to the same thing, of course, although the procedures are a little different.'

His hand made a slight movement, as if he was contemplating touching mine again. If so, he thought better of it. He gave a dry, nervous cough. 'It's a long way to go for what is likely to be little more than a formality. The police have said there were no suspicious circumstances. There are really only two possible verdicts. In my own view, there is only one sensible verdict and that is Death by Misadventure.' His face took on a bleak expression: 'There is the other one, of course. But frankly there is not a scrap of evidence for it.'

'Of course there isn't,' I said. 'Daddy was his usual self just before he left. Quite cheerful in fact. And I've spoken to his friend Ivan Jensen. Ivan was the last person to see him before he drove north. He said my father was very much looking forward to the trip.'

'Quite.' Blake's eyes flickered in the direction of the ticking clock on the wall behind me. In that long silence its every stroke felt like a little stab of cold wire.

My hour was almost up.

'I'll let them know you'll be attending, then,' he said in a rather distant, disapproving voice.

I thanked him and left.

9

A novel about a death but the language seems itself dead. False. Of course there is the gleaming of style ('the blanched graveyard on the low headland' – that's not bad) but basically it's the Lit Fic style. A package sold in that bright noisy jostling shopping mall where the tastiest candy is at Updike's. Bored, the writer skipped some pages about the narrator's friend Blanche.

10

Scotland lay below me like a piece of shattered crockery, broken against a dark blue surface.

On that short connecting flight from Edinburgh to Wick I gazed down keenly at the northern edge of those fragments, for it was there that my father had met his mysterious and lonely death.

What I saw below me matched the map I'd stared at, numbly, for far too long. The coastline had a splintered look, all jagged peninsulas and bright sharp inlets. In the distant haze I could make out the jigsaw puzzle outline of Cape Wrath, where the land ended and beyond was nothing but the great grey wastes of the Atlantic.

Somewhere down there, not that far from that jigsaw puzzle piece, my father had died. His body was found just outside a place called Tongue, a name which tasted bitter to me when all the circumstances of his dying were mute.

I went on staring until the plane turned to make its descent. It was one of those crisp, sharp, cloudless spring days and the lochs slid by below, getting closer, slivers of lapis lazuli which briefly blazed with reflected sunlight. Like a dark attendant soul the plane's shadow skimmed the desolate moorland below.

The captain's voice broke into my thoughts; we would soon be landing. Nervously I ran my hand over the brushed-steel buckle of my seat belt, checking once again that it was fastened properly.

The plane tilted and began to drop. Below me, in that dark town clustered around a shining river, stood the building where I could at last begin to try and unlock the enigma of my father's sudden and peculiar end.

11

To read this manuscript now is a bitter and bleak experience. Its falsity shines from every paragraph. For now the story is over. 'Really over,' as a character might say in a 'realist' novel about 'real life'. The story is over since it ended as all stories end. The writer's heart knotted at the knowledge. He felt a slight breathlessness.

12

The Sheriff's Court in Wick is in a big dark stone building on the main road which runs through the town centre. The architecture, classical in its solidity and appearance, seemed heavy with authority and tradition. It was only a short journey there from the airport. I paid the taxi driver and went inside and explained my business to the grey-haired woman at reception.

Court number one was almost entirely empty. It lacked windows and was filled with artificial light which poured out of harsh fluorescent strips. Everything – the panelled walls, the dock, the witness stand – was surfaced by a light pinewood. It was bright as the furniture section of a department store.

In the well of the court a woman who I took to be a stenographer waited by her machine, reading a paperback. The public gallery contained just two figures: in the front row, head bowed as if asleep, was a long-haired young man in a leather jacket. Two rows behind him sat a uniformed police officer with fiery red hair.

I sat down some rows behind the policeman and waited. A clock on the wall above me ticked softly. It felt like being in a small theatre at the matinee performance of a deeply unpopular play.

The minutes passed with excruciating slowness. No one else was coming; that much was obvious.

A small commotion behind the pinewood door to the left of the judge's bench began the proceedings. A muffled, echoing clatter preceded the sudden opening of the door. A dark-suited usher entered and solemnly commanded us to stand. Through the open door came the Procurator Fiscal, or rather, as he immediately explained once he was seated, the Acting District Procurator Fiscal. The incumbent was indisposed. The substitute District Procurator Fiscal was a tall, wiry man with snowy hair; he might have been Edward Blake's twin, had it not been for the light Highland accent.

His manner was brisk and to the point, as though he was late for an appointment. 'We are here to inquire into the death of Jonathan Charles Henry Tain in Sutherland on October 17th or 18th last year.'

It was odd to hear my father identified like that. His middle names were hereditary accretions he'd quietly dropped in adult life, and no one ever called him Jonathan. He was always 'Jon'.

Sutherland, the place where my father had died, was the name of that sprawling region of moor and rocky coast which on the map is North-West Scotland. For reasons unknown my father had been visiting it when his life abruptly ended. I had no idea what he'd gone there for, and no one else did either. His friend Ivan's guess was the most plausible – dad was a geologist and he was there to pursue some private line of research. It was, after all, good country for a geologist, rich in crumbling shorelines and exposed, rain-denuded rock.

I'd also wondered why the Fatal Accident Inquiry was being held so far from where my father had died. Edward Blake had gently explained to me that in the vast, under-populated stretches of the northern Highlands and Islands, this was actually the closest office of the region's District Procurator Fiscal.

'I believe Inspector Boston has a statement to make.'

'I have, sir.'

The policeman stood and made his way to the witness stand, where he was sworn in. Inspector Donald Boston looked as if he was in his early thirties, perhaps five years older than me. His red hair was dense and wiry and his face was splashed with freckles. Unlike a lot of police officers, he looked trim and fit. He had a rather steely, warrior-like appearance; I could imagine the inspector in a kilt, storming down a misty hillside two hundred years ago, a fearsome dirk gleaming in his raised hand. That effect was tempered by the reading glasses he put on, which added intelligence to those rough indigenous features.

'At 7.50 a.m. on the morning of October 18th last year I received a telephone call from Iain Campbell of Sea View House, Tongue. He informed me that having gone out early fishing he had noticed what appeared to be a body lying on the ground in the old graveyard. I should perhaps explain that this graveyard lies some distance from Tongue itself, and is situated on the other side of the estuary, north of Achuvoldrach, close to the A838. I have a witness statement from Mr Campbell together with a map and some photographs of the site which I wish to submit to this Inquiry. The location where Mr Tain's body was found is marked with a cross.'

There was silence as the court usher collected these items and passed them up to the Procurator Fiscal. He examined them for two or three minutes, then put them down. 'Proceed, inspector.'

The inspector's accent was very different to the Procurator Fiscal's and I found myself tipping my head forwards a little, trying to catch every word. An Edinburgh accent was like an only faintly distorted version of standard English, perfectly comprehensible to a nicely brought up girl like me. But Inspector Boston's way of speaking was altogether different: his words were deeper and muddier, brewed in a dark, gale-swept region, guttural and resonant and harsh. His words seemed to drag and dip, as if wind-battered, shaped by a force that was reluctant to let them go.

He had driven out to the graveyard, he said. A parked car stood by the entrance, empty. Towards the centre of the graveyard, which stood on an exposed ledge of land, he was able to see a dark shape resting at the foot of one of the graves. Approaching it, he saw that it was the figure of a man. From the pallor of the face he guessed that the man was deceased. This was confirmed by checking his pulse.

It wasn't anyone he recognised. He knew everyone who lived and worked in the area and this was no one local. A man with a slim, refined face, in his late fifties perhaps. Expensive-looking shoes, a mid-length dark cotton coat, designer jeans. He guessed it was someone from the south – Edinburgh, Glasgow, or south of the border. He'd evidently been dead for some hours. Rigor mortis had set in. The face looked as if it had been carved out of wood. The dead man's eyes were closed. He almost looked as if he'd been asleep when he died.

A bottle of whisky, almost empty, stood upright at the man's side. It was resting on the rim of the small pedestal of the gravestone by the prone figure. (The Inspector saw the brand and it won his approval. A good, smoky West Highland malt.)

The grave itself was a granite plinth dedicated to a matriarch of Tongue who had died in 1857. A conclusion had already formed in the inspector's mind: the man had drunk too much whisky and had slumped unconscious on to the grass. The night which had just passed had been well below zero. Death from exposure. From time to time it happened in these parts.

Such a conclusion was premature, however. Appearances – it was the banal starting point of any investigation – could be misleading. Inspector Boston walked a little way from the dead man, as if stepping away from his hearing, and telephoned for assistance.

While he was waiting for the arrival of the police doctor and the forensic investigators, Boston made an inspection of the scene. It was a cold morning and the grass was stiff with frost. He noted that the only footprints were his own. He did a slow circuit of the cemetery, observing nothing out of the ordinary. The car parked at the entrance was unlocked. It presumably belonged to the dead man. Staring at the registration number, Boston contacted the police national computer and asked for owner details and all other data held on file.

The glove compartment contained a plastic card with details of the car rescue service my father subscribed to, together with a music CD. Another music CD was in the deck. The boot held a sleeping roll, a folded tent, a muddy pair of walking boots, an umbrella, a kagool and a travel bag. The inspector unzipped the travel bag and rummaged inside. Clothes, a small transistor radio, a powerful flashlight. A couple of books. One was a small, battered paperback edition of *Romeo and Juliet*; the other one of Darwin's lesser-known books.

There was nothing that supplied any clues as to why the probable proprietor of these items was now lying dead some two hundred metres away. Nor was a later, more exhaustive search of any more assistance. I could verify the accuracy of those conclusions, for these possessions, including the car, had in due course been passed on to the dead man's next of kin, namely his only child. Me.

The minutes went by. The inspector lingered by the gate, his senses balanced in that strange, almost spiritual calm which had become familiar to him in such circumstances. He absorbed the solitude and silence of this place of death; the inertia. It was like being on an empty stage before the theatre opened. Pleasure was the wrong word to describe this feeling; but his senses were heightened, yet very controlled. He felt acutely the pressure of the significance that a death – abrupt, unexpected, as yet unexplained – laid upon an ordinary day. He felt his own mortality at these times. It was an unexpected gift. So much policing was a matter of dull, boring routine, but just occasionally the profession led you into life's mysteries; its depths and hard burning intensities.

Boston recalled how his father sometimes dryly remarked that he should have been a philosophy professor, not a policeman. He might have smiled at the memory of his father's view of him as an unworldly dreamer, but this was not the time or the place for levity. He pushed these reflections away and became the sober professional once again, dispassionately scrutinising the scene.

The sun had begun to gild the hilltops as a new day began. A lorry rolled by on the A road into Tongue. A hawk, no more than a scrap of darkness, whirled to one side overhead, very high. And then the calm cracked and the mood leaked away: he saw the doctor's blue Audi coming down the highway.

Dr Millar emerged from his car and at once saw the body. 'Your thoughts, laddie,' he said gruffly.

'Drank himself into oblivion. Died of exposure. Possibly an accident, possibly suicide. No obvious signs of it being homicide.' He added: 'He's not from round here.'

Dr Millar snorted. 'Even though this place would drive anyone to drink. Ach, well, let's take a closer look.'

Inspector Boston had known Dr Millar since he'd first joined the force twelve years earlier. Millar enjoyed cultivating an eccentric, curmudgeonly image – he was fond of polka dot bow-ties whose dots were of the same colour as his pink cheeks. A surge of wiry white hair rose from his scalp like a frozen wave. But beneath the veneer of grumpiness and oddity – and perhaps a reluctance to stay within the weekly units of alcohol limit that he solemnly recommended to his male patients – he was a shrewd, competent and experienced physician. When Fiona had first begun to display the symptoms of her illness, it was Millar they'd relied on for an authoritative, and as it turned out all-too-accurate diagnosis.

Millar knelt over the body. It required little of his attention. The spark of life was gone. He groaned as he stood up again. 'My knees are killing me,' he remarked, straightening.

Boston waited for his verdict.

'Died somewhere between five and eight hours ago, probably. Exposure seems a very likely explanation. Five below zero last night. But we'll leave firm conclusions to the post-mortem, eh laddie?'

As Boston agreed he heard vehicles approaching. Two police cars and a white van. Blue and white tape was stretched along the side of the cemetery that was accessible from the nearby main road. A police car blocked the access road, with a constable to turn away the public. Soon the graveyard was dense with a bustle of activity and loud voices and the crackling of radios. The forensic team took photographs; the gravestone by the dead man was dusted for fingerprints. The cemetery was subjected to a meticulous search, but yielded nothing. The dead man's wallet confirmed his identity as the owner of the car. The process began of contacting his next of kin.

The hours passed. Inspector Boston stayed until the end. He was in charge of the investigation, since it had been agreed that this was not a case for the murder squad. The forensic team departed with their photographs and samples. A private ambulance with darkened windows came to remove the body to Thurso, where the post-mortem would be performed. By mid-afternoon the sun was beginning to slip behind the hills. A constable removed the tape, leaving a scrap flapping on a fencepost where he'd been unable to untangle the knot.

The long day was done.

13

As the writer re-reads this ancient text he finds he's forgotten most of the characters. He can barely remember the plot. All those minor characters; that back-story padding. Dull, attention-seeking prose. He goes on reading.

14

'As a result of my investigation I concluded that Dr Tain had died as a result of exposure. It appears that he had consumed sufficient whisky and painkillers to induce a state of semi-consciousness. I understand that Dr Millar will be making a statement about the post-mortem results. It is my belief from the evidence at the scene of death and the medical report that the deceased fell asleep, probably on the previous evening, after dark. He lay there all night and died as a consequence of his exposure to the very low temperature prevailing during that night.'

'And you find no evidence of third-party involvement?'

'None, sir.'

'Is it your belief that Dr Tain intended to kill himself?'

'I found no evidence whatever to support such a conclusion.'

'No note in the car, or elsewhere?'

'There was none in the car, and none was found at his home or workplace. Those who were closest to him state that he was in a good frame of mind prior to his trip to Scotland. I might add that Dr Tain had no history of depression or mental illness. His death came as a great shock to everyone who knew him.'

The Procurator Fiscal's lips tightened. 'Quite,' he said. 'Thank you, inspector.'

Inspector Boston gave a slight bow and returned to his seat in the public gallery. My attention switched to the young man in the front row, who had been scribbling into a notebook. I determined to find out who he was, and why he was interested in my father.

Dr Millar appeared from the rear of the court and took the witness stand. His plump cheeks quivering, he reiterated what the inspector had said about the alcohol and tablets, only in much greater detail, and larded with medical phraseology. I learned that my father's liver was in excellent condition and there was no evidence of alcoholism. The amount of whisky he'd drunk was quite out of the ordinary, for I knew that he barely touched spirits. He'd been given a bottle of Laphroaig on his fiftieth birthday and it remained in his drinks cabinet, only half drunk, all those years later. Nor was he addicted to painkillers.

The doctor's evidence concluded. Now it was my turn. The Procurator Fiscal spoke my name and I went forwards. The questioning was perfunctory, though sympathetic in tone. I attested to my father's good humour, to the enthusiasm with which he'd looked forward to his trip to Scotland. I explained that it was not unusual for him to go away on trips alone since his retirement. He was a geologist; he was still actively engaged in his profession, despite having given up teaching. He was on numerous boards and editorial committees. He regularly attended conferences. He travelled, internationally. In the past five years he'd been to Shanghai, the United States and Mumbai. His contribution to his field of study was widely acknowledged and respected. He was the author of several books and innumerable articles. Though he was a widower his days were filled with activity. His journey to Scotland would undoubtedly have been in relation to one of his various academic interests, though as a non-geologist I was unable to identify it.

I was thanked for my contribution and offered some formal

condolences. I returned to the public gallery. I noticed that the man in the front row had barely scribbled a word during my evidence; I felt a little chastened.

An adjournment was announced, for the Acting District Procurator Fiscal to retire and consider his verdict.

We stood while he exited the courtroom. I then sat down again, uncertain whether or not to join the others who were leaving.

'May I show you where the canteen is, Miss Tain?'

It was Inspector Boston, looking down at me. He seemed to understand my uncertainty, explaining that I need not fear missing the verdict; the usher would text him when the Procurator Fiscal was about to return.

The canteen was a bleak, bright room with grey plastic chairs clustered around fake marble Formica tables big enough to accommodate a jury taking a lunch break. It was almost deserted. A grey-haired woman spooned a bowl of lurid tomato soup, and the young man in the leather jacket scrutinised his smart phone.

'Who is that guy?' I asked, when the inspector returned with two lattes.

'I don't know.'

'He's been taking notes. I wondered why.'

'I'll go and ask.'

He returned. 'Nothing sinister. He's a reporter. Writing a piece for the *Highland Gazette*. He said he'd be happy to interview you about your father. But if you'd rather not then he won't bother you. He said he'd leave it up to you.'

'I'd rather not,' I said. I didn't want my name in the papers. 'Talking about my father isn't going to help me understand why his life ended the way it did, is it?'

The inspector looked across the table at me. 'Aye, in the absence of third-party involvement, publicity is probably futile, I admit.' He pronounced 'futile' to rhyme with 'Bootle'. He said: 'Did ye go to Tongue?'

'To the graveyard? No. I didn't see much point. It wasn't anywhere special to dad. To my way of thinking what happened there might have happened anywhere. Why do you think my father died there, inspector?'

My companion laid his mobile phone on the table top and sipped his coffee. He scrutinised me again. 'May I be frank with you, Miss Tain?'

'Please do be.'

'My job was to investigate the circumstances of your father's death. In particular, to decide whether or not a crime had been committed. I found no evidence of one. My task stopped there. I did not have the mandate or the resources to pursue the matter further. The purpose of your father's presence at the graveyard, for example.'

He put his coffee cup down. 'This is what people often don't understand. The Law is concerned with criminal intention. That is not necessarily the same thing as motive. A man may kill his wife, for example. The law wishes to know did he *intend* to kill her? His motive – anger, jealousy, what you will – is a secondary issue. Similarly, the Law is not, in general, concerned with consequences. It is the primary conscious intention of the criminal action that a court punishes. This is why conspiracy to murder is regarded as seriously as murder itself.'

He paused and finished his coffee. 'I'm sorry. I'm jumping in too deep. I feel very sorry for your ordeal. I just wanted you to understand the nature of my investigation.'

I smiled. 'I have no reason to doubt your professionalism. None at all.'

I knew what he was skirting around the vexed question of why my father, whose drinking was moderate, had consumed what was, for him, a prodigious quantity of whisky, washed down with a fistful of analgesics.

The inspector's mobile phone trembled and began to emit a series of loud hums. He glanced down at the screen. 'That was quick,' he said. He escorted me back to the courtroom and sat next to me.

The Acting District Procurator Fiscal's verdict was just as Edward Blake had predicted: misadventure. There were a few words about 'an unfortunate accident' and 'a combination of alcohol and barbiturates with unforeseen and tragic consequences' and then it was all over. We all stood as he glided out of the room. The reporter glanced across at Inspector Boston, who gave a little shake of his head.

As we left, the usher began switching off the lights. The little drama was over.

Inspector Boston accompanied me to the corridor outside. 'I'm driving back to Sutherland now. I'll be happy to give you a lift to the airport. It's no distance.'

I accepted his offer and he led me to the back of the Sheriff's Court. His patrol car was parked alongside a prison van.

We hardly spoke in the car. The inspector asked how I was feeling and I said: 'I don't feel any closer to understanding what happened.'

He did not reply but looked thoughtful. He dropped me at the terminal entrance and turned and looked me in the face. 'Look for the unhappiness, Miss Tain. Look for the unhappiness.' He added: 'And if you ever come to Tongue and need my help' – I deduced this was a euphemism for *and would like to see where your father's body was found* – 'I'd be happy to assist.'

I thanked him and said goodbye.

In the departure lounge I sipped an orange juice and reflected on the inspector's words. Unhappiness. The prefix 'un' – that deadly nullifying prefix which converted happiness into its absence, its opposite, something worse because it had been tasted and then snatched away. Was that what my father's death was all about?

Although the thought left me sad, angry and baffled, I was inclined to think it was. And it was only later, when I was on the final leg of the journey back to London, that I allowed myself to open my handbag and take out something which I had mentioned to no one, not even Blanche. Had I done so it might have led to a very different verdict.

The flight was half empty and the two seats beside me were deserted. I saw myself in the window, my square face and short hair giving me a boyish appearance. I raised my hand and flattened it, hooding my face against the cabin light. I stared through my image at the darkening land sliding past below. Far beneath this big throbbing droning winged metal tube England was a dark rippled mass sprinkled with tiny dots of light. I had no idea where we were but I guessed we were passing over some bleak swathe of the Midlands. Landing time at Heathrow was only twenty minutes away.

I glanced away and considered for the hundredth time the postcard which I'd taken out and now held in my hand. On one side it showed a view labelled 'Loch Morar'. It showed an expanse of water which might have been almost any Scottish loch. The foreground was a hillside bursting with sprigs of purple heather, with a distant blue lake edged by smooth, bare mountains.

On the other side was an Elizabeth II stamp postmarked 'Fort William', my handwritten name and address, and a blank space for the message. Conventionally it would have been filled with three or four sentences celebrating the weather, or the scenery, or the food. Instead it was empty, apart from one, neatly written word. Though the card was unsigned, there was no question that it was my father's handwriting: I recognised the simple unlooped 's' and the swinging tail of the 'y'.

The word was *Sorry*.

It told me that what had happened out there in that lonely graveyard was pre-determined. It was no unfortunate accident. It was perhaps not quite suicide, and yet my father had planned never to return from that long, lonely journey north.

He had wanted me to know that, and he had wanted to apologise for what he was about to do, even though he had chosen to provide no explanation.

Look for the unhappiness, the inspector had said. He may have been right but I hardly knew where to look. I always felt close to my father but now I knew there was a part of him I never knew at all.

The captain announced we'd shortly be landing and a stewardess came down the aisle to check that all seatbelts had been fastened. The plane sank over west London. By now rain was lashing the fuselage. The M25 was a slow blurry sparkling river of red and white dots. Then hard-edged brightly lit sheds and warehouses rushed into view and the jet's tyres thumped against the runway.

15

The story is over. It ended earlier in the month. Now it is 23 November and already they are playing 'Jingle Bells' in the supermarket. The song fills the aisles where the writer takes goods from the shelves: bananas, potatoes, tomatoes, red onions, sourdough bread. The Christmas music makes him think of the end of *The Man Who Fell to Earth*. Seen one weekday afternoon that summer at a cinema in Esher. A stopping train from Waterloo. The little empty platform. On the return waiting there, buffeted by the fast trains moving past in a blur.

16

In some ways my new job with Orlando Publishing didn't change much from my earlier employment with Ace Books – I greeted visitors, I smiled, I answered phones, I took messages. Mike Spark was an easygoing boss to work for. He was in his forties, with greying hair and an amiable manner. He had a wife he adored and twins aged six. He never once came on to me, which I appreciated.

The new job did have two differences though. Firstly, I didn't have to travel quite so far. I got off each day at Warren Street, then walked through the wide, placid Bloomsbury streets to the Orlando offices near the British Museum. Secondly, I now had an entrée into the exciting side of publishing. At Ace I never met any authors apart from very minor ones, and then only to tell them which floor to go to for their meeting. All Ace did was TV tie-ins, thrillers by D-list authors, cheap cookery books and pot-boiler war books. *Death on the Somme* and *Agony at Stalingrad* were just two of the scissors-and-paste straight-to-paperback titles which had no hope whatever of being reviewed anywhere, least of all in the serious Sundays or the *Times Literary Supplement*. But at Orlando I was in with the big boys and girls. Famous writers would sometimes briefly drift past in the corridor. In my first week I spotted [deleted, imaginary encounters with commercially successful 'literary' novelists].

I bobbed alongside Mike as he networked the crowded rooms – mostly ours but sometimes other big name London publishers. Before too long I found myself in rooms fuelled with big goblets of white wine and raucous with conversation, alongside real live famous authors. Sometimes [more imaginary encounters, deleted].

Most of the time I was dealing with smaller fry, not the kind of writers I swooned over each weekend when I read the Saturday *Guardian Revue*. There was, for example, Harry Stansted (real name: Fred Bott), who was the author of a series of thrillers which sold in quantities large enough to require book-signing tours. Fred was plump, middle-aged, and very reliable: every December he delivered a new manuscript featuring the latest adventures of his hero Wild Blackstone. Blackstone is the kind of muscular hero who can garrotte a man with a paper handkerchief and cross the Sahara nourished by nothing more than the apple in his pocket and his SAS training. The prose was basic but snappy and Fred had a great gift for suspense. I'd done a tour of the UK with him and we'd got on marvellously. But then writers liked me: Mike said it was because I was small and attractive and bubbly and made authors seem big and important. He added with a smile, 'Even the total shits.'

Fred made me laugh, not always intentionally. Admirers of the fearless and indestructible Wild Blackstone might have been surprised by the time on a book tour I had an urgent phone call from his creator. Fred was in the next room of our hotel: 'You must come this minute, Jane! Come at once!' I rushed there and banged on the door. 'Come in!' he shrieked.

Fred was standing on a chair, trembling, His face was chalk-white. He looked terrified.

'I just saw a mouse,' he sobbed. 'It went under my bed.'

I helped him down from the chair and guided him out of the room. While he waited in my room I packed his things. He insisted on moving to a different hotel. I often wondered if this incident provided the germ of the following year's Wild Blackstone thriller, in which Wild encounters a giant mutant rat in the ruins of an Aztec temple. The rat is terminated with a knife and Blackstone goes on to eliminate the swarthy terrorist fiends who, plotting to release their prodigies into the streets of the West's capital cities, have obscenely projected radiation on to caged vermin.

Not all writers were as nice as Fred, who was cheerfully self-deprecating about what he wrote. There was the utterly obnoxious literary novelist Jake T. Amos, arrogant, with the table manners of a pig. There was the sleek, charming and compulsively libidinous Andrew McPherson, widely praised for his sensitive portraits of women. There was squeaky-voiced Solomon Speight, winner of the Barking Prize, who regarded himself as the planet's top novelist and whose monstrous, throbbing ego required a regular, vigorous massage. I humoured them as far as was humanly possible, though with each of these three superstars I had to remove their wandering hairy hands from my knee and make it clear that our relationship would be strictly professional.

I didn't require a lover: I already had [deleted].

17

Later on this November day the writer looks for some music to play now that the story is over. Bach doesn't help – at least not that Cantata. It brings it all back. Even the Goldberg variations can't do it. *Journey Through the Past*. No, that's not it. Joan Baez? Too piercing and painful, those particular songs. On Brian Eno's *Film Music 1976-2020* he comes across the five minutes and nineteen seconds of 'Under'. It's not a song he understands but the melody pulls him in and there are moments in the lyrics which seem to catch where he is today. Snow; destruction; a force pulling you down. But you do not go under. You remain. You think it through. You make a stand. You endure. So: a song about resisting some obscure catastrophe – and an accompanying annihilation. At any rate a song he chooses to interpret as being about survival and endurance. A thought occurs. Perhaps song writing is itself what allows the singer to survive.

18

Darling Alec, with the hazel eyes and the jet black curly hair and the sweet soft lilt of an Irish accent. The writer frowns. It's hard to believe that he wrote this crap. A desperate attempt to create a 'character' and supply a back story. The narrator first meets him at a book launch. They're together five years. Lots of detail. Padding. A sister in Galway. The sister's story. To be sure, it's the emerald oil... Fetch leprechauns – lots of them.

19

In the evenings, alone, the writer returns to Netflix and *Ozark*. He's reached the third season. It gets him through the hours. Later he goes to bed and reads. He listens to the midnight news headlines, then switches off the radio and continues reading. Alone.

20

The end came suddenly, horribly, unexpectedly. And it was so conventional, so clichéd, so utterly and heart-rendingly banal. I was in Kent on a signing-tour with Annette Laval, whose sagas of family life in Surrey between the wars sell by the bucket load. Her core readership is women aged over fifty. Her novels are formulaic but very readable. There's always an extended family living in a big mock-Tudor mansion in the countryside outside Guildford. Father works in the City, mother is bored, the children are at a difficult age. Most of the time the sun shines. The South Downs frame the action. Storms, lightning and heavy rain only occur at moments of extreme emotional tension – I calculated every twelfth chapter. Mother has a fling with a gardener, or the chauffeur, or sometimes the husband of a close friend. Father encounters scarlet-lipped temptresses in the City but usually resists. The children get into scrapes. The local police are family men, big and kind and understanding.

There are always two back stories, usually involving infidelity or larceny. There are brothers-in-law and sisters-in-law and picnics on Box Hill. Sometimes there are illicit-but-not-explicit tumbles in the undergrowth. Just occasionally there is a bastard (who tragically dies of 'flu aged eleven months, or who returns from Australia nursing a terrible secret, sun-browned and sixty).

At the end all the loose endings are neatly wrapped, everyone rises above their domestic catastrophes, and large inheritances opportunely arrive. The middle-class nuclear family is strengthened and renewed. The endings are upbeat and feelgood. And tens of thousands of women loved the formula and wanted more.

I liked Annette. She was a big, jolly, generous-hearted woman. Despite her arthritis and her bad hips she was always happy to sit behind a table and sign hundreds of copies for her fans. The big problem was always trying to stop her talking. She would have chatted to each fan for twenty minutes if I'd let her. I had to be very firm. 'Annette,' I'd say. 'You still have sixty-five people waiting in the queue. And some of them have walking sticks.'

It was last autumn and we were in Broadstairs promoting her new novel, *Mrs Willoughby's Confession*. We were two-thirds of the way through a five-day tour in Kent. We'd done Rochester, Faversham, Whitstable and Margate. Annette was doing a lunchtime signing in Broadstairs and a later one in Deal. Tomorrow we looped back for an evening signing in Canterbury, then the next morning we returned to London. Annette lived in an exclusive apartment black in a posh development in Islington. She had a companion, Moira. 'And like Muriel Spark,' she'd hiss, if she detected a questioning hesitation when an interviewer asked about her private life, '*I am not a lesbian*.' The enigmatic and elusive Moira never accompanied her on signing tours. She didn't even turn up for launch parties. There were times I wondered if she even existed.

After breakfast I accompanied Annette for a stroll along the front. She was keen to visit the Dickens Museum – Dickens was her favourite writer – but it turned out to be closed. 'Pity,' she said. 'I've heard they do the most marvellous Dickens mugs. Ah well, another time, Jane, eh?'

Instead, she decided to walk out to the sea's edge. We descended the long flight of steps that leads down from the promenade to the little protected curl of sandy beach known as Viking Bay.

Annette clung to the railing all the way but just a few steps from the beach she trod on a sliver of seaweed and slipped. She gave a gasp of surprise as she fell, then screamed in pain as her rib cage crunched against the hard stone edge of a step.

At the base of that cliff I couldn't get a signal on my phone, so I had to sprint back to the top to phone for an ambulance. Then I ran back down to comfort her.

Poor Annette's face was contorted with pain. 'Damn fool thing to do,' she whispered.

Fortunately a paramedic was soon on the scene and gave her painkillers. When the ambulance crew arrived they decided it was too risky carrying her back up the steps on a stretcher – Annette was, after all, quite a large woman. More paramedics arrived and four strong men carried the stretcher across the sand to the far side of the bay, where the ambulance could reverse down a ramp.

She was whisked off to hospital.

21

The writer began to assemble material on his desk which would help him to write about this story's end. Templates, perhaps. Examples of how aftermaths were dealt with. The first book which came to mind was *The Great Fire of London*, by Jacques Roubaud. He'd bought a copy in the Foyles bookshop on the South Bank when Roubaud had given a reading there some years ago. Gabriel Josipovici was in the small audience. He recognised him, having in the recent past attended a talk by him. Also present was Britain's first book blogger. But he had no idea what the blogger looked like. Perhaps now it is also time to read *Robert Browning* by Pamela Neville-Sington. The writer had read very little of Browning's poetry and that was many years ago. He'd only bought the book because the subtitle intrigued and interested him, and because a new hardback priced at £20 but remaindered at £4.99

was irresistible. His collection of books by and about poets was almost as substantial as that part of his library devoted to fiction. He'd decided that if he lived past 85 he would throw out all his fiction and dedicate his final years to poetry. He'd always liked the way Thomas Hardy had packed in the novel-writing racket and switched exclusively to verse. *The Great Fire of London*. Roubaud had autographed his copy. He'd read the book shortly afterwards. But the years had passed and now he remembered little of the book.

22

On the bus, travelling along the bright canyons of fried chicken outlets and convenience stores, I wondered again about Annette and Moira. It was impossible to tell if they were or if they weren't (and I still don't know). It made me think of the Marxist lecturer at York who kept insisting that novels were nothing but machines to sedate the bourgeoise. Novels lied, he insisted. They gave you rounded characters and neat endings. Robinson Crusoe escapes from his island and returns at last to England, a wealthy man. Gulliver survives his extraordinary adventures and ends up home again in England, a property-owning recluse with a family and a stable filled with horses. Marriage can be a prize (Jane Austen, Charlotte Brontë, Charles Dickens) but even when the golden prize turns out to be a hollow thing (*Middlemarch*), Dorothea is allowed a second chance with sexy Ladislaw. In the end, everything was explained, wrapped up, sentimentalized. *Middlemarch* was no better than a Mills and Boon romance. It was as formulaic as any thriller. The novel – there was no getting away from it – was dead. It was a defunct art form. It lingered on, a mild sedative for the middle classes.

How shocking these ideas seemed! I remember my intake of breath as the lecturer said that Ian Fleming was just as good as George Eliot, and both authors, though extreme reactionaries, shed great light on the capitalist crises of their time. (I remember he also quoted something by Trotsky, which I've forgotten.) He kept talking about *contradiction* and *the dialectic* and while his abstractions kept me scribbling on my notepad I noticed that this slim, dashing, bearded figure embodied its own sartorial contradiction – a smart pin-striped jacket over a pair of raggedy blue jeans.

Life, he asserted (raising his fist like someone at a rally), wasn't like it was in novels. People's characters were messy and unknowable. Lives were filled with ambiguity, mystery and irresolution. And society itself was unstable, tugged at by the clash of class interests, quivering with unresolved contradictions.

Well, yes and no.

His words were persuasive yet I wasn't persuaded, for reasons I could not entirely articulate. It wasn't that I *entirely* disagreed with him. But I loved *Middlemarch*. And I knew that what people who bought novels wanted was a page-turner. There had to be something – a situation or a mystery – that engaged their interest and made them want to read on. Even Shakespeare manipulated plot. And even *Hamlet* was a play written to cash in on a popular genre – revenge tragedy.

People, most of the time, were not interested in the contradictions of society. People want to know about other people and their secret lives – their thoughts, their passions, their hidden boiling emotions.

It wasn't just what other people wanted in a novel, it was what *I* wanted. And when I looked around the well-stocked tables in Waterstone's it seemed to me that the novel, far from being dead, was thriving.

When I got off the bus on Kingsland Road it had just started to spit with rain. I pulled my collar up and hurried to [deleted].

I went up the short flight of stairs to the big communal front door and let myself in. Then I slipped my Yale key into the door bearing the number two and went inside. The door opened into the living room, which was heavy with the odour of recently consumed curry. Plastic takeaway trays were strewn across the low coffee table and I felt a sudden pang of hunger. It was hours since I'd last eaten, and that had just been a ham sandwich on the train.

I crossed the room and opened the door on to the short corridor beyond, with the kitchen on the left, bathroom opposite and bedroom at the far end. The kitchen door was open and I could see a clutter of dishes and glasses on the sink.

Alec had a small TV in his bedroom and it was on because I could hear the murmur of voices. The door was slightly ajar and I was about to push it open when I froze. One of the voices was Alec's.

The other was a woman's.

The woman's voice sounded vaguely familiar, but I couldn't think who it might be. She said something and I heard Alec's laughter.

My pulse accelerated and began to hammer in my head. I felt my heart turn to mush. I opened the door and it was every bit as bad as I'd suddenly thought it might be.

They were in bed together, naked. They'd obviously recently had sex. The woman was sat up in bed, her back resting on an upended pillow. Her large breasts were framed by her arms. In one hand she was holding a glass of white wine.

Alec was barely visible. I could just see the top of his head resting on the pillow, the mass of black curls stark against the white cotton.

The woman looked across the bed at me. 'Oh fuck,' she said softly.

Alec, whose eyes were closed, didn't understand.

A smile appeared on his face. 'You've got to give me time to get my strength back,' he said. 'I'm not superman.'

I saw who the woman was.

Vanessa Smith.

23

The writer tried to remember who Vanessa Smith was. He had given birth to this woman and now he couldn't remember anything about her. A shamefully neglected creature, shut away in all these years in a cold filing cabinet. But soon he will find out more.

34

Like me, Vanessa Smith was a publicist. I saw her around from time to time at launch parties. She worked for Harry Blue, a one-man-band publisher who made a very good living publishing true-life crime titles, with a sprinkling of celebrity memoirs and books about members of the royal family. Harry Blue titles were slick and trashy and had a high scandal or violence content. It was niche marketing but a very profitable one. The bigger houses eschewed the grimy end of the market; this material was regarded as beyond vulgar.

We'd been introduced and had talked once or twice but only at a very superficial level. I'd never warmed to her. She was a bit tarty. She wore loud, short skirts and lots of make-up. She liked displaying her ample cleavage. Her complexion was unnatural and indicated lots of time spent at a tanning salon. Her plump legs were usually encased in lacy stockings and her high-heeled shoes were at the leopard-skin fuck-me end of the style range. Men were drawn to her and her easy promise. She had a reputation, although it tended to involve public figures rather than the minnows of the publishing world. She was supposed to have notched up three Booker Prize winners and a minor member of the royal family. (Two of the Booker names I could believe in but the third left me highly sceptical.)

A memory flashed into my mind. Alec chatting to Vanessa Smith at a launch party six months earlier. I couldn't remember the book – I went to so many publishers' parties that they were mostly a blur. The memorable ones were those in unusual locations. It must have been one of the unmemorable ones. But I did remember seeing Alec in conversation with her, and being surprised. I think he'd simply gone off to get me another mineral water and had taken a long time to return. And when I looked again, he wasn't talking to her but to my boss, Mike. I never even spoke to Alec about it. It was one of those trivial, momentary things that are not worth mentioning and which sink down into memory's dense, muddy residue.

Vanessa Smith prodded Alec. '*She's back*,' she hissed.

Odd, how characters hiss like kettles – the old-fashioned kind sold with a red exterior option, which you put on the gas ring, and which spurt a thin squeal of sound when the water is boiling.

'You said she wouldn't be back until Friday.'

The reality of the situation finally hit home. Alec emerged from beneath the duvet and sat up. He stared at me in disbelief and horror.

This is reminiscent of a scene from *Sliding Doors*. The writer had seen the movie at least three times. So this was probably the main influence on this scene – although as a plot device this is surely incredibly hackneyed. But then it does occur in Hackney.

My whole body seemed charged with a motion which was part nausea, part fire. It surged through me, the blood roaring in my head. In the midst of it I felt a strange calm. I didn't feel inclined to shriek or hurl abuse. There were no words that seemed suitable. I felt sick with shock.

Alec and Vanessa continued to stare at me, as if they waiting for me to make a speech.

I said very quietly, my voice trembling, 'Goodbye, Alec.'

Then I closed the door and hurried away. I knew I would never return to this place, ever.

I slammed the front door behind me and ran down the steps. I was thirty yards down the road when I heard him scream my name.

I didn't look back.

The weather was like the twelfth chapter of an Annette Laval saga. The rain came down in torrents. A gale was blowing through the trees, scattering great frantic fluttering masses of leaves. Thunder exploded overhead, close. Its ragged echo shuddered across the neighbourhood. It was answered by the sudden nervous flicker of lightning over Islington.

Within a couple of minutes my clothes were sodden. I hurried into the first side street and then began to run. At the end I turned and took the next street. I kept on, zig-zagging eastward. My chest felt tight.

I slowed down and glanced back. I was afraid that Alec would chase after me but the street was empty. A line of cast iron bollards blocked off the street and beyond it there were bushes growing in the road. I realised I'd reached De Beauvoir Square. Apart from a passing minicab, it was deserted.

I knew where I was now. It was here, in this windswept rain-battered empty space that I finally gave way to the torrent of emotion boiling in my chest. I began to weep, uncontrollably. Tears cascaded down my hot cheeks.

I walked on down the wet dark desolate streets until at last I came to London Fields. There, a big red double-decker bus loomed out of the night, destination Walthamstow and Chingford. It stopped at a bus stop to let passengers on and off, and I ran to board it. I sank into its muggy warmth, feeling my skirt squelch beneath me.

Thirty minutes later I was relaxing in a hot bath, with a scented candle and a large gin and tonic. My landline kept ringing but I hadn't bothered to disconnect the Answer Phone. It rang several times that night and then stopped. I recognised all too well that muffled, importuning voice.

In the morning, without listening to a single one, I deleted all messages.

29

The writer's heart thudded at the sight of the obituary. Afterwards he went to get his copy of T.S. Eliot's *Collected Poems*. He quickly located the two lines he was looking for.

In Chapter Eight the narrator tells her close friend Blanche about Alec. Blanche sympathises. The narrator changes the locks on the two doors that access her upstairs flat on Orford Road, Walthamstow. She blocks all Alec's calls and messages. She changes her Facebook entry to Not in a Relationship. Blanche has an idea. There is more gruesome dialogue, of the kind which inflates contemporary fiction.

31

'Listen, darling. Thomas and I are off for the weekend to a hotel at the glorious seaside. Why don't you come too? I'm sure they'll have a room for you.'

I hesitated. 'I don't want to be a party pooper,' I said. 'I wouldn't want to spoil your romantic weekend.'

Blanche laughed. 'Fat chance of that. If I know Thomas he'll slip his laptop in at the last minute and then say he has to stay at the hotel and work. I'll tell you what: let me phone the hotel and see if they've got a room for you.'

'Where is it?'

32

Southend.

33

The reader learns that *Blanche's reason for choosing it had been whimsical: that it couldn't really be as bad as its reputation.* But the real reason was that the writer had spent a few days there. That experience could be used to pad out the tale with some local colour.

34

The four-star hotel on the seafront was more than adequate. I had a seaview room on the same floor as theirs. We dined in the hotel restaurant, serenaded by a guitar-playing singer our own age. The food was excellent and the Damien Rice impersonations weren't bad either. Our vocalist invited requests from diners so after the starter Blanche went over and with a sardonic smile asked him to play anything by Leonard Cohen for her friend (pointing across the room at me). Sadly – or mercifully – this merchant of melancholy had yet to be heard of in that part of Essex, so I had to make do with a Dylan number instead. Not that a song about the imminence of death ('Knockin' on Heaven's Door') was really quite what I needed either.

35

This all happened. Except that it was not thin, fictitious Blanche who walked across the crowded room to ask for anything by Leonard Cohen but the writer. But now he hadn't listened to Cohen for quite some time – not since the singer had died. Now the writer preferred listening to Van Morrison, Lana Del Rey and Taylor Swift.

36

In the morning I woke early to the sun rising over the Thames estuary. Kent was a low, misty mass which, directly opposite the hotel, took shape as a line of big grey rectangular structures clustered around a giant chimney. If you ignored this distant oil refinery you might almost have thought you were somewhere more exotic. Two palm trees in front of the hotel were silhouetted against the glittering estuary, where a score of small anchored cabin cruisers bobbed restlessly offshore. Westward, about a mile away, the pier stretched out to a fuzzy, indistinct terminus. It bore there a shape resembling the tilted hull of a shipwreck.

37

The writer thought: This is okay, as descriptions go. If you like realism. There's a certain elegance there. Updike would have done much better, of course. A crisper turn of phrase, a protruding metaphor designed to catch the reader's attention, with a syrup of glowing adjectives poured across all of it. The writer read the next seven sentences.

38

After breakfast Blanche and I set off to walk into town. Thomas, as she'd predicted, said he had work to do. He'd received emails. There was a project he was working on, and he had to get it finished before he went to Berlin in two weeks time. We left him to it, and I had to admit I didn't mind at all. I needed to pour my heart out to Blanche. I needed her support.

39

Dead language, used to entice the reader into thinking that there is some solidity below the barren words. The writer continues reading.

40

After a brisk walk of a little over a mile we came to the Happidrome and Neptune's Fish Bar and the first amusement arcades. We passed a casino with an onion dome roof, and a line of soaring slender metal structures which rose out of the seafront walk like frozen rocket trails. Beyond lay the pier head.

'Oh God.' Blanche had noticed what I hadn't. On the far side of the road beside the seafront walk a shrine had been constructed. Bunches of flowers were tied to a lamp post, with more heaped at the base. There were candles in jam jars and, worst of all, a teddy bear. A photograph taped to the lamp post showed the face of a smiling child.

I felt sick. It looked like a boy had been run down and killed at this spot.

We hurried on, lost for words.

41

The writer had entirely forgotten that little shrine. Incorporated as local colour. Realism. A story there he'd never know. *Lost for words*. Not in this text. The words flowed smoothly, sealing up the cracks. Surges of banal prose rearranged the scenery boards.

42

We reached the entrance to the pier.

'Let's go to the end,' said Blanche, so we bought return tickets and boarded the next train. At that time of the morning there were only seven other passengers, which meant we had a complete compartment to ourselves.

The doors were shut and we were alone.

43

'Girl talk' about Alec and men in general. Blanche talks about Thomas. Deleted, deleted, deleted. Delete this, too:

I laughed: 'You're awful.'
'I try to be, darling.'

44

26 November. Restlessly searching for more music, the writer settles for Arvo Pärt's *Cantus in memoriam Benjamin Britten*. He turns the volume up.

45

The little blue train jerked away from the platform of the dark, windowless, enclosed station and soon burst out into sunlight. A powder-blue sea shone below the pier, turning a darker shade as we left the creamy shoreline behind.

We fell silent and stared out at the view.

The train rattled gently on. It took over ten minutes to get to the end. And even this wasn't the end. Beyond the terminus and its quaint miniature station, the pier continued. The boardwalk led on to a strange-looking building, then turned ninety degrees left. At the end of this extension was the lifeboat station. An RNLI flag moved sluggishly in the breeze.

Blanche and I sauntered on, our shadows distended by the low winter sun. The sea slopped noisily against the stanchions, which were scabbed with orange rust. Some of them looked disturbingly anorexic.

What from the shore had looked like a shipwreck turned out to be a slice of futuristic architecture – a wedge of big spiky triangles linked by sheets of plate glass. Through its metal ribs could be seen the silhouettes of people sat at tables, drinking coffee and gazing out across a dazzling silver surface. We walked past it and went on to the lifeboat station. There was even a stub of pier beyond this. Here, it finally came to an end. The sea was now dark green. It seemed faintly ominous, full of secrets.

46

The writer had forgotten some of these details of the journey, which his two imaginary women briefly occupied. Southend Pier. Another place he was unlikely ever to visit again. Once, years earlier, he'd sailed off the pier in a cabin cruiser with a friend, his friend's parents and their large Alsatian dog. They cruised the same stretch of water as the one where Marlow began his tale. They passed the navigation buoy marking the site of the Chapman lighthouse. They anchored off Southend and as the tide went out discovered they were on the side of a softly sloping bank of mud. The cabin cruiser sank into it and tilted. But as the water went on sinking the vessel did not tip over. In the morning, afloat again, they moved off.

47

A big ancient cast iron bell hung from a scaffold, its tongue gone, a relic of pre-radar days of fog, when it had been necessary to toll a warning as merchant ships made their way past on the journey between the North Sea and the docks of the capital.

I took a snap of Blanche as she clownishly put her head inside the bell.

48

Delete what comes next. The writer finds that his only interest so far is in the scenery, not the plot or the flimsy 'characters'.

49

The next morning, before we left Southend on the dreary, crowded, traffic-light-studded arterial road that leads back to London, we parked near the Royal Hotel and went for a final stroll along the heights above the pier. It was another gorgeous unseasonable day of blue sky and brilliant sunshine. We wandered around the gardens and took a trip on the funicular. We came to a statue of Queen Victoria, mounted on a tall pedestal. The glum-faced monarch was, oddly, pointing out to sea. Her right arm seemed strangely long and muscular and ended with a large male hand, half-clenched, a stone forefinger levelled against the distant hazy outline of Kent. I wondered if a straight line drawn on a map would follow the direction of that monstrous finger all the way to Broadstairs. But the unravelling of my life which had originated there shrank in significance with the much greater blow that was to follow.

50

Suspense. Tease the reader with little mysteries. But always supply revelations. Nobody likes loose endings or unanswered questions, do they? Any literary agent will tell you that.

51

At the end of that week, I went to Waterloo station and boarded a fast train to Portsmouth Harbour. It was a Friday evening and the train was packed. I didn't know it, but that weekend would be the last time I ever saw my father.

52

And so on. The narrator's father dies three weeks after the rupture with Alec. It's his death which supplies the axis of the plot's rotation.

53

Chapter Nine begins with some information dumping about the narrator's background. Before reading it the writer looks up Violette Szabo on the internet. The poem in the film *Carve Her Name With Pride* made an enormous impression upon him when he first saw it. This morning it was misty outside and cold in the house. He turns the heating on in the kitchen and makes coffee. Then he returns to the information.

54

The Tain family home is a detached Edwardian house in Warblington. This is a small, obscure parish on the Hampshire coast, within a few miles of the eastern extremity of the county. Warblington is cut in two by the A27, the fast dual carriageway that connects Portsmouth with Chichester. Even with sound-fencing, there's always the low, distant hum of speeding motor vehicles in the background. As a resident you get used to it.

North of the road, Warblington amounts to nothing more than streets of modern residential housing, a secondary school, a convenience store, and a couple of desolate platforms where South Coast Mainline trains stop with surprising frequency. This is commuter belt territory, with fast connections to London

Waterloo, Brighton, Gatwick Airport and London Victoria.

Old Warblington has all the appearance of a soporific rural backwater, while being close to all the benefits and amenities of urban society. Between the shoreline and the dual carriageway it's almost all farmland and commons. Ringed by water meadows and tranquility, old Warblington has what little history there is in these parts. There are the remains of a Roman villa buried beneath the grassy roundabout that connects a slip road on the edge of the village to the A27. There's a medieval church and, nearby, a slender, towering finger of red brick and stone visible for miles around. This is all that remains of a Tudor castle. Elizabeth I stayed briefly at Warblington Castle on one of the last royal progresses of her reign. Later, as a minor royalist stronghold, the castle was duly blown up and levelled during the English civil war. A solitary octagonal turret was deliberately spared, left as a navigation aid for shipping.

Not much has ever happened in Warblington since those times, although if you talk to some of the oldest residents they remember the time that the ebullient movie director Ken Russell came. He arrived with a film crew and hit Warblington like a tornado. Russell was making a film of The Who's rock opera *Tommy*, with Jack Nicholson and Elton John. Then, having shot some scenes using the church and the Tudor turret, Russell and his crew departed. The commotion over, Warblington returned to its traditional stupor.

55

The writer used Warblington because he'd once known it well. He kept meaning to go back to hunt for the grave of Rosemary Tonks, who was supposedly buried in the churchyard there. He reads on, deleting swathes of Jane Tain's childhood. Her existence is thinning with each day that passes. What's left is the local colour.

56

The sun always seemed to shine. The beach was safe because the coastline here isn't the English Channel, merely a muddy estuary separating the mainland from Hayling Island. Although on a map they bear the terrifying name of Sweare Deep, the waters here are shallow and tranquil. No one local ever uses that name – it's commonly known, not entirely accurately, as Langstone Harbour.

The estuary doesn't have waves: they are choked at birth by banks of mud that break the surface like big brown whales. The high tide sluggishly laps a slender strip of shingle before receding over a vast expanse of mud and bristling weeds. Out there, in the deep channels, the weekend yachting fraternity park their slender white hulls.

Half a mile eastward there was once a ramshackle wooden pier, and I remember swimming off it when I was about ten or eleven years old. But the soupy water, full of sediment, never warmed, and when you lowered your legs your feet sank into six inches of slimy mud. When the pier was demolished nobody really missed it. For us children the fun of the foreshore lay not in the water but in the open fields and a triangular piece of woodland known as Barn Wood. As a small child it seemed to me like a vast forest, though it was really just a skimpy copse, at its widest only forty or fifty yards of well-spaced blackthorn, and around two hundred yards in length.

57

Fictitious Jane remembers her fictitious mother and her fictitious father. The writer deletes a few more paragraphs.

58

My father was a more remote figure, commuting each day on a fast train to Waterloo. At first his teaching schedule at UCL was rigorous and demanding, but after he made a name for himself and was promoted to Professor he had more time off. He wasn't always at home because of his geological interests, which sent him off round the world, investigating remote locations, or simply attending conferences.

It was not until I was in my twenties that I felt able to ask my mother why I was an only child. It was not long before she died, and we already knew what was wrong with her. With sadness in her eyes, her voice very low, she told me that I was a twin. My sister had died the day after she was born. There had been complications and she was too weak to survive. She was buried in the local churchyard but there was no gravestone. It seemed morbid, she explained, to mourn for a child that young, its personality a complete blank. She and my father had blocked off their grief and channelled all their love into me, the tiny survivor. After that tragedy they had not felt inclined to try again. One child was enough.

I was stunned by this revelation. For a time I was haunted by the thought of my absent twin and what it would have been like to grow up alongside my double. But it is hard to mourn for a ghost which is formless, without even the wisp of an identity. Soon the shock and the brooding ebbed and went.

My parents took me to see where my deceased sister had been buried, but when we reached the place they realised they were uncertain. They had deliberately not made a shrine of the site; deliberately not perpetuated the rituals of mourning. Now, all these years later, they couldn't remember. The grave was somewhere in one of the plots by the east wall but exactly which one was obscure. Of course it would always be possible to get the church to examine the cemetery records... I agreed this would be futile. I must not let my tiny sister's ghost become too tangible or it might reach out and drag me down to a place I didn't want to go. The three of us hugged each other, and I said: 'Thank you both for telling me this.' And then we walked back home and never spoke of it again.

59

The writer had completely forgotten Jane's dead twin. Strange. It occurs to him that this unpublished manuscript is about death. But the story and the manner in which it is told is an unintentional concealment of the reality it purports to dramatise.

My father came in his car to collect me from the station.

'No Alec?'

'Not this weekend, daddy. He's busy.'

I didn't want to talk about what had happened. It was too seedy and banal. If I'd told Dad he'd have wanted to spend the weekend talking about it and offering me advice.

Back at the house he had a stew cooking for his hungry daughter. I ate a bowlful, washed down with a glass of red wine. Then, exhausted by everything, emotionally drained, I went to bed. To compound my fatigue I'd just started my period.

61

The writer smiles mirthlessly at that last bloody sentence. A sentence designed to please an agent. A calculated pitch at the women's market.

62

When I woke next morning the sun was splashing against the pale curtains in my room. My window looked south, towards Hayling Island. The estuary was bronzed and shining, and the water meadows looked summer-lush. I could see my father at the end of the garden, burning leaves. A pillar of lazy blue smoke rose over the trees beyond, which bordered Pook Lane.

I dressed, made myself a mug of tea, and walked down the garden to the far end. Whereas my father had wanted to buy the house for its size – it had six bedrooms, four receptions, and derelict stables on the west side – my mother, a keen gardener, had been attracted by its acre of land. Since her death, the garden had been neglected. My father employed a man to come round once a month to keep the weeds in check and the lawns mowed, and that was all. The once radiant flowerbeds were bare.

'Sleep well?'

'Perfectly.' I sipped my tea and looked at the heap of burning leaves. At its base was a mass of gently crackling sheets of paper. They looked like documents. Next to the bonfire was the material for a second, unlit one: a pile of shattered furniture. Wooden drawers were piled around an upended armchair. The armchair covering seemed dimly familiar.

My father smiled. 'Spring cleaning. I'm getting rid of a lot of old files. And I'm sorting out the house. There's too much junk. Mustn't leave you a house full of rubbish to sort once I've popped off, eh?'

I chided him: 'Don't be morbid, daddy.'

63

The writer deletes these paragraphs and the ones that follow. And arrives at a brief description of the father.

64

I thought my father looked good. His dark hair was flecked with silver strands and gave him a distinguished look. That he was an Emeritus Professor would not have surprised anyone. But he looked younger than he actually was. Unlike many of his contemporaries, he hadn't suffered from hair loss, and apart from the wrinkles he was still recognisably the figure I'd seen in old photographs of his university days.

65

Delete, move on. Fictitious father and imaginary daughter go for a walk, they have lunch in the next village, which exists. They return along an actual foreshore, refracted through prose.

66

The tide had receded, leaving a lumpy carpet of glistening seaweed along the walkway by the Gatsby houses with their huge lawns. We dipped down on to the wet shingle and trudged westward in silence. Far away, rising out of the blue haze of

Portsea Island, the faint silvery outline of the Spinnaker Tower resembled the ghost of a giant quill pen.

I could say that my father and I trudged back along that beach in silence but in truth I can no longer remember every hour of that weekend. I am joining the dots of what we did together for the last time, father and daughter. Between those dots lie the ellipses of all that's forgotten. It isn't as if I haven't tried very hard to remember. After my father's sudden, shocking death, I went back over the events of that weekend, searching for clues to his behaviour. Was his mind at that point made up? It may have been, but I still can't be entirely sure.

Was he saying goodbye to me? He might have been – but again, doubt and disbelief erode my certainties. I prefer to think that what was raised that weekend was no more than a possibility. A coin had been flipped into the air and it might have fallen either way. In one possible future my father never falls asleep in that lonely place in the far north. He wanders slowly back to his car and drives, a little unsteadily, with foolish recklessness and disregard for others, to the nearest B & B. And there he sleeps off his *Angst* and in the morning sets off south, back to Hampshire. Nothing having happened, there is then no story to tell.

I do remember, vividly, that when we reached the slender tip of Barn Wood (the dark ancient remnants of the original barn rotting quietly beside the rushes of some swampy ground north of the path) my father halted.

'Let's go back this way,' he said, indicating the path that diverged from the one leading straight back to Warblington. 'We can call in on your mother on the way.'

I suppose my father always had a slightly macabre sense of humour. But perhaps it was merely a blunt tool to conceal pain. I knew what he meant: we'd continue along the foreshore until we came to the path that led across a field into the far corner of the large graveyard south of the church. Here, in a plot just a stone's throw from the water's edge, was my mother's grave.

We approached it and stood before it. The gravestone was plain and simply bore her name GILLIAN TAIN and birth and death dates. Although it was one of the newer graves in the row the passage of time had already begun to tarnish it. Coin-sized patches of yellow and amber lichen had begun to colonise the stonework.

'You look after it very well,' I said, admiring the trimmed grass and the pot with a single fresh rose. None of the other graves were this kempt.

'I do my best. When I'm abroad I pay the gardener to keep it up to scratch.'

It was then that he mentioned he was going away to Scotland. 'I haven't quite sorted out the details. But I might be away quite a while. And up there among the mountains you can't get a signal, so don't expect to hear from me and don't worry if all you get is silence.'

'Take care.'

'I always have done.'

It was true. As a geologist my father had spent months of his life in some of the remotest places on earth but he'd never had a serious mishap. He always said the worst place was way beyond Alice Springs – day after day in the desert, the heat incredible, the sun blinding, with no water apart from the jerrycans in his 4X4. Out there you were a long way from help.

The shadow cast by my mother's grave slanted over the gravel path. My father said, 'Did I ever tell you there are two slots left here? One's for me. The other is for you, if you want it.'

'*Daddy!*' I said, shocked. 'I think burial is, well, old fashioned. Cremation will do nicely for me. But do we *really* have to talk about this?'

'Suit yourself. But I want to be buried here. It's in my will. I just thought you ought to know.'

'I won't forget, I promise.'

Afterwards, of course, this brief exchange came back to haunt me. But in itself I attached no significance to it. My father was a scientist. He could be briskly matter of fact about material things. Death was a natural process: he attached no divine significance to it. Of course it was ironic that he wanted to be buried in a churchyard, but I understood this was an aesthetic choice, not a religious one.

67

What a feast of information dumping and 'character' painting is found in those lines! Delete, delete, delete. Next: some padding about the long dead mother.

68

The same wasn't true of my mother. She was a churchgoer and came here to St Thomas's every Sunday. It wasn't something she ever talked about. Her religious beliefs were quiet, private ones.

I normally came to my mother's grave once a year, around the time of her dying. I always found it disturbing to think of the image of her body, slowly mouldering in this deep, filled-in pit. I'd never been able to forget her funeral, held on a bright cold day just like this one. I remembered the curious lime-green coconut matting draped over the open grave and the small yellow digger parked nearby, which had been used to scoop it out. I suppose I'd been expecting a gravedigger with a shovel and a caustic wit, like the one in *Hamlet*. In the event there wasn't one. The vicar uttered his monologue in the silken, easy tones of someone who'd performed it many times before, and for whom the words had lost all meaning. Then we all trooped away, leaving the gleaming coffin resting beside the tastefully covered trench. It would be lowered later, when no one was present. I felt cheated and angry. My expectations of what a funeral should be had been shaped by movies and TV dramas, and this one flouted the entertainment conventions.

69

Delete, delete, delete. Onwards. What, you may wonder, did mother die of? The next paragraph will enlighten you.

70

I never found that her grave was the right place to remember my mother. In memory she was still alive. In memory she was always as before the cancer thinned her and stripped her of her auburn hair. I remembered [fictitious memories of fictitious Mother deleted].

That bright Saturday we [deleted].

That weekend my father did not seem depressed or unable to cope. Besides, it was nearly eight years since she'd died. He had learned to live without her. Her going had not robbed him of the will to live. My father showed no signs of being a man debilitated by grief or mourning. That last weekend he seemed much as he'd always seemed over the years. We went back to the house and in the evening we ate monkfish washed down with a bottle of Muscadet. Next day we [deleted].

What I most remember about that last weekend is how *calming* it was. Home was supposed to be like this: a refuge for a child to seek warmth, protection and comfort. And this is how I remember it: convivial, casual, very ordinary and everyday. I sensed nothing of what was to come.

That Sunday evening my father drove me the short distance to Havant station to catch a fast train to Waterloo. We kissed goodbye in the light shining from the station entrance. He seemed in fine spirits. I waved goodbye and he drove off into the dark.

I went through the ticket barrier and over the footbridge. The train came in, half empty. I boarded it and never saw my father again.

71

Buffy St Marie singing 'Now You've Been Gone for a Long Time'; Buffy St Marie singing 'Bells'.

72

The writer decided that since the story was over it was now time to get rid of the things which he'd kept. They could go to one of the local charity shops. Quite why he'd kept them at all was open to question. Some had strong associations – a place or a date or a performance, occasionally more than one of those things. But they were now no real use to him. They could not now be shared with the only person who might want to see them. That boxed set of five long playing records of *Die Meistersinger von Nürnberg*, directed by Wilhelm Furtwängler. Live-Aufnahme von 1943 aus dem Festspielhaus Bayreuth. He barely remembered the performance of this opera at the London Coliseum that year. That had been sung in English and the Furtwängler record was of course in German. For him that Coliseum performance was less memorable than *Don Giovanni*, which he'd seen at the same venue, alone, that autumn. And there was no real point in hanging on to the huge Brockhaus Illustrated Dictionary English-German, German-English, bought for him in München on 2 July of that year. That could also go to the charity shop. He would never learn German, not now. He'd once made an effort, at the Goethe Institute in Manchester. But his heart wasn't in it. He never went back to Germany or for that matter back to Austria. He never returned to Canada. Afterwards, when he went abroad, it was to Spain, France or Italy and, just once, Greece – a holiday in Crete – and, later, the United States.

73

Now, two weekends after the inquest, I was on my way back to Havant station. Oddly, it was when I arrived here that the first searing shock of bereavement always abruptly, startlingly returned. It was concentrated and sharp. It speared my heart and made it ache. Tears welled up in my eyes. I was so used to walking through the ticket hallway and out into the street and seeing the parental Citroën parked in the pick-up bays beyond the taxi rank.

That tradition was gone forever. I was an orphan, bereft of family. Now I had to turn right to where the drivers sat with their newspapers, huddled behind the wheels of a line of stationary taxis.

'Where to, love?'

74

A disintegrating copy of *Nicholson's London Guide.* Annotated.
The date 21 May written inside the cover. Lamb & Flag. Strand
Palace 24-26 May. Bluenose 16 June 2766. Leaving Finchley 2777
G.D. Above map 1 an address: 9 Princes Gardens. Above map 2:
40 S. Molton St. Below it: Duke of Wellington 94a Crawford
Street. Above map 3: Camden Arms. Above map 5: Golden Lion,
Fulham. Above map 6: Williamson's Tavern, west side, Bow Lane.
Inside the back cover: 435-7141 ext. 592. Arden & Beckett.
Osborne *Luther* Brecht *Galileo*. Phone at 4pm, meet at 5pm. Until
8pm Polish Library. *Luthe*r: 8.30 CURZON. The writer recognises
his own handwriting but he no longer understands all that he
wrote. He remembers the car and the mileage but not what 'G.D.'
represents. The addresses no longer mean anything. Nor does the
phone number. And those pubs – he remembers being inside two
of them. Were the others simply possibilities? He throws the
guide in the bin.

75

Ten minutes later [deleted] as the taxi turned in the driveway and
drove away, its headlights slashing the dark outlines of hedges
and sycamores, it was odd to stand before The Vicarage – my
parents had kept the original name – and see it all in darkness.
  To someone of a nervous disposition that big unlit house
marooned in an acre of dark restless rustling growths might have
seemed a place of fear. It looked like the classic haunted house.
But it was not fearful to me. My father had supplied me with a
cautious, sceptical, level-headed scientific outlook on life. I'd
often wandered around the gardens in the dark with him, as we
hunted for bats, or investigated the behaviour of pale fluttering
moths, or waited to see if we could see one of the snuffling
badgers that lived in the neighbourhood.
  I was not afraid of big gloomy rustling bushes or looming trees
with outstretched limbs that sometimes gave out low groans as if
in pain. The sudden scuttling of a formless creature dashing

across the lawn did not make me jump. I knew this garden intimately. I knew if you stood here long enough the inky blackness of night drained away and in the pale half light everything returned to the familiarity of the daylight hours. I had the names of all the trees and bushes and plants, and above, in the bowl of night, I knew the sparkling constellations too. Glancing upward I saw at once the stark unmissable outline of the Plough and the fuzzy cluster of the Pleiades. If my father had not been a geologist he would, I think, have been an astronomer. He loved stargazing and had done since he'd been a boy. And it was his interest in astronomy which helped him towards his great geological discovery, the one that made his name.

As I approached the front door and stood in the porch I was bathed in the sudden illumination of the security light. Inside, I stepped over the drift of letters scattered across the doormat, and put my bag down.

The house was deathly silent apart from the steady ticking of the grandfather clock in the hall. It was another reminder of how everything had changed. My parents both loved music and there was usually something low and soothing playing in the background from one of the various boom boxes or compact music centres that were plugged in around the house. I grew up to a Mozart and Chopin soundtrack.

Now the house was cold and desolate and cheerless. I went through to the main living room where the thermostat was located. I'd left it set to 18, enough to stop the pipes from freezing up. Now I swirled the dial to 25 and soon I could hear the low roaring of gas as the boiler engaged with its new instruction. I went on round the house, turning on lights. Returning to the living room, which was already starting to warm up, I put on some Nocturnes, for the sake of auld lang syne.

I'd eaten a sandwich at Waterloo and now I was hungry again. I warmed up a can of tomato soup. I finished reading the copy of the *Evening Standard* I'd picked up on the train and then I went to bed.

It is hard to imagine Joseph Conrad at a literary festival or stroking his beard and sleekly smiling at a line of book-buyers keen for him to autograph their copies of *Nostromo*.

I had visitors arriving in the afternoon, which gave me the morning to start work on the house. I'd had several meetings with Edward Blake and now probate was almost finished. My father had left everything to me, apart from his geology books. Those he had assigned to his best friend, Ivan Jensen. It was Ivan and his wife who I was expecting later.

I needed to clear out the contents of the house, and then sell it. I'd decided not to keep it on. I had no use for a large house in Hampshire. My centre of gravity was London. Selling it made more sense than hanging on to it and being lumbered with gas, electricity and water bills. Besides, at best I'd only visit at weekends, and I couldn't afford to rent a flat, own a house, and travel regularly by tube and train between the two. My salary was relatively modest, and there was the ever-present risk of redundancy. The internet's chill wind was blowing through publishing. Bookshops were struggling, sales were declining, advances were shrinking. Orlando Books had already started cutting staff. The editors were the first to go.

I'd had five estate agents round to value the property but their sale price estimates varied enormously. Before the house was ready to sell, probate had to be completed and I had to get rid of all the clutter my parents had accumulated over the past three decades. I wandered from room to room, making a brief inventory of the contents. I looked in the twin garage and the outhouses, noting the score of tins of paint, the jam jars containing all kinds of metallic oddments, the rusting shears and all my mother's other gardening tools. I even remembered to carry the biggest stepladder upstairs and open it up beneath the loft hatch. I raised the square of wood and shone my flashlight. It revealed a light switch, which I flicked on. At once a solitary bare bulb came on, illuminating a loft jam-packed with clutter. There were tea boxes and objects which might have been paintings, loosely covered with blankets. There were half a dozen plump suitcases, the old-fashioned sort, before wheels. A glimpse of pink indicated my ancient tricycle, with stabilisers and a white plastic basket which I used to transport my favourite doll, Mandy. I could see the dark outline of my old dolls house and a pair of pale plastic horses harnessed to a Barbie carriage.

I shone the torch into the dark spaces which the bulb couldn't reach. Pale crossbeams showed, hung with extraordinarily dense ribbons of cobweb. The loft seemed to contain even more junk than the house or the outbuildings, and my heart sank. I knew at some point I'd need to clamber up here and work my way through this mass of dusty leftovers. It was not a task I relished. I closed the hatch and descended, feeling a little depressed at the scale of my task.

Instead, my house clearance began with my father's bedroom. I'd already disposed of his clothes. In those first few blinding weeks of grief after his death I'd felt bewildered by it but also angry. Getting rid of his suits, his shirts, his shoes, was therapeutic. I filled up two large bags, stuffed some smaller items in a rucksack, and made regular trips up Pook Lane and over the footbridge that crossed the dual carriageway. At the end of the other half of Pook Lane (which had been severed by the building of the A27) there was a convenience store with parking bays. At the back of the bays were industrial-size recycling containers. I stuffed my father's clothes into the mouth of the big yellow one, which belonged to the Air Ambulance charity.

This brisk walk was good for me. But I'd hardly made an impression on the house: it remained crammed with family furniture and possessions. I could have just paid a house clearance firm to empty the rooms, but that would have seemed like a violation. Besides, I had the tiny and tentative hope that somewhere in this house might lie the clue to my father's final journey. His visit to Scotland did not add up. If he'd really gone on a geological field trip I'd have expected him to take tools and maps. There would surely have been some clue to his purpose. But when he died the boot of his car contained no rock samples. He hadn't bothered to take hammers or chisels. He'd taken his camera, but when I downloaded it on my laptop the most recent photographs had been taken before he'd ever gone to Scotland. They were of sunsets over Hayling Island. And the Ordnance Survey maps he'd taken were basic tourist ones. He hadn't even annotated them in his usual manner, drawing lines and arrows and writing instructions to himself.

There was another small mystery associated with his trip to Scotland that had arrived in the post at the vicarage a fortnight after his death. I planned to talk to Ivan Jensen about it to see what light he might be able to shed on the matter. But that was for later. For the present I had plenty to keep me occupied.

If the vicarage contained a Rosebud, I'd find it.

78

Clutter. The *Citizen Kane* allusion. The reader is being prepared. The plot has had a brisk rub of varnish. The writer gets up from his desk, leaving the text floating in suspension on the shining screen. His gaze falls on a particular shelf in the study. He wonders whether to dispose of that ancient Faber paperback edition of *Four Quartets*. An early memento. A gift, containing two autographs; two identities. The single woman; the wife. The spine is cracked and the pages loose. The title page is stained by a surge of spilled black ink. A number of passages in the book are underlined. He glances through this ruined book. On one page

There is no end, but addition: the trailing
consequence of further days and hours

and three pages later

People change, and smile: but the agony abides.

I was in no hurry. I could take my time and strip the house bare at my own leisure. My father had left me almost the entire estate, including his capital. I was now no longer modestly comfortable but very well off. When the vicarage was sold I could afford to buy my own place in London. But for the moment I was happy to stay where I was, in my rented apartment in Walthamstow.

As I wandered from room to room I felt a certain bleak satisfaction in the reflection that Alec [delete reflections about her faithless lover].

The other consolation was Alec's silence. After that brief flurry of unanswered messages he'd given up. Perhaps he knew me too well to know that I could possibly ever forgive him. Call it the Tain genes. There was a streak of stubborn, unyielding principle in me that I recognised in my father's character. I could remember odd times in the past (small-scale episodes in restaurants or shops, and all to do with service and attitude) when my mother, flexible and pragmatic, had counselled acceptance but my father had insisted on absolute rejection.

The only other person to benefit from my father's will was his best friend, Ivan Jensen. He'd been left daddy's library, to dispose of as he wished. I did not resent this bequest. Ivan was my father's oldest and closest friend. They'd met at the University of Birmingham in the late 1960s, where they were both enrolled as undergraduates studying for a B.Sc. in Geology. When they graduated Ivan got a job with BP working on oil rigs, and my father continued his studies at the University of East Anglia, where he did an M.Sc. Though their paths had diverged – Ivan rose high in the oil business, while my father remained in academia – they'd remained great friends. They'd both married in the same summer, 1979, and their wives had also become great friends. Miranda Jensen, like my mother, adored gardening, and like my mother she was a quiet Anglican attached to a hard-headed scientist utterly indifferent to religion. The Jensens had no children, and I'd been on many holidays with them and my parents. I was practically their adopted daughter, and in my younger days saw a lot of them. They lived in a village outside Guildford, in a big mock-Tudor detached house with a garden even bigger than ours, with the added bonus of an outdoor swimming pool. Ivan was on a stupendous salary and Miranda, like my own mother, was a primary school teacher. I have memories of [deleted].

80

Back stories. Information dumping. Oiling the plot. Adding layers to the characterisation. It can all go, this text. It's dead. It can't be rewritten or somehow rescued. It is what it is and what it is isn't worth saving. It's like stepping into Waterstone's and looking at the fiction paperbacks in little piles on the tables. Their bright jackets draped with clusters of dead shining words of praise and inside the machine-perfect plots. All those tidy last chapters designed to distract you from the one true ragged ending. And in bed, alone, continuing to read the Handke novel, the writer comes to an observation: 'criticism could be an art in its own right, the art of finding the right angle from which to look at a work'.

81

After my father's death I stayed with the Jensens several times. Ivan was plainly very upset by daddy's sudden demise. He was baffled by it. 'It's all a terrible accident,' he kept repeating, his eyes red. Miranda, too, was pale and shocked. But they pulled themselves together, and together, the three of us, we talked and talked about the quirkiness of life, and how brutal and unfair it can be.

On this day the arrival of Ivan and Miranda Jensen raised my sunken spirits. Ivan and Miranda were wonderfully unpretentious people. By the time they pulled into the driveway it was lunchtime.

82

A dull competence. Dead words strung like beads on a wire.

83

I'd spent the morning dismantling the parental double bed (which dad had kept after mum died). It was a pinewood kit bed from a chic bed manufacturer who advertised in *Time Out* thirty years ago. By noon it was no more than a pile of lengths of sun-bleached wood, with a little heap of nuts and bolts. I planned to burn it, since I couldn't imagine anyone who'd want it. The idea of burning it also carried the pleasing weight of ritual significance, for this was surely the bed where I'd been conceived.

The honk of a car horn told me that Ivan and Miranda had arrived, and I skipped down to meet them.

84

At moments of emotional extremity the writer turned to poetry, not prose.

85

I made them coffee and we sat in the sun-drenched living room and chatted. I'd fixed a light lunch of baguettes, cold meats and salad. After it, Miranda, who insisted on doing something to help, went off to [delete, delete, delete].

86

Save the last dance for me, no, it can't be. The writer knows that dance is done.

87

[deleted] my father's library. This was a large room at the back of the house. It contained a large desk, two grey filing cabinets and four walls of floor-to-ceiling bookshelves crammed with a lifetime's purchases. They were three-quarters geology and about ten per cent general science. The rest were miscellaneous oddities:

travel books, memoirs, biographies.

Ivan had brought some boxes in from his car. I'd asked him to take my father's bequest literally, and rid me of the entire collection. Ivan had happily obliged me, even though it must have been a slightly annoying request. Having hundreds of books dumped on you is not necessarily a joy. But Ivan had always been a relaxed, amiable person (much more so than my father, who could at times be quite intense, focused and inward-looking – especially when engaged with a matter he felt he must resolve). Ivan explained he'd sort the books into three: the ones he wanted to keep for himself, the ones which were worth donating to a university library, and the ones which could be unloaded on a charity shop. Oxfam was the best bet, he explained: they made sure every book donated that wasn't obviously mainstream was looked at by someone capable of valuing it. This suited me: I doubted if my father really had any rare books, but even if he had I was happy for Oxfam to get the money.

I left Ivan to start sorting through the books and went back upstairs to do more work in my father's bedroom. I began by [delete].

The three of us worked at our various tasks until five, then [delete, up to the scene in the restaurant].

It was only when we were there, sat at our table overlooking the harbour and drinking a fine New Zealand Cabernet Sauvignon, that I brought up the matter that had been troubling me ever since I'd first picked up the letter from the mat and tore it open. I produced my father's last Visa statement, sent posthumously, and passed it to Ivan.

'Take a look at those last three transactions,' I said. 'Tell me if you notice anything.'

Puzzled, Ivan glanced quickly at the itemised list.

'Three hotels. A night spent at each on his way north.' He frowned. 'It looks straightforward enough to me. Although I suppose the route is a bit peculiar. Norwich, Cromer, Harrogate. It's not exactly the quickest way to get to Scotland by car.'

'That's one mystery, certainly. But it's not the biggest one.' I persisted. 'Look at the dates.'

Ivan said: 'I still don't see anything unusual, frankly.'

'It's the dog,' I said. 'The dog that didn't bark in the night, or however it goes. Look at what *isn't there*.'

At last Ivan understood. 'Ah, I think I see what you're getting at.'

88

In *Ozark* season three at the end of the seventh episode there was a song which jolted the writer into searching online for the name of the singer and the song. It turned out to be Dion's 'Only You Know'. He watched it on YouTube. Firstly, Dion singing it live. Then the original studio recording. Then the cover version by the Arctic Monkeys. Then the acoustic version sung by Alex Turner.

89

The obituary. The writer came across it online. His heart thudding, he read it.

90

'I hope so. Because there are two days missing. There's no hotel payment for the final two nights before he died. Which raises the question: where did he stay?'

Ivan said: 'A Bed and Breakfast, maybe. Or perhaps he camped out – there was a tent and a sleeping bag in the boot of the car, you know. Or maybe he just crashed out in the car in a lay-by somewhere. Maybe that's what he planned to do the night he died.'

'Well, possibly,' I said. 'I suppose we'll never know. I just feel I wish I understood what dad was up to. I find it hard to believe it was some kind of research trip. I just don't see a scrap of evidence for that. You know he was always bringing back rock samples. But this time he'd collected nothing. And what was he up to staying at those hotels in those places?'

Ivan's frown deepened. 'I wish I knew. He did his M.Sc. at UEA, so he knew Norwich well. Maybe he was visiting friends. And Cromer is just up the road. Frankly, I find Harrogate a bit more perplexing. But I know your dad had an old friend who used to live there. He was called Mark. But he was killed in an accident twenty years ago. Your father went to the funeral.' Ivan paused. 'Maybe he just dropped by at his grave to pay his respects. Assuming there is a grave, that is.'

'I've never heard of Mark,' I said.

'You wouldn't remember. You were just a child when Mark died. He was originally at Birmingham when we were there, although I didn't know him very well. He was studying English, I think. Mark and your father used to go jogging together.'

91

Jogging. It used to be called jogging. But the writer knows that nowadays the term is running. Nobody jogs any more: they run. In those days you put on a T-shirt, a pair of shorts and some plimsolls. Now runners wear branded gear and expensive stylish running shoes. They run listening to music on headphones or ear buds. Many have devices strapped to an arm to record the distance run, speed, average speed, heartbeat and other information. The writer never knew anyone called Mark or anyone who went to Birmingham. Perhaps he was thinking of Bill, who he had lost touch with. Bill was an enthusiastic runner. Bill persuaded the writer to run with him round a nearby oval-shaped running track. Some days they ran instead to the main motor vehicle entrance to the campus and back. He has quite vivid memories of Bill. His drawl; his pale smooth face. Bill liked to talk about sex. Later he had what would now be called mental health issues. After some years of correspondence they lost touch. At one point Bill sent him a copy of *The Imitation of Christ*, advising him to aspire to perfection. Bill was surely being ironic. Soon afterwards Bill had a meltdown and some time after that their correspondence ceased. He knew that with Bill long gone from his life he'd go no more a-jogging.

'You said Mark died in an accident. What kind?'

'Hit by a car, I think. I seem to remember it was a hit and run. The police never traced the driver.'

Miranda [deleted].

Her words were no sooner spoken when there was a commotion in the street. Someone out there screamed [deleted].

Back at the vicarage we went to bed. Ivan and Miranda were in the guest room on the other side of the house. My own room faced due south. I put the light out and went and stood by the window, gazing out at the darkness. A car came down Pook Lane from the dead-end by the footbridge. Its headlights turned the hedgerow into a dark low mass speckled with hundreds of shining points of light. Then the car came to the sharp bend, and swerved round it to go past the vicarage. The beam from the headlights cut across the trees at the end of the garden and that was when I saw the man. He was standing beside a tree, looking towards the house. I caught a brief glimpse of a pair of jeans and a jacket with a hood which was pulled down low over the man's forehead.

The car drove past and [deleted].

My heart beat wildly at what I'd just witnessed. Was this [deleted].

I stood by the window, uncertain what to do. I continued to stare out. Although for a moment it seemed as if he was looking directly at me, I doubted if the intruder in the garden could really see me, since there was no light on in my room.

I waited there for five minutes, feeling every second thudding past in my blood. I could detect no movement. No one crossed the lawn.

I walked to my bedroom door and opened it. At the far end of the corridor I could see a strip of light beneath the guest room door.

I was halfway towards it when I heard Miranda cry out. It was followed by more low moans.

I suddenly realised the meaning of that sound, and flushed at the thought of how close I'd been to knocking on their door. I retreated hurriedly to my room.

I told myself not to worry about a break-in. The alarm system was switched on, and Ivan's car was parked in the drive. Anyone watching must be aware that the house was occupied. A burglar would surely prefer to come back when the house was empty.

I went back to the window and watched for another five minutes. Still nothing. Eventually I decided to get into bed. I lay there for what seemed a long time, ears alert for the noise of splintering glass and wood. But apart from the distant ticking of the grandfather clock downstairs the house was silent.

At some point I woke to the muffled unmistakable throaty roar of a motor bike starting. It seemed not far away, and then it quickly faded into the night. I was too fuddled with fatigue to find significance in this. I turned in my bed and slipped into a deep sleep.

93

The writer needed to read some Kafka again. *The Castle*. The parable of a man shut out. Because when someone dies they shut you out of their life for good – and for what is not good. Thinking about this on the last day of this month he reflects that perhaps he has always been shut out. He thinks of the salaried employment he failed to obtain. He remembers all those rejection slips. Each rejection was an incitement to get closer to what the market wanted. The market. A homely term for those big corporations in their office blocks. Where the gatekeepers spend their days. Team workers.

94

'Zombies?' I said. 'You know I *hate* zombies.'

'Yeah, me too, ducky. But the fact is people buy this shit. The other fact is that we sell it. And the other fact is that Norman has gone down with 'flu and no one else can do it.'

'That's a lot of facts,' I said. 'There's a Charles Dickens quote I should probably bash you with, but sadly I've forgotten it.'

'You bloody literary types. You just don't belong in publishing. Here's another fact. You don't have an author tour for another five weeks. So congratulations, Jane Tain. You have just won five nights in the Midlands and the chance to meet some interesting people.'

'That's what I'm afraid of,' I said. 'Fifteen-year-olds with spots, a lot of piercings and some very strange shades of lipstick.'

'You can do it, baby. And just be grateful it's not vampires. Vampire fans, some of them, can be very creepy. The men in particular. They dream of getting their teeth into a tasty young virgin like you.'

'Oooh, you are awful,' I said in my best laced-with-sarcasm voice.

It was Monday and I was back at work. This kind of badinage was par for the course in the publicity department of Orlando Publishing. Mike Spark hid himself behind a constant spray of quips, puns and cynicism. But he was good at his job and everyone in the office liked him. He wasn't a creep where women were concerned – always a bonus in an industry not short of libidinous middle-aged men and attractive women in their twenties. Nor was he as brutal as he tried to appear and he was always very flexible about time off. Mike had been very kind to me after dad died.

I grimaced as he pressed the publicity pack into my hands. 'You'll need this, too,' he said, and winked.

It was a copy of the book I'd be promoting: Grant Montgomery's *The Island Walkers*. It was the seventh in a series which had started with *The City Walkers* (zombies take over London) and had achieved great success with *The Switzerland Walkers* (Swiss bankers infected by a mutant plague destroy the economy of the West – which Mike quipped was 'not fantasy but neo-realism'). This last novel had been adapted (rather radically) and filmed as *Undead in Detroit*. It had become what is politely known as 'a cult classic'.

Montgomery had done what Orlando required of him, supplying a new manuscript at the rate of one a year. I glanced at the plot outline of the latest title. It was about a secret government laboratory on a remote island off Scotland. A virus turns most of the local population into zombies. The uninfected hero and his uninfected woman try to find a way off the island to warn the outside world, only to discover that the government already knows and is determined to obliterate it with a small nuclear device.

I sighed to myself and turned to the profile of Grant Montgomery.

95

Glumly, the writer recognised where these derivative paragraphs came from. The jokey tone, the prose. He was trying to emulate Iain Banks. What he was after was popularity, readers, commercial success. A pact with the devil. An attempt to be the kind of writer he wasn't.

96

The day before I'd woken late, pleasantly surprised to find that the house was still intact. No one had broken in overnight. Ivan was in the kitchen in his dressing gown, standing beside two mugs and a boiling kettle.

'Can I do you a tea, too?' he smiled.

'Please.'

I told him about the man I'd seen and he looked troubled. 'You should have told me. I'd have gone down the garden and taken a look.'

'Bad idea, Ivan. He might have had a knife. Or worse.'

'When I'm dressed, let's go down and take a look.'

But there were no clues at the spot where the man had been. In a novel there would have been footprints or some carelessly dropped item. Life is more opaque.

I remembered the motorbike in the night.

'It might have been someone casing the joint,' Ivan said.

I agreed this was the likeliest explanation and later, leaving my visitors to continue with their tasks, I walked up Pook Lane. I rang the bell at the home of the Frosts. A middle-aged couple lived there: Dr Frost, who worked at a practice in Emsworth, and his wife Mary. There'd lived here almost as long as my parents. I knew Dr Frost, as he was our family doctor. His wife answered the door and invited me in, but I declined. I quickly explained about the intruder, and asked her to make sure the neighbours knew. If people could keep an eye on the vicarage I said I'd be grateful.

'Of course, my dear, of course. We'll be happy to. One of us walks past every day with the dog, so we'll be sure to keep an eye out.'

After that errand I retraced my steps and went down to the farm to the house where Harry lived.

97

Harry? The writer struggled to remember who Harry was. A fictitious villager in a real place. A 'character' he'd presumably liquidated in the deletion of Warblington padding.

98

He opened the door himself, red-faced and ebullient.

99

Harry, the writer saw, was like the wasp which George Orwell once cut in two. The head half went on feeding even though its stomach was open to the world and its wings gone. It would never fly again. Harry, though he didn't know it, was a dead man talking.

100

Harry invited me in, but once again I declined, explaining I had visitors. I quickly explained my purpose.

'Will do, Jane. And if I catch the bastard I shall jolly well pepper him with my shotgun.'

'Please don't. Just call the police.'

He shook his head. 'The rozzers are bloody useless. A bit of on-the-spot justice never hurt anyone. Thank God the government is finally beginning to understand this. You know it makes my blood boil what I read in the papers. This country's gone soft.'

101

Too easy prey, *Daily Mail* readers. It's lazy comedy.

102

Back at the vicarage my roast beef and potatoes were browning nicely in the oven [deleted].

Later, Miranda returned her gardening tools to the shed, and Ivan loaded six boxes of books into the boot of their car. 'I'm afraid I've only sorted some of them,' he said ruefully.

[deleted]

They took me to Havant station to catch a fast train to London and then headed off to the A3.

103

An old *London A-Z*, the spine broken, some pages heavily marked, others loose. At the end, on the penultimate page and the inside cover, a list of drinking venues, some with comments. London Airport Terminal One bar; bar in Kilburn cinema; pub in Rupert Street opposite theatre; Golden Lion; King of Bohemia; Jack Straw's Castle; Ship & Shovel (after TS Eliot); Joiners Arms; Old Caledonia; Lamb & Flag; The Spice of Life (before Scofield); one opposite Duke of York (twice); Sherlock Holmes (pass through); The Grapes (after *Luther*); The Brecknock + neighbouring pub; after Parliament Hill Fields: p. 28; between the Needle and Strand; after Spice of Life & tickets – the class one; one by Old Vic (The Gun and Powder); The Marquis of Granby on Charlotte Street; the Heather & Phil pub – with globes on ceiling; the one by Kentish Town tube – (The Assembly [indecipherable]). At the end of the list the words COMPILED in THE JOINERS ARMS – after which Keats house pub + The Flask near Highgate. The writer has no memory of those times spent at these locations or of any conversations held there. He throws the *A-Z* out.

104

I must be frank. Birmingham, Manchester, Sheffield, Nottingham and Leicester do not feature in my list of the world's fifty finest cities. Or even Europe's. But on the positive side, they contain more people who buy zombie books than you might expect. Admittedly most of them are under thirty. They also tend to be male, thin, pale, and wear black jeans and black T-shirts. Most wear glasses, many with coloured frames. Zombie fiction readers plainly spend too many hours a day in front of a small screen. But that's the early twenty-first century for you.

Grant Montgomery was better than I might have expected. He was thirty-seven years old and really rather dishy. He had a firm jaw, blue eyes, beautifully cut auburn hair, and a snappy brown suit with a crisp floral shirt.

'Jane is a huge fan of yours,' Mike said when he introduced us. 'She totally, totally adores zombie novels.'

'Thanks, Mike,' I said.

This exchange naturally passed completely over the head of Grant Montgomery. But he was okay. He was genuine. Grant wasn't turning his stuff out to make money. He genuinely cared about zombies. He was passionate about the genre. He seemed to have read everything in Zombieworld. The novels, the mashups, the mock non-fiction guides to surviving a Zombie apocalypse. The critical studies which referenced Freud and Marx. The whole caboodle. And to a true believer, loquacity is no problem. Grant never seemed to grasp that Mike was being ironic, and that my knowledge of the genre had been gleaned in two days of intensive, very fragmentary reading.

I'd dipped into Grant's zombie series, and I'd almost finished reading the new book. I managed to sound authoritative and interested enough to fool him. And I didn't particularly want to hurt his feelings by telling him that deep down I felt all genre fiction – crime, thrillers, fantasy, whatever – was rubbish. It was, at its best, beautifully crafted, brilliantly written, and very readable. No one should underestimate the skill or authorial drive behind genre at its best. But in the end it was all escapist. It took you away from your life and its difficulties and problems. It was great for a two-hour flight on a jet or a train journey from London to York. But it wasn't deep. It was deeply, deeply shallow. In the end F. Scott Fitzgerald and the serious literary novelists would always be better than the best genre writer. Because, like all good artists, Fitzgerald took you into the heart of your reality. He didn't sedate you, he woke you up. He agonized about his art. He was never untroubled by it. Like Kafka, he didn't sleep so well.

The Midlands zombie tour was a breeze. We travelled first class and stayed at good hotels. The bookshops where Grant did his signings were all competently managed and did what they were supposed to do. I sat smiling at Grant's side and helped him to get rid of the most ardent kind of fan. The fans themselves were okay – a bit on the outré side, but then a lot of them were teenagers. They were still working out their shit (as Mike would have said).

We shifted a lot of hardbacks. Orlando would be pleased. And in any case it was all tax deductible. That was the wonderful thing about the publicity lifestyle: everything about it could be signed off as a legitimate business expense.

After each signing it was my task to take Grant out for a meal. He favoured curries, which was scarcely my own idea of fine cuisine. But publicists can't be choosers. I chose mild. I smiled my way through chicken korma and Bombay potato and messes of spinach. I crunched on peppery poppadoms and tried hard not to sneeze. In Sheffield he told me I had wonderful eyes. By Leicester he wanted to marry me. I said, brutally, 'That's the Tiger beer talking.'

Grant was a gentleman. He made his dignified approaches, which I rejected with a diplomacy I'd learned from previous tours. Grant was rueful but he was neither dejected, insulted nor angry. I liked him for that. Novelists are a strange breed. Commercial success can so often inflate their intrinsic vanity and self-regard. And Grant certainly had a following. I was startled by the lengths of the queues and by the curious popularity of this weird sub-genre. Rampaging mobs of diseased, flesh-hungry corpses – an odd basis for a narrative. The fashion for cute mashups of the literary classics – *Tess of the Zombie World*, *Zombie-Dick*, *Great Zombie Expectations* – I found wearisome and predictable. Read one and you've read the lot. The tricks are tiresome. Thankfully, though he liked this stuff, Grant had never felt the urge to try his hand at it.

The tour was a success. A lot of copies of *The Island Walkers* were shifted, the fans were pleased, the author was pleased. I said goodbye to Grant Montgomery at the taxi rank outside Euston station. He formally shook my hand, then, impulsively bobbed forwards and kissed me.

'If you ever change your mind...' he said wistfully, before the taxi took him away.

I blew him a kiss in return. I liked Grant but I wasn't in love with him. I never would be, I knew. He had the looks but the spark wasn't there. Still, it had been fun. More fun than I'd expected.

When I met Blanche next day for our weekly lunch in Covent Garden she rolled her eyes. 'He looks *gorgeous*,' she said, eyeing Grant's publicity photograph. I'd cruelly taken the pack along to mock it. Zombies – ghastly people. But Blanche wasn't interested in hearing about people in bookshops. She downed her second glass of wine and kept staring at the smiling face of Grant Montgomery.

'You should have shagged him. I know I would have done in your situation. One in the eye for Alec.'

I sighed. 'Did you have to mention him?'

Alec I was forgetting. Alec was receding into my past far quicker than I'd expected. I felt oddly liberated by his absence. The hurt had ebbed. My life was back on track.

'I'm off men,' I reiterated. 'And I don't miss not having one in my bed.'

Blanche grimaced. 'Get thee to a nunnery,' she retorted.

We said goodbye and I walked back to Bloomsbury.

And then it happened.

74

Desperate stuff, slick as journalism. This was a manuscript fit only for the Recycle Bin. Delete. Transfer. Then click on *Empty Recycle Bin*. The writer read on, to see what horrors of language and form came next.

I went past the underground station, crossed Long Acre and headed up Neal Street. I was cutting across Seven Dials, threading my way between the crawling traffic, when someone shouted my name. At first I didn't react – Jane is a common name and I'd been fooled in the past by thinking someone was calling out to me in the street when in fact they were addressing another woman called Jane. In any case I wasn't entirely sure I'd heard correctly. There was building work going on nearby (there is always building work going on nearby in central London). The high-pitched whining of cutting machinery shredded what little peace and quiet existed above London's permanent soundtrack of the internal combustion engine.

'Jane!'

Second time round there could be no mistake. I knew that voice all too well. He was crossing from a road on the right and reached the monument on the little traffic island at the centre of Seven Dials at the same moment as me.

He grinned at me. 'How are you doing?'

It was Alec. I felt numb with shock. A black cab lunged at us and I moved on to the steps at the base of the monument. Alec joined me and we stood, face to face, marooned on our concrete island. Black cabs circled slowly like hungry sharks.

'I'm fine,' I said, going into automatic-politeness mode.

'I'm on my way to Soho,' he said. 'A meeting with a litigation lawyer. Business, you know. Fancy meeting you like this.' His jet-black curly hair framed a suddenly serious expression. 'It must be destiny.'

'There's no such thing,' I said.

'Listen, Jane, darling. I know I've been a complete fool and a total shit. But take me back. Please. I love you. I loved you more than I've ever loved you.' He reached out and took hold of my arm.

I tore it free.

'Don't touch me!' I hissed.

107

That red kettle is on the boil again…

108

'Don't you *dare*.'

'I'm sorry.' He looked suddenly downcast. 'I do love you, you know.'

I snorted: 'Does Vanessa know this?'

'That cow? I haven't seen her for months. It was only that one time, you know. That one bloody time.'

He was lying, I was certain of it.

'She threw herself at me. I was weak. I was very, very stupid. Must I be punished forever because of one miserable lapse?'

'Listen, Alec. I really don't want to hear your excuses. I must be off or I'll be late for work.'

'Let's meet for a drink later. We need to talk.' He looked at me pleadingly.

I said: 'I have nothing to talk to you about, Alec. Ever.'

There was a gap in the traffic and I darted between a white van and a taxi and made it to the next street.

Alec ran after me and caught me up. He bobbed alongside me.

'Please go away, Alec. Otherwise I shall tell people I'm being harassed.'

His face was wild. 'For God's sake, Jane. I love you. Doesn't that mean anything to you?'

'In a word: no.'

He gave up and stood still, while I continued towards Bloomsbury.

'I'll phone you,' he shouted after me. 'We absolutely have to talk.

Don't ignore me, doll. Don't do that to me.'

'I'm not your doll,' I said, without turning round. I don't know if he heard me. I didn't look back until I reached New Oxford Street. Only then, having crossed to the British Museum side, did I dare to glance back.

He'd gone.

That evening [deleted].

My silence seemed to work. In the days that followed [deleted].

At the weekend I [deleted].

And then, next day, I had the phone call from Ivan Jensen and my world turned upside down again.

109

The writer quickly read the obituary and then slowly re-read it.

110

'I found something in one of your father's books. I think you should see it. Can you come to my office after work?'

The oil company that Ivan worked for occupied a massive tower block on the South Bank. It was little more than twenty minutes' walk from Orlando Books. I took a short cut through Covent Garden and then took the pedestrian bridge from Embankment tube station.

Ivan's secretary came down to reception and took me to his office on the eighteenth floor.

Ivan greeted me and led me through the small reception area into his inner sanctum. As is often the case, life was an imitation of a movie. The view through the big plate glass windows was impressive. Nearby, the luminous pods of the London Eye slowly rotated in the night. Across the river pricks of light shone in the offices of Whitehall. Miniature cars and buses crawled over Westminster Bridge.

'Here. Use these.' Ivan handed me a massive pair of binoculars.

The clock face of Big Ben filled the lenses. I dropped my gaze to the Stranger's Bar, which was deserted. It was too cold and too windy for MPs to want to linger out there beside the river.

I put the binoculars down. 'So, I take it you've discovered something interesting, Ivan.'

He smiled wryly. 'Something like that. I found these tucked inside your father's *Road Atlas of Great Britain*. This wasn't the Atlas that was found in his car, by the way.'

He invited me to sit down by his desk, and laid several sheets of A4 on the wooden surface.

111

Suspense. Mysteries to be solved. The pulse of contemporary fiction.

112

The first sheet was a monochrome photocopy of the British isles, with the word 'ROUTE' written on it in blue biro. I moved my face closer to make out the place names. A line of blue ink connected Warblington, London, Norwich, Cromer, Harrogate, Bracorina and Tongue.

This was plainly the route he'd taken to Scotland. It connected with the hotel receipts. But I felt a sudden chill at the realisation that there was no route drawn for a return journey – unless, of course, the plan had been to retrace every stage of the journey. This seemed unlikely, bearing in mind its zigzag route. I remembered the postcard of Loch Morar. That fitted, too, both in relation to the route and the indication that there'd be no return journey. My hand started to tremble and I quickly put the sheet down.

Ivan observed the change in me. 'Would you like a whisky or a brandy? You look as if you could do with a shot of something. This stuff is good for you when you've had a shock.'

I waved the suggestion away. 'No, I'll be fine, thanks.'

I picked up the second sheet. It was handwritten and consisted of a short list of addresses and places.

113

The story is over because now there is only one of them left.

114

44 Cavendish Avenue, N3.
20 West Parade, Norwich.
137 Earlham Road, Norwich.
Elm Hill.
Cathedral.
Hotel de Paris, Cromer.
47 Burnside Road, New Park, Harrogate.
Bracorina.
Graveyard, Tongue.
Dove Cottage.

115

The penultimate place listed had a bleak finality about it. I felt my heart flutter hotly inside the cage of my ribs. But the addresses meant nothing to me at all.

A little shakily I put the sheet down and turned to the next one. It consisted of two scanned colour photographs. Oddly, they were exactly square in format, redolent of a long defunct format. The grain was a little coarse and fuzzy.

The first showed a narrow cobbled street with people shopping. In the middle distance, the focus of the photographer, was a woman, her long black hair extending to her shoulder. She was wearing a dark coat and white trousers, and holding a large orange carrier bag. She'd turned to look back at the camera. The houses on the street looked very old.

The second photograph showed a young man standing on a grassy pathway high above a huge lake. He seemed vaguely familiar but I couldn't attach a name.

It must have been a hot day because his denim shirt was drawn back, exposing his slim stomach and chest. Denim jeans enclosed his slender legs and he was wearing sunglasses. He was looking out over the water. In the background were bulbous mountains, which receded into a blue haze.

The final sheet supplied a clue as to the identity of this second photograph. It was the photocopy of part of an Ordnance Survey map. It showed a landscape devoid of roads or settlements, running along the northern edge of a lake. The place was easily identifiable, because, though cut off at the waist, the top half of the upper case letters made it easily decipherable: LOCH MORAR. A line in red ballpoint had been drawn along the dots of a marked path, ending with a cross. The marked path continued on beyond the cross to the edge of the frame. The site of the cross seemed without distinction: a bulge of brown contour lines, bunched together, indicating a sharply rising landscape.

'His final journey,' I said. 'It obviously possessed some kind of logic. But what that was is beyond me. I don't associate those places with my father, and I don't know who is in the photographs. Do you?'

Ivan looked uncomfortable. While I was scrutinising this little collection of papers he'd gone over to a wooden cabinet by the wall and pulled down a hatch. Inside was a line of bottles and some chunky tumblers. He poured himself a generous slug of whisky. He drank some and said,' What do you know about your father's life before he met your mother?'

I didn't understand the question. I said: 'Where he was born. Where he grew up. The usual stuff. I've seen the family albums.'

'I was thinking of his student years.'

I frowned. 'Very little. Well, nothing really. Apart from where he studied.'

'Let me put the question in a different way. Does the name Alexandra Pendleton mean anything to you?'

My frown deepened. 'It means nothing at all.'

Ivan gave a little sigh. He drank some more whisky. He looked me in the eyes.

'Your father met her when he went off to the University of East Anglia to do his M.Sc. He was twenty-three and she was eighteen. She was a first-year student of English Literature. She was his girlfriend. They lived together.'

'My God,' I said. 'I never knew.'

Ivan said: 'There's no reason why you should. It was all a very long time ago. Before your father met your mother.'

'So what's she got to do with this?' I pointed at the sheets of A4 lying on his desk.

'The second address listed is where they lived. A room in a ground floor rented flat. I stayed with them a couple of times. There were a couple of other rooms, each with a student in. Guys. I can't even remember their names. Your father and Alexandra were the only couple.' He refilled his glass. 'They lived there for about eight months. Then the lease ran out and they moved to Cromer for the summer. Then Alexandra got a job and they stayed on until the following year. Then they split up and your father went to Canada.'

'This is all very unexpected, Ivan,' I said. I felt a little numb. Hollow and cold inside, suddenly. I'd never really thought about any woman being in my father's life before my mother. They'd had a long, happy, loving marriage; there had never been any hint of infidelities on either side. I didn't associate either of them romantically with anyone else but each other.

Ivan picked up the sheets. 'I can't make a lot of sense out of these, to be honest. The London address means nothing. Elm Hill is in Norwich, and although I guess "Cathedral" refers to the Norwich one, I don't understand their significance. Although one of the photographs shows him on Elm Hill.'

He pointed.

'That's my father?' I was incredulous. 'I thought it was a woman. His hair is so long.'

Ivan gave a dry smile. He ran the palm of his hand over the bald gleaming dome of his head. 'Hard though it may now be to imagine, I too once had hair down to my shoulder. Fashion is a powerful thing. Especially when you are young.' He added: 'Both photographs are of your father.'

Of course. I knew the figure standing on the path seemed familiar. I'd seen photographs of my father in his twenties, I just found them hard to relate to the much older man who I'd grown up alongside. Also, like everyone else in that generation, he dressed in denim and was slimmer back then.

A new thought occurred to me. 'So who took the photographs? And why were they so special?'

Ivan stared at the shards of white light trapped in the thick base of his tumbler. 'I've been thinking the same thing. I guess they were taken by Alexandra. I think Jon must have been reliving something. He was going back into the deep past.'

He stared out across the river. We sat in silence for a while.

Ivan looked melancholy, now. 'It's what people do in middle age,' he said. 'I've done it myself – gone back to the houses I lived in when I was a child. Looked at my first school. It's about going back to the place you were at before your life really began. It's about seeing all those choices which stretched out ahead of you which you weren't aware of at the time.' He added: 'I don't understand half of your father's itinerary. Just bits of it. It was something very, very private. He didn't tell you and he didn't tell me.'

'What's with the Scotland angle? Is there nothing you can say about that?'

'Tongue means nothing to me at all. But I think Loch Morar is where Jon did some research for his B.Sc. He must have been twenty. He went off alone with nothing for company but a tent. I remember him saying it was beautiful out there. Why it was so special I really have no idea. I'm not aware he had company. And your father went to many places on his own, researching geology. Frankly I can't see why Morar particularly mattered.'

'But Alexandra Pendleton might know?'

'She might. If you can find her. I expect she got married and changed her name. She might even be dead by now.'

'The University might know what happened to her.'

'If they did they wouldn't tell you. The best you could do would be to put a notice in their alumni magazine. But my guess is that Alexandra wouldn't be involved in an alumni society. She never graduated, you know. After that year with your dad, she dropped out. She was always very scathing about academic life. She was restless.'

It was my turn to lapse into silence. The situation seemed hopeless.

'To be honest, Jane, I don't think anyone is going to understand what was going on in your father's mind on that drive to Scotland. Or why he went to those places. Like I said, it was something very personal. Something he didn't feel he could share with either his daughter or his oldest friend.'

'That might be true, Ivan. But he wasn't completely silent about his intentions.'

I reached into my handbag and took out my father's postcard. 'Promise me you won't mention this to a soul. Apart from Miranda, obviously.'

He took it, looked at the picture, turned it over, and gasped in surprise. Ivan did not need to be told who it was from: like me, he recognised the handwriting.

'My God. When did he send you this?'

'It arrived two days after he died.'

'Jesus.'

Ivan shook his head. His eyes filled with tears.

'I don't know what to say, Jane.'

'You don't need to say anything. I just wanted you to know. But I guess you're right. Neither of us is ever going to know what was going on inside his head.'

Ivan contemplated his glass, then filled it again. 'Sorry,' he said. 'I [deleted].

I watched Ivan dab away his tears. I felt my own eyes brimming.

'I just remembered,' he said. 'I have something for you.'

He reached into a drawer in his desk. 'You can keep this. It might help.'

It was a glossy black and white photograph. Unlike the ones of my father, this one was more conventional in format; postcard-sized.

It showed three young people with, in the background, what at first sight looked like pyramids with windows in. But the pyramids were terraced and had what looked like big square low chimneys rising out of them.

'University plain,' Ivan said. 'The famous UEA ziggurats. That's me on the right. The couple are your father and Alexandra.'

I couldn't help but smile at the figure of Ivan. What he'd said was true: he had a surge of hair down to his shoulders. To my surprise it was blond. He wasn't wearing glasses then, either.

My father resembled the figure in those other two photographs, except that his luxuriant black hair seemed even longer. It spilled over his shoulders and lapped his upper arm. His other arm embraced Alexandra Pendleton.

She was stunningly beautiful. She had high cheekbones and the eyes of an enchantress. She looked like a cross between a princess and a gypsy fortune-teller. There was no question that she was the embodiment of the Age of Aquarius. She wore a long floral dress that ran down almost to her ankles. Her dark hair was parted in the middle and ran down almost to her waist.

I was reminded of someone, and it hit me who I was thinking of. Alexandra was that woman who haunted the paintings of the pre-Raphaelites. She was a dreamy Arthurian princess, a creature woven of wide-eyed longing, no denizen of a vulgar everyday industrial world. She was hauntingly weird. She was the Lady of Shalott's daughter.

'I forget who took the photograph, or how I ended up with it. Some friend of Alexandra's, I think. Anyway, keep it. If you want to take this thing further, it might be useful.'

I gave Ivan a hug. 'Thank you,' I said.

116

Alexandra Pendleton. That's what the writer called her. A four-syllable first name to match the real one. Her surname invoked in 'Pendleton'. He hardly ever thought about *Alexandra*. Despite all that time together. Despite all those mornings of waking up by her side. Despite [deleted].

117

At the end of that week I went to spend a night at Blanche and Thomas's. They were holding a dinner party and I was invited to stay over – an invitation I happily accepted. Blanche's voice had a voluptuous tone to it as she told me on the phone that [deleted].

They lived on the same street where Sylvia Plath ended her life. That might have meant more to me if I'd been a fan but though I'd worked my way through her *Collected Poems* they didn't engage me. I admired the cold brilliance of Plath's verse and its ingenuity with language. But the *Thanatos* was too explicit, too suffocating. She made the death-drive dangerously seductive. I felt the volume needed to display a health warning, like a pack of cigarettes. If I'd had to choose a suicidal poet, it would have been Anne Sexton. Sexton spoke to me as a woman who'd loved life. In the end it hadn't been enough for her, the love, the sex, and everything else. But at least she'd given it a go. Whereas the Plath-Hughes soap opera I found faintly repellent. And though I liked *Crow*, I never really warmed to Hughes. The womanising was wearisomely predictable: *I'm a big sensitive poet. Fuck me*. Big hairy-chested Lawrentian brutes who liked fishing were very much not my cup of tea.

The frisson of passing that blue plaque on their street soon faded. Ironically, the plaque was for Yeats, not Plath. Two famous poets at the same address was a veritable surplus of cultural connection. Naturally neither Blanche nor Thomas had read either writer. That didn't surprise me. Nobody read poetry anymore, except for people who wrote it. And sometimes I felt that half the population of Britain was writing poetry. I understood all too well why agents put up a sign reading NO POETRY OR SCIENCE FICTION. There was no money in poetry, and skiffy was a niche market requiring a profound grasp of the primitive intellects and desires of thirteen-year-old boys.

I went straight from Bloomsbury to Fitzroy Road, via the Northern Line. I took the footbridge from Chalk Farm tube. This was a route I'd done many times before. I always enjoyed visiting Blanche at home. Camden High Street was close and the neighbourhood had a real buzz. Then there was Primrose Hill. It was fun to stroll to the top and look south over the sprawl of London. Everything seemed so close from up there: Canary Wharf and the Shard and St Paul's and the London Eye. On a bright clear day, with a good pair of binoculars, I could probably have seen Ivan looking back at me from his office window.

The house that Blanche and Thomas lived in was fabulous. It was about halfway down the street. They rented out the basement to a woman barrister, and kept the other three floors for themselves. Downstairs there was a front room which Thomas used as an office, and beyond that a massive through lounge which looked out on to a long, thin strip of garden. A short flight of steps took you down to a spacious kitchen and dining area. Some Liszt was tinkling gently in the background as Blanche let me in, beaming.

118

Re-reading this desperate text the writer was struck by the coincidence. Driving down the A1 a month earlier he'd switched on Classic FM. He'd caught some music which was instantly familiar. The melody was that of one of the tracks on *Recent Songs* – 'Came So Far for Beauty' – and he was sure he must be listening to an album of orchestrations of Leonard Cohen songs. But when it ended the announcer said that the piece had been Liszt's Liebstraum No. 3.

119

'Darling! So good of you to come!' She winked. 'Wait till [deleted].

She took my overnight bag and coat up to my room and [deleted].

I was given a glass of champagne and introductions were made. There were three couples, including [deleted].

The evening drew to a close and [deleted].

Thomas went off to bed, leaving Blanche to load the dishwasher. I [deleted].

I'd never mentioned my father's postcard and I still didn't tell her, but I showed her the photograph which Ivan had given me. Blanche's eyes widened: 'My God. What a woman this Alexandra Pendleton was. She looks like a fucking witch. A beautiful, beautiful witch.'

'Ivan thinks she's the key to what happened. I'm trying to find her.'

I told Blanche [deleted].

I discovered that there were three Alexandra Pendletons living in Britain – one in Devon, one in Cardiff and one in Northumberland. A website offered me their full postal addresses in return for a small fee, so I paid up and obtained the data. I sent the same short letter to each address, explaining that I was the daughter of Jon Tain and I was anxious to trace the Alexandra Pendleton who had been his close friend at the University of East Anglia. I enclose a stamped addressed envelope, as well as my mobile phone number and my work email address.

There were nine Alexandra Pendletons on Facebook, so I contacted them through my own Facebook page, asking to be a friend. If one of them was the woman I was after my surname might ring a bell. I wasn't hopeful, though. Not all of them displayed their faces but the ones that did looked far too young. If she was still alive Alexandra Pendleton would be fifty-nine or sixty years old. People of that generation were rarely on Facebook, unless they had children who'd alerted them to its wonders. My own father had never had a Facebook account, and [deleted].

'I'm not hopeful,' I said, raising my voice above the sudden roaring and shaking of the dishwasher. 'Ivan's probably right. She'll be married, with a different name. Or long dead.'

'Worth a try, all the same,' Blanche said. 'I suppose.' She gazed mournfully at her empty flute. 'Is it really worth it, though? I mean, face facts, darling. Your daddy's dead. It was an accident. End of. Does it really matter why he drove all the way to the north of Scotland, stopping off at those addresses on the way? I mean, if it was some sort of personal odyssey it was his odyssey, not yours. Can't you just forget it and move on? [deleted]

I realised Blanche was more than a little tipsy. Her face was suffused with colour.

[deleted] she whispered. Her eyelids hung down heavily. She looked close to sleep.

'Good luck with that,' I said dryly. Blanche didn't understand. Her head tipped forward.

'There is one other thing,' I said. 'I've decided to drive to

Scotland. Following the same route that dad took. Calling in at those addresses and ending up at the graveyard outside Tongue.'

Blanche raised her face. She looked shocked. Her eyes blazed. 'You're crazy,' she said. 'Don't do it.'

120

Those old anthologies of love poetry. *Modern Love Poems* selected by John Smith, published in the Pocket Poets series by Studio Vista, Blue Star House, Highgate Hill, London N19. Paul Dehn, 'At the Dark Hour'. *Scottish Love Poems: A Personal Anthology*, chosen by Antonia Fraser, Penguin Books, Harmondsworth, Middlesex, made and printed by Richard Clay (The Chaucer Press), Ltd, Bungay, Suffolk. Alexander Scott, 'A Rondel of Luve'. *English Love Poems*, chosen by John Betjeman and Geoffrey Taylor, Faber and Faber Limited, 24 Russell Square, London W.C.1. Emily Brontë, 'Remembrance'. Years later the writer drove past the printing works in Bungay. It was on the way to the final place visited by the narrator of *The Rings of Saturn* before 'Clara' came in the car to collect him and take him home. The writer, who liked graves and graveyards, had been all over East Anglia making pilgrimages. Sebald, of course. (An unforgettable day, for a deer had jumped unexpectedly out from roadside undergrowth and a collision had only been narrowly avoided.) Fitzgerald. Elizabeth Smart. Doreen Carwithen. Several others.

121

Ivan Jensen said much the same thing when I told him, though [deleted]. But then it was those qualities which had made my father what he was. Without them he'd never have written the book that made his name.

When I say that, I mean within the realms of science. And when I say the realms of science, I mean the specific field of geology. And geology isn't sexy. There are no celebrity geologists – not yet, anyway. Nevertheless, within that scientific category, and among

88

its specialists and leading figures, my father had a global reputation. He was thirty-two when he published the book that catapulted Dr Jon Tain from the obscurity of a junior teaching post at UCL to international status. Even today the book is not particularly well known to anyone who isn't a geologist, but it remains, as they say, seminal. *On the Origin of Certain Terrestrial Craters* by J. Tain resulted in a paradigm shift. And the way in which my father came to write his book perfectly exemplified Kuhn's thesis, as set out in *The Structure of Scientific Revolutions*. There was problem solving and empirical investigation but there was also serendipity.

My father hadn't even been particularly interested in craters when he started writing his Ph.D. His original thesis title had been 'A study of Cretaceous regional metamorphism in the northern Monashee Mountains' – the kind of research which essentially involved testing, confirming and expanding existing geological knowledge. It was the type of project designed to confirm that the doctoral researcher was knowledgeable, competent and able to enlarge, albeit in a very small way, the sum of human knowledge.

Having graduated with an M.Sc. in Geology from UEA, my father applied for, and was granted, a Commonwealth Scholarship. This funded two years of research in Canada. He flew out to Vancouver and settled into a new life, sans Alexandra, at the University of British Columbia. And it was there, doing some work in the Special Collections Division, that he stumbled on the monograph that changed his professional life.

My father once told me that in a strange way it was music that ignited his interest in craters. When he first arrived in Vancouver the song that all the radio stations were playing was Lynyrd Skynyrd's 'Sweet Home Alabama'. They loved it in Canada for reasons of irony – it was a retort to Canada's very own Neil Young and his two less-than-complimentary songs about the Deep South. Popular music lodged the name Alabama in my father's mind – a place he vaguely associated with the Civil Rights movement and nothing else. Then, late one night in the fall of that year, the radio played Ella Fitzgerald and Louis Armstrong singing 'Stars Fell on

Alabama', which not only put that name again into his mind but also made him wonder about the song title.

My father did a little research and discovered it was probably borrowed from a travel memoir by Carl Carmer. The title of Carmer's book refers to a legendary shower of meteorites which were observed in Alabama on the night of November 12-13, 1833. A contemporary account described how thousands of luminous bodies shot across the firmament in every direction, hour after hour. It was a still and cloudless night and the spectacle evoked awe and wonder among the watchers of the night.

My father also came across the claim that 'Stars Fell on Alabama' was inspired by the Hodges meteorite. This event attracted worldwide attention because it involved an incredibly rare occurrence: a meteorite the size of a large pineapple which struck a house, penetrating the roof and striking someone inside. The victim was Ann Elizabeth Hodges and she lived in Oak Grove, Alabama. It happened in the early afternoon at the end of November, 1954. As most of the meteor burned up on its descent it created a fireball which was visible across three states. The impact of the meteorite, lessened by its small size and impact with the roof of the house and a piece of furniture, left Ann Hodges with massive bruising to her hip but not seriously hurt. It was a bizarre and highly unusual episode, but it had nothing at all to do with the song. That had been penned twenty years earlier, in the golden age of jazz.

That might have been the end of the matter. But when he came to return Carmer's book he happened to notice on the shelf above a companion volume on Alabama. It bore the less than mouth-watering title, *Accounts of a State Geologist*. The author was Eugene Allen Smith and the book had been privately published in 1903. My father flipped through the monograph. It smelled of age and disuse. How it had ended up on the shelves of the Special Collections Division of the University of British Columbia was anybody's guess. The monograph was barely one-hundred pages long and supplied a dry-as-dust summary of the state of geological knowledge about Alabama at the end of the nineteenth century. The title of one short chapter caught my father's eye:

'The Enigma of Wetumpka'. He stood in the deserted stacks and read the chapter's entire seven pages.

Wetumpka is a small town some twenty-five miles north of Montgomery, just above the fork of Interstate 65 south of Birmingham and Interstate 85 from Atlanta. What attracted the attention of Eugene Allen Smith, Alabama state geologist, was the unusual terrain east of the settlement. He described it as 'structurally disturbed' but found it impossible to explain the disturbance. The layers of rock here are bent over and twisted in different directions in a manner quite different to the other rock layers in the area. Smith's own geological mapping had demonstrated that this geological disturbance indicated an epicentre somewhere in the hills east of Wetumpka. The rocks in the very centre of these hills were a chaos of disturbed and mixed formations quite unlike the relatively ordered horizontal rock formations of the surrounding region. Eugene Allen Smith pronounced himself 'stumped'. Nowhere else in Alabama had a geology like this. This disturbed surface was quite simply inexplicable.

My father said he felt his pulse quicken. Geology, so far in his life and developing career, was a matter of received traditions. It was the purest of pure science. Geology, as a discipline, did not encourage speculation. It was pure empiricism. It was quite literally the hardest of science. What could be harder or more tangible than rock?

My father put the book back on the shelf (no one was allowed to borrow books – at best you could take them to read in a carrel). He went back to his rented room, on the first floor of a house on Vancouver's Larch Street. He took home a takeaway burger and fries and drank a couple of beers. He listened to an LP – as he recalled Elton John's *Captain Fantastic and the Brown Dirt Cowboy*. He went to bed and slept.

He slept well. And he dreamed a dream. His dream was a swirl of meteorites scarring the sky and fireballs and a ball ricocheting around a dream house, bouncing merrily from wall to wall like a rubbery-textured cartoon creature. And then the sky was clear again, and a single fiery giant fell across it. It hit the ground, wrenching the earth upward. A spout of swirling colours merged with a bright crystal firmament.

In the morning, remembering his dream, he went back to Special Collections and ordered some geological maps of Elmore County. He took another look at the fairly rudimentary illustration of Wetumpka's anarchic rock formations in *Accounts of a State Geologist*. He stared hard at the layout of the surrounding hills. He felt his pulse quicken, his heart begin to pound. Was it possible? Was it remotely credible? Could the violent fracturing of the earth's surface east of Wetumpka possibly have been the result of a meteor strike? No, not a meteor – something much bigger. An asteroid. Was that horseshoe arrangement of hillsides in fact the remnants of a crater?

Common sense said No. His geological training said No. He'd absorbed the conventional wisdom on craters during his B.Sc. course. Craters have many causes. There are the man-made ones which are the consequence of mining, or war, or nuclear testing. There are natural craters which result from erosion or subsidence. But the biggest cause of all the craters found on the earth's surface is volcanic activity. Volcanoes create craters. They spew out lava which solidifies around the molten core. Or they explode. The phenomenon has been observed for hundreds of years.

As for impact craters resulting from one celestial object colliding with another, you can see those on the moon, copiously. But on earth? No way. There was no evidence. The very idea was regarded as outlandish and absurd. Celestial objects burned up in the stratosphere. Nothing of any significance ever hit earth. At best, what got through to the earth's crust was mere debris, tiny and insignificant. Orthodox geology disdained the notion of impact craters on earth.

When the maps arrived, my father scrutinised them intently. He felt excited by what he saw. But he was also frustrated by his prior commitment to the focus of his Ph.D. He had to get Cretaceous regional metamorphism in the northern Monashee Mountains out of the way first. Only a doctorate and a teaching post would provide the solid foundation he needed to take this matter further. So that is what he did. Like his hero, Charles Darwin, he delayed.

He scribbled his thoughts on Wetumpka in a notebook and set it aside. It would be some time before he returned to the subject. In fact it wasn't until he'd left Canada, graduated and found work at UCL that he was able to return to the idea roughly sketched out in that little blue reporter's notebook.

He did do one thing, though. He told me he still had unspent money from his scholarship, so he blew it on a flight to Birmingham, Alabama. There he rented a car, drove down to Wetumpka, and spent a couple of days criss-crossing the disturbed land to the east of the town. He took some black and white snapshots on his little Kodak camera. He put them with the other material. Then he put it all in a shoebox and saved it for another time.

In Alabama, they revered his name. At my father's memorial service, which was full of geologists, colleagues and old students, I'd been introduced to Bob Schrader, a big, genial American academic. He told me they were building a Visitor Center at the Wetumpka crater site, and he'd be honoured if I'd represent my late father at the opening. I promised that I would.

122

The writer had forgotten all that research he'd done. The information dumping was blatant. But it helped to explain who Jon Tain was. His character was being enlarged for the reader.

123

I could have spent the rest of that weekend with Blanche and [deleted]. I dressed, had a quick coffee, scribbled a note, and let myself out. I took the Northern Line to Waterloo and by early afternoon was down at the vicarage. [deleted]

After a snack lunch I took my father's car out of the garage [deleted]. It was a six-year-old Audi, with a lot of mileage on the clock. [deleted]

Now, suddenly, I had a use for it. To charge the battery, I drove it to [deleted].

In what remained of that weekend I began clearing more furniture from the house. I planned to strip the vicarage room by room, until it was empty. Only then would I [deleted].

On the Sunday night I returned by train to London. I had four days of work ahead of me, then I'd be back in Warblington, ready to begin my little adventure [deleted].

Ivan and Blanche both agreed that re-tracing my father's final route was a futile undertaking. Well, maybe it was. But unless I attempted it, I'd never know.

124

The writer owned three editions of *The Oxford Book of English Verse*, all bought second-hand. They were the 1931 impression of the 1900 edition edited by Arthur Quiller-Couch, the 1979 reprint of the 1974 Book Club Associates edition edited by Helen Gardner, and the 1999 edition edited by Christopher Ricks. When the writer went to look for them, so that he could write a paragraph beginning 'The writer owned three editions of *The Oxford Book of English Verse*' he found them wedged between *Wormholes* and *Poet in New York*. Having written the paragraph the writer returned the books to the shelf in the room upstairs. Next he began drinking a glass of red wine. His current favourite – a Fairtrade organic 2020 Malbec from Argentina, purchased in his local Co-op.

125

It was raining heavily when I set off early that Friday morning [deleted]. The wipers struggled to flick away the slithering torrent that blurred my view of the road ahead.

I took a minor road north out of Emsworth and joined the A3 just as it started its gentle ascent of the South Downs. I kept to the slow lane. In my attempt to replicate my father's journey I'd taken the two CDs which were in the car when he died. One was a compilation disc he'd made himself. The other was a country rock album by Lucinda Williams. I'd listened to them while driving but they seemed to offer no particular clues to his state of mind, so after one listen I'd left them in the car. Now I forced myself to listen to them repeatedly. I began with the Williams record. Country rock wasn't a genre I particularly liked but by the third listen the album started to grow on me. The songs seemed to be addressed to both a past love and a current love, and about change and the passage of time. Their melancholy timbre seemed apt for a day of rain and desolation.

The first half of the journey to London was all green hillsides and forest. By the Hindhead tunnel the rain had eased off and after Guildford it stopped altogether. The traffic, light until then, suddenly became much heavier. The dual carriageway widened to three lanes. The woodland faded; the views became greyer, more developed. I turned off on to the M25 and headed north, as far as the M1 interchange. There I turned off towards central London.

My father never bothered with SatNav. He said that as a geologist he was used to maps and he didn't need a machine to tell him how to get from A to B. As I was doing it his way, I'd planned my route in advance. I had the lineaments of the route jotted down on a pad on the seat beside me. The M1 took me to the North Circular, and then it was just a mile or so to the turn-off to Finchley. I plunged off into a grid of residential streets and stopped. I quickly located where I was using my father's A-Z. I drove on and found myself on Cavendish Avenue. The road was solidly parked on both sides so I drove on and squeezed into a space on the next street. I locked the car and walked back to my goal.

Number 44 was at the far end. It was one of a pair of semi-detached houses, which looked Victorian in appearance. They were different to the other mixed styles on the street. Each of the houses had an original porch, and bay windows projected from both the ground and first floors. Number 44 was the one on the right. Both houses had had their front gardens concreted over, for parking.

I took a deep breath and walked up to the front door of number 44 and rang the bell. It opened and a woman my own age stood there.

'Excuse me,' I said, my heart beginning to thump. 'I'm

enquiring after Jon Tain. I believe he came here towards the end of last year.'

The woman frowned. 'Who?'

'Jon Tain,' I said. 'Middle-aged, grey hair. A geologist. He came here.'

'I think you've got the wrong address, love. Nobody called Jon Tain has anything to do with this house. I should know, I've lived here three years.'

We stared at each other.

'I'm sorry, I can't help you.'

I felt she was telling the truth. Her puzzlement seemed quite genuine. [deleted]

I walked back to the Audi. Suddenly my plan seemed as pointless as Blanche and Ivan had said. Somehow I thought these addresses would unlock a mystery. Instead I'd failed at my first attempt. I could almost hear Blanche's mocking laughter at my wild goose chase. 'Finchley,' she'd say. 'What [deleted].

My punctured spirits were turned a little flatter by the sight of something tucked under my wipers. It was a little square of polythene containing a fold of paper. It was headed FIXED PENALTY NOTICE. It informed me that I had parked in a Controlled Parking Zone without displaying a valid permit and I was therefore liable to a penalty under section something of the something something Act. Irritably I stuffed the notice into the glove compartment and edged out of my parking spot. I indignantly reflected that I must have been gone from the car about three minutes. This was not turning out well at all. I just hoped it wasn't an omen.

Next stop: Norwich.

126

Scenes and images from films. *The Romantic Englishwoman.* Seen at a cinema somewhere in downtown Ottawa. All the writer remembers now is the fantasy scene, where a lorry crashes into a café's tables and chairs. So much memory is scraps. All those odd scraps of verse. Robert Browning could not recite from memory any of his own poems. Scraps, bits, orts. Those two lines of John Clare's.

I sleep with thee, and wake with thee,
And yet thou art not there.

The writer considered devoting a year exclusively to reading poetry and books about poets and their work. No fiction at all. It reminded him that he hadn't yet read Jonathan Bate's biography of Clare, which he'd bought remaindered in Bookthrift at £9.99.

127

The St Giles House Hotel was at the heart of the city. I parked the car in the hotel car park and checked into my room. [deleted]

In the morning I was the first guest down for breakfast. Afterwards I strolled to Elm Hill, which was only a short walk away. I easily found the spot where my father had stood when he'd been photographed all those years ago. Oddly, the little narrow cobbled street looked identical. The passage of the years seemed to have changed nothing. The shop on the corner in the foreground had the same yellow walls. The one-way street sign was identical. The manhole cover set in the carriageway was still there. Even the billowing tree in the background didn't seem to have grown. I took some photographs on the digital camera I'd brought with me. Then I walked on to the Cathedral.

I came to Tombland and entered the Cathedral precinct by the tall open archway. My father had written the word 'Cathedral' but it meant nothing to Ivan and it meant nothing to me. I gazed at the exterior of the building, feeling nothing. It seemed pointless going inside, so I returned to the hotel and checked out.

I drove half a mile along Earlham Road and [deleted]. I parked and got out. A small sign said PRIVATE ROAD. Across the surface were laid a series of thin speed humps which had the camber and density of a car tyre. They were big enough to trip an unwary pedestrian and I stepped carefully across these protruding tarmac ribs as I walked down the road.

Another oddity of this street: there were no lamp posts.

After the heavy traffic on the Earlham Road it was suddenly peaceful. The racket of motor vehicles faded behind me. The houses here were mostly big and detached, and were half-hidden behind billowing hedges and clusters of pines. Unlike the other residential streets nearby there was no uniform design to them. They had evidently been built at very different times. Thirties mock-Tudor stood alongside black-slated Victorian villas. One home seemed to be entirely constructed out of curving glass: a contemporary eco-house, evidently. To underline its credentials a white electric car stood parked in the drive. The interior of this intriguing house was blanked out by screens and blinds.

Halfway down it and I realised that the road was a cul-de-sac. That explained the absence of traffic. The only other pedestrian was a child, a small boy with a silver scooter. He came towards me and said: 'What do you want?'

'I've come to look at a house,' I replied. I smiled and kept walking.

The boy scooted along beside me. His face looked very serious as he manoeuvred himself over each road hump. He had the earnest, unabashed directness that children are capable of.

'Why do you want to look at a house?'

'Because it's where my father once lived.'

'When did he live here? Was it before the war?'

His question startled me. I wondered which war he meant but thought it better not to ask. It might divert our conversation into matters of history, and it was quite a short road.

'He lived here before I was born,' I said.

'Why did he live on this road?'

'Because he was a student,'

'What's a student?'

'Someone who studies. It's a bit like going to school.'

'I go to school. My teacher is Miss Ball. I like her very much. She smells of biscuits. I like biscuits.'

'*Jonathan!*'

A woman a few years older than me was calling from the entrance to a driveway behind us.

'I think your mummy wants you.'

'That's not my mummy. She's dead. That's my daddy's girlfriend. She's called Laura. She gave me this scooter. She's quite nice.'

He scooted off.

I walked on. There was a short row of decrepit wooden lock-up garages which seemed out of keeping with the smooth affluence of the rest of the street. A mass of ivy had colonised one of the doors and spread snakelike across the roofs.

Number twenty was the next house.

The tone of this quiet, affluent street seemed to dip sharply at this point. The house seemed bleak and a little shabby. Number twenty had no hedge, merely a lawn which was long overdue for cutting.

I walked slowly past, staring. The ground floor windows had drawn curtains. From its faded appearance I deduced that all these years later it was still being rented out to students. There were two floors, and dormer windows set into the roof. A house like this could pack in a lot of students.

I turned back and paused a little while longer. At least I knew not to waste my time ringing the front doorbell. My father hadn't been here for over thirty years. This was a house of mystery, haunted by his younger self and the remote, spectral figure of Alexandra Pendleton. This was the house where they'd lived together for a year. They must have emerged from that front door and walked up and down this road many, many times. Now, whatever it was they'd shared, was dust.

I wondered again about that witchy figure in Ivan's photograph. She was still elusive. Before I'd left London I'd had two of my letters back: each sender acknowledged the name but explained they had never been to the University of East Anglia, and had never heard of Jon Tain. No matter. Not all of the possibilities had yet been explored.

I walked back to the end of the road. I passed the Audi and turned left on to Earlham Road. The other address on my father's list was a little further along. A couple of minutes later I was there. This was a much smaller house, terraced, in a much less attractive setting. Traffic poured by all the time. But like the house on West

Parade it looked neglected. The shapeless privet hedge at the front was completely out of control and rose to the height of a single decker bus. The scrap of lawn behind it was similarly unkempt. What this place's connection was with my father was more obscure, since Ivan insisted it wasn't somewhere he'd ever lived. [deleted]

It started to rain. I turned and hurried back to the car, then drove on to Cromer.

128

Half-enjoyable prose, from a private perspective, the writer thought. Serviceable. But for all that, false.

129

[deleted]
    The Hotel de Paris is spectacularly sited on rising ground overlooking the North Sea and the town pier but its name and architecture are the only lingering signs of a lost age of opulence. Affluent Victorians and Edwardians came here in that [deleted].

I was shown to a small room at the rear. It was dark but clean. The ambiance was Edwardian, with faded nineteen-seventies trimmings. [deleted]

Gulls screamed overhead.

I felt paralysed by depression. This trip was a bad idea. What was I up to, exactly?

I [deleted].

Then walked back to the hotel along the windswept esplanade, beside a dark, boiling sea.

What was I up to? I was searching for answers. That was the [deleted].

The day was louring and drizzly. Fenland was ditches and desolation. [deleted]

The drive to Harrogate was too long, too dreary. [deleted]

I found the hotel – it was big and old and close to the centre of town – but I didn't check in immediately. I needed to get 47

Burnside Road out of the way first. It was the last house address on my itinerary.

New Park was only ten minutes' drive away. I went along streets lined with houses constructed out of soot-dark stone. Harrogate seemed affluent but somehow grim. I didn't warm to it. It seemed suffused with the same grey banality as the sky which had hung over me on the long drive from Norfolk.

[deleted] 47 Burnside Road was the odd one out. It was a street of modern housing, and number 47 was just like all the others around it. The afternoon was dying but I guessed there was still just about enough light for a photograph.

It was a semi-detached house with a short drive, a garage, and a small, trim lawn. [deleted] big flickering rectangles of lurid colour, spilling quick splashes of light across motionless figures in armchairs.

[deleted] I drove away [deleted].

Tomorrow I planned to be down early for the start of breakfast and then off on the long drive to Morar.

As I drifted off to sleep [deleted].

130

Scotland didn't really begin for me until after Glasgow.

Up until then it was a day of motorways and grey conurbations and drizzle. I stopped at service stations to take a break and pump myself full of coffee. Then on, to the next one two hours down the road. Every service station seems the same – the crowded car park, the people coming and going between the rows of vehicles, the bright garish caverns filled with people eating fast food, buying fizzy drinks, or lingering at news stands. The seasons don't exist here. Here it is always summer, warm and bright and desolate for [deleted].

The dim memory of a poem about motorcyclists [deleted].

Glasgow, the environs. I drove under gantries bearing big blue signs with names and road numbers. They were supported by big grey jointed legs that suddenly reminded me of passing beneath a Louise Bourgeois spider in the Turbine Hall at Tate Modern.

The city rose up north of the river, lacklustre and dull, a clutter of low off-white office blocks and grey urban sprawl.

Glasgow was where [deleted].

The author was the crime novelist Hamish S. Campbell. He lives in Kirkwall, in Orkney, where most of his novels are set. His first book, *The Brodgar Killing*, was snapped up by a TV company and turned him into a minor star of the British crime firmament. Another dozen books followed starring his hero, Inspector 'Big' Billy Brown. To popular sales could be added critical acclaim. Hamish's prose sparkled, and his landscape descriptions were magnificent. The scenes in his fiction became an Orkney tourist attraction. When Hollywood made a movie out of *Scapa, Scalpel, Skull* his sales doubled.

[deleted] He was a big, jolly man with a Father Christmas beard and twinkling eyes. He was perpetually buoyant. He adored meeting his fans. Orlando liked him because he always delivered on time, and he always agreed to any promotional activities we suggested. [deleted]

Hamish's most recent book – the one he was promoting – was *Stacks and Stiffs*. Nobody at Orlando much liked the title. How many would readers would understand that by stacks Hamish was referring to needles of rock off the Orkney coast? But then nobody had liked *Scapa, Scalpel, Skull* and that was his biggest selling title. When authors start to achieve big sales you don't mess with them too much. [deleted] one elderly publishing figure who was still bruised years afterwards from having to deal with Iris Murdoch and her furious haughty opinion that not a single word of her manuscript should or could ever be trimmed, revised or in any way improved.

[deleted]

Everywhere was filled with restless leaves which clattered along the pavements and wrapped themselves, slippery and half-decomposed, on kerbs and steps. Each gust brought a new tumble of curled brittle yellow scraps. [deleted] Next day Hamish went back to his home in Kirkwall. He was already halfway through his next book, *Old Man D*.

[deleted]

131

The writer remembers his Graham Greene phase. Novel after novel. But there was only one title that truly mattered to him. A bitter, bleak London ending, even though *A story has no beginning or end.*

132

It was only when I reached Loch Lomond that I started to feel free of a residual, lingering sense of futility and depression that the dark urban wastes of Glasgow had only exacerbated.

133

Cumbersome. A heaviness. Lubberliness. Unsatisfactory. Bosh. Infelicitous. Inadequate. Not up to scratch. Awkward. Ponderous. Ungainly. Foozled.

134

At first from the road you only catch glimpses of the loch, flickering dully in gaps between the trees. Then, finally, the route takes you along the shoreline, and you can see across to the other side, a great expanse of dark blue water, metallic in sheen, reflecting the light of a gloomy sky.

That bleakness embedded in the heart of the highlands grew denser, balder, more uncompromising, the further north I went. The windscreen clicked and shimmered with sudden brief showers, intense, momentary, gone. The wet tarmac shone with silver.

Glencoe was a valley of desolation, walled in by great protuberances of bare swelling mountainside, rounded off by the hands of giants. Boulder-strewn, all it lacked was meteorite impact craters to make it truly lunar. An illusion swiftly shattered by the sight of water. The mountainsides were clouded with mist, the peaks vanished into dense dark cloud. Rain began to spatter on the windscreen again. The valley began to gleam like metal. Lochs and lochans fractured the smooth folds of the weathered braes. I glimpsed narrow burns as they tumbled and frothed.

135

Such style! All told not a bad effort at 'literary fiction', the writer thought.

136

The rain stopped. I was finally out of that rolling slate waste. Scotland became green again.

A swirl of dark flakes against the sky came closer. They moved together. Now I could see it was a flock of gulls, wheeling in from the coast. A sign said BALLACHULISH.

Loch Leven came into view. In my father's road map the road turned sharp right here and followed the shoreline to the end, then curled back along the north side. Now there was a bridge across the narrows. On the far side was the ragged mouth of the Great Glen. Here the highway followed the shore, all the way to Fort William.

The town's name – I'd spent a few minutes on Wikipedia while planning my trip – invokes England's military suppression of Scottish insurgency. The fort is long gone and today there's just small-town sprawl, softened by a backdrop of rolling hills. I found a supermarket and went in to buy provisions for the next day – a bottle of water, orange juice, a pack of sandwiches, a couple of bananas, chocolate. I had a long walk ahead of me on the morrow. I secreted my purchases in the boot then drove on to a hotel with a restaurant which had a ninety per cent approval rating on Trip Advisor. It lived up to expectation and I tucked into [deleted].

By the time I left Fort William it was dusk and lights were beginning to twinkle amidst the dark environs of the town. A little way outside town I turned left on to the Mallaig road.

Soon it was night. My headlight beams caught the gorse at the side of the winding, twisting road. The route followed the coastline but there were no glimpses of the sea – just a tunnel of trees and wilderness. [deleted]

Place names slipped by until at last I reached the sign indicating the side road to Bracora and Loch Morar. I turned off the A road down a narrow lane. I passed under a small viaduct and soon met another road. Turning right, my headlights played across a dark, unending space of water. This must be the shallow, western end of the loch, I decided. I passed a boathouse and a church and followed the road as it went up and down a series of switchback hills. The darkness of the night was now absolute, broken only by occasional glimpses of whitewashed cottages.

At last I came to a sign bearing the word LEDAIG and under it a smaller sign: B & B. The top sign was decorated with the profile of a hand, its forefinger extended to point the way along a driveway which descended to the pale outline of a house built on a broad ledge some twenty metres below the line of the road. I manoeuvred the car down the bumpy surface to a gravelled area alongside the house. Another car was parked there, visible in the pair of illuminated carriage lights attached to the wall.

I pulled in alongside the Skoda estate. A dog was barking furiously inside the house.

By the time I'd taken my overnight bag out of the car the front door had opened. A middle-aged woman stood there, smiling.

I said [deleted].

I unpacked a few things, freshened up, then went back downstairs.

Moments later one of the outstanding mysteries of my father's last journey was solved, and I discovered that the effort spent on retracing his route had not been wasted.

137

One story halts, a new one starts. The writer will only ever be a very small part of it, in Chapter One. Most of the story will occur without him. He will never know how it ends. A retrospective reflection, from the month that followed.

138

The MacLeods were waiting for me in their living room. Mrs MacLeod poured me a cup of tea.

'So, Miss Tain. I suppose your relative must have liked it here, to recommend it.'

I sipped my tea.

'My relative?'

'Aye, Mr Tain. He stayed with us last year. He had a car like yours, too.'

My heart churned. 'Jon Tain. Was that his name?'

'Aye, it was. A lovely man.'

'Was that last October?'

Mrs MacLeod frowned. 'Donald – the book.'

Her husband went over to a dresser lined with ornamental plates depicting pagodas and small arched bridges. He opened a drawer and came back with a rectangular book bound in black. He passed it to his wife. She thumbed through it until she found what she was searching for.

'Aye, he stayed two nights in October.'

'The fifteenth and the sixteenth,' I said dully.

'Aye, that's correct.'

'That was my father. Jon Tain was my father.'

Mrs MacLeod frowned. She was alert to the resonance of the past tense.

139

The plot hots up!

140

'He died in an accident. Soon after he stayed with you. You did not see it in the papers?'

Mrs MacLeod looked shocked. 'You poor thing. I had no idea. We lead a quiet life out here. Donald and I dinna bother with the news. We used to buy the local paper once a week, but it closed down. As for the wider world... It doesn't affect how things are round here. This is a very quiet place. But what a dreadful thing to happen. I'm so sorry.'

I said [deleted].

'An accident, you say,' contributed Mr MacLeod.

'He died of exposure,' I said. [deleted] 'What I'd really like to find out is what he was doing here, at Loch Morar. You see, I had no idea he'd stayed with you. His credit card statement lists payments to the hotels he stayed at on his drive north, but you are not listed. I am guessing he paid cash?'

Mrs MacLeod glanced at her black book again. 'Aye, he paid cash.' She smiled: 'We dinna have a machine for cards, I'm afraid. Payment has to be in cash or by cheque. We tell people that when they book.'

I remembered. 'So you do,' I agreed.

'I think we can help you, dear. About what your father was doing here. He told us [deleted]. He stayed with us two nights, just so that he could spend a day walking along the loch and back.'

'Which is my plan, too. You see I knew he was coming here. He left an itinerary of his route. But I'm still not too sure what exactly it was he was coming back for. I know he'd camped out by the loch years ago when he was a student. He was a geologist, you see. He was doing some research for his degree.'

'Aye, he told us he was a geologist. Isn't that so, Donald?'

'That he did.'

141

Och aye, the Scotch impersonation is top notch, would ye not say, Mack? I'll tack the High Road and ye...

(Exit, pursued by Paul McCartney singing 'Mull of Kintyre'.)

142

'But he said he was here to remember someone. He said he came here once with someone who was very special to him. A woman.

But he didn't say who she was. He just said he was young and in love.'

'That's what he said,' agreed Mr MacLeod.

143

This should be a film script! Do ye not think?

144

This revelation left me confused. I'd assumed my father had been reliving his days here as a student. Coming back to where his future career began, as it were. But evidently this wasn't the case. And then again there was the photograph of him at the lochside. Unless he'd used a self-timer (did they even exist on cameras in the old days?) someone else had taken that photograph. A woman, it seemed.

Alexandra Pendleton, surely. And yet Ivan Jensen said as far as he knew my father had never been to Scotland with her. The perimeters of their romance did not exceed East Anglia.

Had he come here with my mother?

145

Self-reflexive questions. Always best avoided in a narrator.

146

Not as far as I [deleted].

I went to my room and returned with the photograph of my father and the postcard. I showed them the card first.

They smiled, seeing it. 'Aye, that's the card they sell in all the shops from Mallaig to Fort William,' Mrs MacLeod explained.

I asked where it was taken from. 'Above the kirk. Just down the road. You must have passed it on the way here. It's a bit of a scramble up the hill there, mind.'

I put the card away and passed over the photograph.

'This was taken a long time ago. I believe it shows Loch Morar.'

Donald MacLeod stared at it for a while. He nodded. 'This was taken up yonder towards Swordlands.'

'Swordlands?' I'd scrutinised the map of Loch Morar a number of times but not come across that name.

'It's an old hunting lodge. But nobody has shoots round here anymore. That all ended a hundred years ago. The house is empty most of the time. The family who own it come here for holidays, but at most once a year. If you walk along the north shore path you can see it below you, by the lochside. There's a small pier. It's only accessible by boat. I'd say your father's photograph was taken this side of Swordlands.' He jabbed a finger at the image: 'You see the outline of those mountains? That's across from the bay where Swordlands is. I recognise the pattern of the woodland. This picture was taken from the path. Probably from where it turns and goes inland and round the back of the Swordlands estate.'

'That's where I plan to go tomorrow. To walk as far as the point where the picture was taken. To try and find the exact spot.'

Mr MacLeod smiled. 'I doubt you'll manage that. The path twists and turns and follows the line of the bays. I've walked it many times. Your photograph was taken before you reach Swordlands but the precise spot won't be easy to find.'

I smiled. 'I shall do my best. Which reminds me...' [deleted]

147

Mr MacLeod smiled. The writer smiled blankly and bleakly at such smiles. Far too much smiling; far too many behavioural spasms.

148

I slept soundly and woke to my 7.15 alarm.

By eight I was downstairs, tucking into [deleted].

By nine I was on my way. [deleted]

It was a gorgeous day of sunshine and cloudless sky. I walked a short distance along a tree-lined bridleway which was broad enough for a vehicle but embedded with rocks. It soon opened out into a flat grassy space as big as a football pitch. It ran alongside the loch, separated from it by a narrow strip of pebbles. Here, the loch was wide and shallow and surrounded by wooded shoreline and short promontories. The bulk of the loch lay out of sight, beyond a headland. I crossed this deserted green space and walked towards a gravel path on the far side. It curled up around the headland and vanished from view.

Beyond, the path climbed rising ground, looping round miniature ravines cut by streams which bubbled out of the steep, mountainous slopes to the north. From here the path levelled out, following the line of the loch shore along a ledge high above its gleaming surface. On one side the ground fell away sharply, dense with ferns and thistles. On the other it climbed abruptly to a towering line of crags. I suddenly felt very small and insignificant: a human ant, picking my way across a giant's landscape. I was alone in this world, apart from a fisherman far away on the far side of the loch. The tiny buzz of an outboard motor came to me across the still air.

I trudged on for an hour, then paused and sat on a rock and drank coffee from the silver thermos which [deleted]. The slight curvature of the loch meant that I still hadn't reached the point where I could see to the eastern end of this vast trench of water. There was also an island in the distance, very close to the shore but plainly inaccessible, except by boat. It seemed swallowed by vegetation; impenetrable.

Refreshed, I continued along the path. A mile further on I came to the ruins of a croft. Its roof and doors had long vanished. All that remained were four crumbling walls and the blank outlines of windows. This desolate abandoned habitation was lapped by tall weeds. It was a forlorn reminder of [deleted].

The path went on, under a blue sky. A pair of cabbage whites fluttered playfully among the ferns. Bracken surged beyond the tumbledown house, a green wave that dropped sharply to the loch. [deleted] The island slipped away behind me.

Time passed. The fiery sun slowly crossed the sky. The loch

surface was a burning, blinding silver. I walked on, alone on an empty planet. [deleted]

I came to a stark, curving headland of rock and grass and sprigs of heather. The landscape was no longer as lush as it had been before. To my left the slope became less steep and the crags had retreated. I stopped and sat on a chair-sized boulder. There were many such boulders dotting this bleak zone. They'd evidently once rolled down from the cliffs above me. I opened up my Ordnance Survey map of the loch to check where I was. I saw that I was almost at my destination: Swordlands, marked only as an anonymous residence, was less than two miles further on.

Once round the headland I felt my spirits surge. Here, the loch broadened out, with a far wide bay, half lost in heat haze, on the other side. The eastern end of the loch was now visible, some three or four miles distant. It was an area of bare rock and emptiness, inaccessible except by boat or a tough hike across the mountains. The path I was on didn't go that far but swung away after Swordlands, going north to the next loch, which was tidal.

Below me the ground no longer fell away quite as sharply as before, and I could see a ledge of rock which protruded out into the water, like a natural pier. [deleted]

I took out my father's photograph. My pulse quickened excitedly as I recognised the contours of the mountains opposite. I was now very close to the spot where the photograph had been taken.

Another few minutes and I believed I'd found it. I was now standing on a bend in the path, directly above the shallow waters which were bisected by a long, low ledge of rock. A few rocks also protruded through the surface of this miniature harbour. The ground shelved away from the path, but only a little way, and then it softened and fell to the lochside in a series of rounded steps.

I rested my digital camera on one of the large boulders beside the path and set the self-timer. As the camera winked red I hurried back and stood by the strip of turf at the edge of the stony track. I half turned and gazed out across the loch, trying to adopt the same profile as my father.

When I looked at the image in the tiny screen I was pleased

with the result. It wasn't an exact match but the similarities were stronger than the differences. His picture had been taken on a camera which produced prints which were not only square but a lot smaller than the standard 6x4 image you get today. The background wasn't the same, because the lens of the camera used to photograph my father had been a cheap wide-angle one. But it didn't matter. This was definitely the place, more or less. It didn't matter that my own image was much sharper – 12 million pixels – or that it was rectangular. I could play with the image later on my laptop – adjusting the contrast, playing with the colour, cropping it.

Mission accomplished. I felt good. And [deleted],

I decided to [deleted].

Some fifty metres above the path was a sunlit ledge in the heather-coated hillside, with an outcrop of [deleted].

From up here the loch looked deep and black and mysterious. I remembered the legend of [deleted].

By the time I'd finished my lunch and drained the thermos [deleted].

Twenty minutes later I'd scrambled up beyond the [deleted].

Above me the sky was a blue bowl, pouring down warmth. I became aware of a tiny cloud of gnats, jostling above the pool.

I loosened my shoes and [deleted].

I basked there like a drowsy seal, absorbing the radiations of that dying hydrogen star ninety million miles above me.

Forty minutes later [deleted].

I glanced across the plateau and was stunned to see [deleted].

I turned back towards the loch. By the time it came into view the waters had turned a rich blue velvet colour. Streaks of foam corrugated the surface: a wind was sweeping in down the eastern valley. Below me the track I'd walked along was clearly outlined along the lowest ridge beside the loch.

I scrambled back down the steep hillside to this path and set off back to Bracora. In the tranquility of the day's end the wind had dropped and I could hear only the remote whispering of streams as they trickled down between rock.

I walked fast through the fading afternoon and [deleted].

Twenty minutes later I was immersed in a hot bath. My long day was done.

'Did you [deleted].

I left at seven thirty the next morning. There was only one place left to go and my little pilgrimage would then be over.

149

It was the line about seals broken by the lean solicitor which had stayed in the writer's mind for many years.

150

I left early because [deleted].

The roads up the west coast split and loop around lochs and down mountain passes and it isn't always obvious from a map which route is quickest. For these local difficulties, blame what happened long ago. The underlying rock – my father's ghost indicates the word *gneisse* – is overlayered with red Torridonian sandstone. More material was dumped into the mix some 500 million years ago, during Cambrian and Ordovician times. The consequences were problematic for twentieth-century road building and driver choices. From Morar I could go via the Isle of Skye, or head back down to Fort William and then curl back north along the A87 to Loch Duich. From there I would meet up with the Skye route, but then there was another choice – cross at Stromeferry and follow the coast to Shieldaig and Glen Torridon, or carry on along the A890 to Achnasheen. Geology made travel in the highlands like an exercise in existentialism, with endless forking paths and parallel possibilities.

I chose Skye because I liked the idea of it. At that time of the year the ferry was half empty. I parked in the vast grey clattering belly of the vessel and went upstairs to watch the view. There's something exhilarating [deleted].

I'd barely registered the outlines of Skye when an announcement requested that car drivers and passengers return to their deck. Fifteen minutes later [deleted].

The Skye Bridge came into view, stunningly beautiful in its delicate, graceful low arc of metal. It might almost have been a gigantic sculpture by an admirer of Barbara Hepworth.

Crossing the bridge, I suddenly remembered [deleted].

Gavin Maxwell bought a house on a remote part of the Scottish coast and raised an otter. The book he wrote about this experience became a surprise best seller, with phenomenal sales. The success of *Ring of Bright Water* was then reinforced by its adaptation into a successful movie.

In retrospect, the dazzling success of the book was easy enough to understand. First off it was the story of a man and his pet. There's a huge market for a well written and original account of someone's relationship with a cute animal. The Brits are sentimentalists; they like their dogs, cats and squeaky ultramarine budgies much more than they like people. But Maxwell also appealed to a market that had little interest in furry quadrupeds with appealing eyes. *Ring of Bright Water* taps that basic human desire to flee from the urban rat race and escape to a cottage buried away in a tranquil rural setting. This book offered the seductive trance of Shangri-La with a dash of gritty DIY interest.

[deleted] I enjoyed the way Maxwell conjured up the experience of starting a new life in a desolate, mega-weathery spot by raw restless poetical Highland waters. [deleted]

But Maxwell's success was toxic. Having created the image of an idyllic life in a remote Scottish paradise, he was stunned when people worked out where it was located. Fans came knock-knock-knocking on Maxwell's door. His success in promoting his paradise brought about its destruction. It all quite literally went up in smoke. Wealth and fame accelerated the unravelling of his exquisite tranquility. Besides, this paradise was always partial and rested on rocky foundations. Maxwell was [deleted].

Later, as everything began to fall apart, Maxwell moved to a new home on a little island, wisely putting water between himself and any unwanted visitors. That little island had been used for some of the bridge supports for the Skye Bridge. Maxwell's old refuge now looked out on to a vision of motor vehicles passing by.

As I came over the brow of the bridge I caught sight of a whitewashed brick house on the island below. I didn't know if this was Maxwell's or whether there was another house out of sight. But it was in about the right place, overlooking Loch Alsh. Somewhere down that coastline were the ruins of Camusfeàrna and a plaque indicating where the author's ashes were buried. [deleted]

A moment later I was past, and back on the mainland again. The highway unrolled smoothly before me to Glen Carron and beyond. And now [deleted].

The journey, not the arrival, matters. This is a morsel of timeless wisdom which I have never found very appetising. Maybe that's because [deleted].

That last leg of the journey north was spectacular but in the end it was all just scenic wallpaper to what awaited me at the end of it. So let me speed up this narrative, cinema-style. Watch me spring out of the car and jerkily fill it up with fuel in less than a second. Watch oncoming traffic race past fast as meteors and clouds rush across the sky like spilt liquid. Watch place names and signposts flicker past in an unreadable blur. Then let the spinning wheel of fate begin to slow down until it delivers me, like a fictional character in pre-*Finnegans Wake* times, back to everyday chronological rectitude.

After [deleted] by a ragged coastline and along rocky valleys and by bare rolling hillsides I came at last to a big sandy bay. This splash of yellow was a shock after a day of slate hillsides and louring peaks. I'd reached the Kyle of Durness, almost at north-west tip of Scotland.

On that very last stretch of road before the graveyard there were just two things of note. Firstly, a sign ahead which pointed to the left and invited the passing traveller to visit SMOO CAVE. I'd never heard of the place. The thought immediately occurred to me that [deleted].

I instantly dismissed the [deleted]. So I drove on.

151

And two lines earlier: *Which is not to be found in our obituaries.*

152

The traffic had been growing lighter and lighter the further north I went. I was now in a region that was only very lightly populated. There was just the occasional whitewashed house visible in some distant fold of hillside. I was driving for as long as ten minutes before ever seeing another vehicle on the road.

I didn't even notice the motorcyclist until [deleted].

I was oblivious of this presence until [deleted] and when I came round this curve the road ahead was empty.

I'd had the distinct and [deleted]. My father's death had involved no one but himself. At the inquest I'd been quietly impressed by Inspector Donald Bolton. He exuded competence. [deleted]

So I refused to read any significance into what had just [deleted].

I remembered a weekend in Lyme Regis [deleted] two bikers cruising up to the esplanade, getting off their massive machines, and removing their helmets. Underneath those sexy visors were a couple of middle-aged wrinkly male faces crowned by a pair of very bald heads. The two bikers lit cigarettes, stared down at Marine Parade (where Jeremy Irons jumps out of a carriage and runs up some steps in *The French Lieutenant's Woman*), then, having given their lungs a good dose of nicotine-soaked smoke, put their helmets back on and returned to their planet. For those two the journey, not the arrival, really *was* all that mattered.

I drove on without incident. [deleted] came over the brow of the hill and saw the estuary directly ahead of me. It had a silvery glitter against which the bridge to Tongue stood out starkly. [deleted] I was at journey's end.

Next, I [deleted]. I knew I was close because I could see the distant graves, scattered across a green mound half a mile away.

[deleted]

I bounced along the rough single-track road to the cemetery gates. To my surprise and dismay there was another car parked there. I'd expected the graveyard to be [deleted].

I parked and entered the cemetery. There was a solitary male figure with his back to me, standing by the final row of graves by the drystone wall which overlooked the estuary. I paused, searching for the obelisk beside which my father had died. Its whereabouts were easy to locate: it was the biggest gravestone in the cemetery, just fifty yards ahead of me, rising above the much smaller graves around it. Some of them were shaped like tables.

I walked across the springy, uncut grass towards it. The memorial was dedicated to the memory of [deleted]. A loving wife and a dutiful mother. The inscription, set in lead, was cut into the plinth at the base. [deleted]

I was now standing at the exact spot where [deleted] In one direction was the estuary and the rising hillsides on the far side, on the other the moor across which I'd just driven. It was starkly beautiful, a landscape stripped down to its fundamentals. A good, if lonely place to die, I supposed.

I stood there, still perplexed about what had brought my father here. He had planned to come – that much was obvious from his itinerary. But what lay behind this as the terminus of his last journey was obscure. It surely couldn't be [deleted]. My last, flimsy hope was that the relevant Alexandra Pendleton would respond to one of my letters or emails, and that she might know. But it was a forlorn [deleted]. I felt numbness merged with melancholy. I'd come all this way but there was no Rosetta Stone to decipher the barrier to understanding.

And then I knew someone was behind me. [deleted]

And then I saw who it was.

153

Drawing on a lifetime of John Braine's experience both as a writer and a book reviewer, this book has become established as a classic guide and manual, it said on the back of his copy of *Writing a Novel.* The clue to a best-seller, the writer read, is a well-constructed story. Every line must have a hook planted to lead the reader on to the next, every chapter must end with a surprise, a predicament, a big hook. Lines and hooks. The writer reflected that it sounded a lot like fishing.

154

[deleted] he said. 'So you have come here after all.'

It was Inspector Boston, the cop from the inquest. It took a moment to recognise him out of uniform. But there was no mistaking that blazing red hair or the deep, slightly gruff voice.

I [deleted].

'Let me show you something,' he said. He let go and [deleted]. He went up to a gravestone which looked fairly new. A vase in front of it held a single red rose. Boston said nothing. He simply pointed at the inscription. [deleted]

The enormity of my error hit me with the force of an explosion. I stared, appalled, at the grave and at the perfect red rose. A trick of the fading sunlight made it seem to shine from within.

[deleted] I said. 'I'm [deleted].

fuelled by an explosive combination of extreme fatigue, stress and an empty stomach. I hadn't eaten anything since leaving Morar, surviving on coffee.

I swayed, and my vision turned milky. The world vanished behind a membrane of whiteness. 'I've gone blind,' I said thickly. Then my legs folded beneath me and I collapsed.

155

That had once happened to the writer. In Africa. At the start of the long aftermath.

156

He [deleted].

The day was going in a last spill of bronze light across the waters.

He [deleted]

As we crossed the causeway I saw that the sun had finally slipped out of sight. [deleted]

I followed Don Boston into his house. We went down the hall to a spacious kitchen at the back of the house. He flicked on the lights and I sat down on a chair while he boiled a kettle.

'I hope you don't mind Earl Grey.'

I managed a [deleted].

'Fiona was a great reader,' he said wryly.

'And you?'

'Not much. A bit of non-fiction. War books. Biographies. I read novels on holiday.'

'Is that her?' There was [deleted].

157

It is impossible to forget but it is possible to attempt not to look back. This requires effort. Remember Eurydice. She lived on in darkness. Orpheus was ripped apart. He sang of his loss as he drifted away down the river, bodiless. But he must in the end have grown weary of his laments. Better to focus on the water ahead and attempt to find something to take your mind off her.

158

Twenty minutes later [deleted].

While he was gone I'd [deleted].

Titles like *Bomber Harris: His Life and Times* and *Berlin: The Downfall* obviously belonged [deleted] to find me holding a copy of *Scapa, Scalpel, Skull.*

[deleted]

This was disingenuous of me. I remembered that last post card. *Sorry,* [deleted].

'Find the happiness, then.'

'Eh?' [deleted]

'Find the happiness he lost. Maybe he [deleted].

'*Le Grand Meaulnes.*'

Don frowned. 'Doesn't ring a bell, to be honest. I was thinking of that huge book about a cake. The one where he remembers everything.'

'Ah, you mean [deleted].

'That's the man.'

'I have to confess I've [deleted].

159

Ozark, start of the fourth season. By now several major characters have been despatched. The teenage daughter seems strangely uninterested in boys or sex.

160

When I woke sunlight was luminous on the ochre [deleted].

The green of the lower hills seemed emerald in intensity. The shining ridges higher were metallic, edged with silvery light. I don't even remember [deleted] the tarmac fraying at the edges. There was a rust-pitted sign that pointed to [deleted].

a scoop of land [deleted] a loch, an ebony strip with a road along the eastern side and a belt of woodland along the opposite shore. It [deleted] the valley ended in a steep, boulder-studded hillside.

[deleted] descended to the loch, which gleamed like varnished wood in the cold sunlight. Its depths seemed infinitely mysterious.

The road [deleted] a field of grass and the ruins of a croft. The southern edge of this rough, abandoned field was lined by ivy-clad yew trees. They leaned a little, misshapen by the wind. Here, a cattle grid was embedded in the road. Beside the grid a sign [deleted] some billowing green rhododendrons [deleted] a grey, square mass of stone crowned with slender Disneyish towers at each corner. [deleted] a pair of terraces with battlements. [deleted]

'It's a Victorian businessman's dream of what a Scottish castle should look like. Built to order in 1870. A completely fake medieval castle. But not [deleted].

The [deleted]. A wintry sun poked its silver light between the horns of a pair of stone unicorns embedded amid that ornamental crust. Its beam was too high to penetrate the well of coldness formed by the enclosing mass of stonework. I shivered and [deleted].

lined with paintings of deer in rugged poses against mountain scenery. It was a room filled with clutter which included, oddly, a spinning wheel. Tall silver-grey mirrors, oval in shape, reflected the blazing logs [deleted].

[deleted]
'You'll see what I mean in a minute.'
[deleted]
The sequence of gardens ended at a door set in a high brick wall. [deleted] hauled me up to a wide ledge dimpled with tiny pools.
'Careful,' he said. [deleted]

Lunch was [deleted].
Time [deleted]
pressed the button of the CD player.
Rod Stewart. *Vagabond Heart*.
Good choice.

161

The Observer's Book of Trees, compiled by Herbert L. Edlin (Frederick Warne & Co Ltd.) Printed in Great Britain by Butler & Tanner Limited, Frome and London. Containing brief annotations on two separate pages, in two different hands. The first: 'pp. 61-63 – Cavendish Ave'. The writer recognises his own handwriting. The pages refer to the entry for Rowan; *Sorbus aucuparia*. It is widely planted in suburban gardens. The juicy berries ripen rapidly through shades of green to scarlet, and in September the birds start to strip them from the tree. Two pages later, in another hand: 'Lest you forget the horse-chestnuts in the Lake District'. Preceding, in the same handwriting, a month and year and a single capital letter. The writer looks at the entry for this tree but there are no annotations or any underlining. The dedication puzzles him. He cannot now remember any horse-chestnuts in the Lake District or what their significance might have been.

162

That night, lying in bed, I [deleted].

Her books were still lined up on the shelves, as if awaiting her return one morning to pick out one of those novels with wrinkled spines, renewing the outlines of half-forgotten characters and a prize-winning event-packed plot which had dissolved shortly after she'd read [deleted]. The blunt fact was inescapable and heavy. This was a Fiona-haunted household and [deleted].

My flight left Wick at 16.30 next day, so [deleted] a fine, pine-scented morning with ragged clouds rushing across a blue sky. A strong wind made the grass on the hillsides shimmer and move like water. Sometimes we [deleted]. Joan Osborne, then The Motels.

Towards the end of our journey [deleted] diversion along a B road north of Loch Scarmclate. [deleted]

This road was narrower and followed an older route across the moorland, occasionally dipping down into hollows and curving round extrusions of rock. Moine rock. The alchemy of time had turned sand and mud from an ancient ocean into these toothy obstructions. At moments like this I felt truly like my father's daughter: I could decipher landscape.

A phrase flashed in my mind: *this vegetable bondage of blood*. A gleaming fragment lodged in the thick residue of a literary education. Pound, was it? I couldn't remember.

163

I couldn't remember. Neither could the narrator's narrator. And why a B road north of Loch Scarmclate? The writer had never been near Loch Scarmclate in his life. He must have been looking at one of his old Ordnance Survey maps. Local colour. Narrative authority. As for the literary quotation. He put it into DuckDuckGo, which instantly vomited 'Commission' by Ezra

Pound. A fine poem, he thought, reading it. (Re-reading it, presumably.) *Go to them whose failure is concealed...* Painfully apt, he thought.

164

As we drove, we [deleted].

When it happened it happened without warning. The car came towards us, head on. The [deleted].

There was a moment which seemed to stretch itself out forever, as if time had the texture of rubber. The [deleted].

The overheated narrative of an impact stayed long enough in my mind [deleted].

That, at least, is the pattern of perception which fallible slippery memory afterwards pressed upon that hot awful flashing moment. Death [deleted] I'd be like the man floating in the pool at the start of *Sunset Boulevard*. [deleted]

No, not *Sunset Boulevard*. Better a trick ending, like 'An Occurrence at Owl Creek Bridge'...

But [deleted].

I winced as [deleted] smacking and slithering along that pitiful slender stretch of indifferent vegetation. I distinctly noticed a giant grey thistle. It rushed at me and slapped my window. Then it broke into fragments. Now everything was moving very fast again, in a colourless world. The [deleted].

And the verge was grey and coarse.

And the moor was white as snow.

And the road ahead was an ebony curve.

165

The writer roamed the internet, using the words 'Ezra Pound'. Pound was proceeding by poetic intuition, and who knows, wrote Christine Brooke-Rose in her *ZBC of Ezra Pound*, now long out of print, his may be the only comprehensible poetry to the twenty-first century, a century she saw little of, at the end, for several years paralysed and blind, dying of a degenerative disease of the nervous system, departing this earth on 21 March 2012, in Cabrières d'Avignon, her prediction unfulfilled of a new economic order, unimaginable, emerging from what she then described as the present apparently irreconcilable dogmas, her final novel *Life, End of* narrated by an octogenarian, Facing death, she considers her experiments with narrative and with the narrative of her life, it says on the cover. It may be, for that matter, she wrote in her *ZBC*, a post-McLuhan age, an age of mixed media and ideogrammic thinking in quick cuts, when we may all be speaking Chinese.

166

[deleted] and the tyre tread gripped the smooth calm untroubled surface. We slowed and [deleted].

I opened the window and sucked in some cool crisp Highland air. I said dryly: [deleted].

Somewhere out there on the moor a bird began a wild, grieving cry. I had no idea what sort of bird it was. The lineaments of landscape I understood; not the creatures that crawled or skipped or flew across it.

We drove on.

167

A tiny pocket-sized paperback, with a green cover. *The Rubáiyát of Omar Khayyám*. Edward Fitzgerald. Illustrations by Edmund J. Sullivan. Bard Books, published by Avon Book Division, The Hearst Corporation, 575 Madison Ave. – N. Y. 22, N. Y. An early gift. With three small homemade bookmarks inserted in the body of the book. The first inserted at Quatrain XI – an irregular rectangle of paper, with an inked-in blue arrow pointing downward at the illustration. It shows a bearded man sat on a grassy hillside, with his arm around the waist of a woman with long dark hair. He is holding a book. Before them a bottle of wine in a basket lies on the ground. A second slip of paper is inserted at Quatrain XX, with an inked-in blue question mark. In the illustration the woman is pouring wine into a drinking horn, which the bearded man is holding out. A third slip of paper is inserted at Quatrain LXXIII, with nine blue dots. The illustration shows a globe containing stars and a crescent moon, surrounded by strings of cloud. The globe floats between a giant human hand and a descending giant fist. In the background are many twinkling stars. The writer wonders whether to throw the book away. He decides to keep it for the present.

168

Back in London there was a message waiting for me. And thankfully it wasn't [deleted].

Dear Jane

I am so sorry to hear about your father Jon's death. It's a great shock, to be honest – even though we hadn't seen each other in decades. We were very close at one time.

You say you'd like to meet me to find out more about his life in those days. I'm very happy to see you but I must warn you that I live in France and hardly ever visit the U.K. If you feel like flying out to Nice for a chat I'll suggest some suitable dates.

Very best wishes,

Alexandra Pendleton

P.S. [deleted]

I clicked on the British Airways website and discovered that there were several flights a day to Nice [deleted].
 I emailed back immediately:

Dear Alexandra

[deleted]

The reply came thirty minutes later [deleted].

And so the matter was decided. I booked a Friday evening flight and two nights in a hotel in the city centre, returning Sunday afternoon. I thought I might as well see a bit of Nice, apart from interrogating my father's ancient *amour*.

[deleted]

'Darling Jane!'

[deleted]

'Don't be ridiculous, Blanche,' I said. 'Nothing happened. Nothing at all.'

[deleted] as wary of each other as two characters in a Jane Austen novel. The pace of our [deleted].

So instead I chattered away about Norwich and Harrogate and the beauty of the highlands, and how once I'd reached the cemetery [deleted]

That week I also had lunch with Ivan Jensen. He, too, was keen to hear how I'd got on in Scotland. With him I was more open [deleted].

'I've also heard from Alexandra Pendleton. *The* Alexandra Pendleton. She was [deleted].

'Give my regards to Alexandra,' he said as he left. He added with a dry smile, 'Assuming she remembers me.'

169

Years later, soon after his marriage, the writer visited the grave of Edward Fitzgerald. A pink marble slab. As he gazed at it three small frogs appeared beside it and attempted to jump it. Their webbed feet desperately tried to get a grip on the smooth sloping side and failed. They fell back into the grass and hopped away. Another year, while travelling in Norfolk, the writer went into a second-hand bookshop in Burnham Market. For £20 he obtained *Letters and Literary Remains of Edward Fitzgerald*, in three volumes, edited by William Aldis Wright. Pubished by Macmillan and Co, London and New York, 1889. Once the possession of G. C.

Moore Smith, who had written his name in black ink, and underneath: July 1890, Cambridge. The internet supplied a skeleton biography. George Charles Moore Smith (3 September 1858 – 7 November 1940) was an English literary scholar. He graduated from St John's College, Cambridge, with a first-class degree in the classics in 1881. He was then employed as an extension lecturer for the University of Cambridge. In 1896 he was made Professor of English Language and Literature at Firth College, Sheffield, and he played a key role in building up the social and academic position of the institution after it became the University of Sheffield in 1905. He retired in 1924. He was the university's honorary librarian from 1896 to 1907, and amassed over 10,000 works for its collections. He was elected a fellow of the British Academy in 1933. He edited *College Plays Performed in the University of Cambridge* (1923), which includes a chronological table of the Latin plays performed by scholars at the university in the sixteenth and seventeenth centuries. The study also contains Moore Smith's 48-page introduction along with an appendix of actor lists. So. He was 31 or 32 when he bought this copy of *Letters and Literary Remains of Edward Fitzgerald*.

170

It rained all that week in London. The kerbstones shone like marble. I went to and fro to Bloomsbury with a new spring in my step, walking a little faster than normal. I felt that my long quest was nearly over. Alexandra Pendleton would have the answers I needed. I bought a couple of traveller's guides to Nice and familiarised myself with the city's streets, geography and attractions.

I travelled light [deleted].

The two-hour flight was uneventful. I listened to music on my headphones (the Webb Sisters, Sigur Rós) and dozed to the thrum of the engine. France passed far below, between wisps of cloud, a patchwork of remote shadowy obscure settlements and quilt-like fields.

Finally we moved over a band of brown baked empty wastes cut and patterned by curling and branching tributaries. The jet turned away and dipped, then abruptly tilted over the silver-splashed Mediterranean.

Nice Airport was almost as quiet as Wick, with hardly anybody around and wide hushed walkways and plate glass walls through which sunlight laid blazing spiky patterns across putty-coloured flooring. The visitor controls for a flight from Heathrow were perfunctory and swift.

The heat hit me the moment I was out of the building.

I did what the guidebooks advised. I bought a ticket for the airport bus to the city centre. It was already waiting in an adjacent bay. I joined the seven other passengers and after five minutes the driver started the engine and set off along the coast road.

The day was rapidly ending and the vanishing sun put a bronze sheen out there where the sky met the Bay of Angels. The road followed the curve of the bay and I gazed out at girls in shorts, roller skating along the promenade. The seafront cafés were busy with people lingering over drinks, engrossed in conversation. Then, glancing at my map, I saw that my stop was coming up. I stood and walked to the front of the bus.

My hotel was three blocks from the seafront. Dragging my tiny suitcase on wheels, I went through a small park and down a street lined with fashion shops. [deleted]

At the end I entered a pedestrianised area full of bars and restaurants. My hotel, named after an American president, was on the far side. I checked in, then went out for a meal. Returning to the restaurants I was startled by how many offered pizzas as a main course. It didn't gel with my previous experience of France. But then I remembered what the guide books had said: Nice was close to the border with Italy. It had Italian aspects, not least where cooking was concerned. So I submitted to the culture and went into one of the restaurants. I sat outside, sheltered by a polythene curtain that separated the table area from the street. I had a pizza with a generous topping of cheese and ham, and a Savoy salad. I washed it down with a small bottle of lager. Then I returned to the hotel for a bath and an early night.

Next morning, after a breakfast of croissants, jam and coffee, I went out. First, I located the restaurant Alexandra had chosen for our rendezvous. It was only five minutes' walk from the hotel. Then I strolled on to the Avenue Jean Médicin, which is Nice's version of London's Oxford Street – but without the traffic. I browsed in clothes shops and bought myself a couple of scarves. Then, wandering around the side streets, I came across a large bookshop and [deleted].

My meeting with Alexandra was fixed for 12.15. I arrived ten minutes early and took my time reading the menu, furtively consulting my pocket dictionary from time to time. In creaky French I explained to the waiter (whose jet-black curly hair and boisterous manner momentarily reminded me [deleted].

The restaurant had looked nondescript from outside – dark dull windows, a gloomy interior, and some sooty pot plants flanking the entrance – but inside it was spacious, with ivy threaded across trellised panels and large brightly-coloured Ali Baba pots. When I'd entered there were just two tables occupied but already it was starting to fill up. Alexandra had said it was very popular – and it was a Saturday.

I'd chosen a seat which gave me a view of the entrance, and having finished with the menu I focused my gaze there. At exactly 12.15 a woman came in alone, who I guessed at once was Alexandra Pendleton. She glanced round the room, saw me, and came over.

Even though we'd never met, I knew it was her and she knew it was me.

She still looked like the woman in the photograph Ivan had given to me. She was tall and slender and still had long jet-black hair that dropped to her shoulders. But the hippy look was gone. Now she was very chic: she wore a navy-blue pleated skirt that ended just above her knees, with a matching jacket. A small silver broach displaying a pair of intertwined roses was pinned to her lapel.

'You must be Jane,' she said. 'In fact, I know you're Jane. You have a quite remarkable resemblance to your father. Jon had those eyes, you know. Your father [deleted].

When the waiter had gone she leaned closer: 'Tell me about

your father's death. I looked up his obituary on the net. It didn't say what he'd died of. It always maddens me when obituaries are like that. Not AIDS, I hope.'

'Goodness,' I laughed. 'Nothing like that.'

I gave her a very brief account of [deleted]. 'He liked to be alone. Solitude never bothered him. He used to say that rock reminded him of bone. Geological formations were the planet's skeleton. You could read the history.' [deleted]

Alexandra nodded. 'I remember. I suppose you know we lived together for a year. He was always making me laugh.'

She looked thoughtful, remembering. 'We used to lie in bed on Saturday afternoons watching *Star Trek*.'

After another pause, she said sharply: 'What sort of accident?'

I stared into the pale lemon-coloured depths of my Picpoul de Pinet. 'He was found dead in a graveyard in the north of Scotland. He died of exposure. It seems he drank a lot of whisky, swallowed some painkillers, and lost consciousness. It was a bitterly cold night and he wasn't found until the next morning.'

'That's awful.'

'The verdict was death by misadventure. The pills weren't enough to kill him. And there was no note. And before he went away he seemed just the same as he always did.'

Alexandra gulped her wine. She looked upset.

I added: [deleted].

Alexandra said in a low voice. 'When things were a bit rocky between us, I was the one who went off to see a shrink. I remember Jon was very much against it. He said psychiatry was a lot of nonsense. I think he was probably right. I was depressed [deleted].

I took out the blue folder from my bag and opened it. 'I wanted to show you these, Alexandra. To see if they mean anything to you.'

Firstly, I showed her the photograph taken at Loch Morar.

She held it up and looked at it closely. 'Yes, that's dear Jon. Looking just as I remember him. But do you know where the photo was taken? It looks like Switzerland.'

'Scotland, actually.'

'Of course. Silly me. The hills are far too low and rounded for Switzerland. It looks gorgeous, though. Whereabouts in Scotland?'

I told her.

She said it must have been after they went their separate ways. 'I never went to Scotland with Jon. In fact, we never went anywhere outside Norfolk. In those days the world was a much bigger place.' [deleted].

She recognised the second photograph. 'That's Norwich! That cobbled street, what was it called? Elm Street? Yes, Elm Street.'

'Elm Hill.'

She mock-tapped her head. 'Old age kicking in again.'

'Did you take the photo?' I asked.

'Me?' Alexandra scrutinised the photo more closely. 'I don't think so. In fact. I'm sure I didn't. We never used to go to Elm Hill. It was a touristy sort of street. There was nothing there for us. No pubs, for a start. Just shops selling souvenirs and antiques and stuff like that.'

She continued gazing at the picture. 'What *is* Jon wearing? He didn't have a leather coat like that when I knew him. He used to go round in a long black coat he bought in an Oxfam shop. It went down almost to his ankles. Very fashionable that gear was – the retreat from Moscow. Napoleon's I mean...'

I wasn't getting anywhere with the photographs, so I produced the itinerary. I passed it across to her. I explained what it meant.

[deleted] 'And a part of me was deeply hurt when Jon married your mother. You see I really wanted to marry him myself back then. That was before I discovered who I really was. So I suppose if I'm honest my silence was a sort of punishment. Revenge. Stupid really.'

She was talking fast, gulping down her wine in a way that reminded me of Blanche. She seemed a little wired. She continued: [deleted].

'That address on Earlham Road. Did you also live there?'

Alexandra picked up the list again and glanced at it. 'Doesn't mean a thing, I'm afraid. I never lived on that street, neither did your father.' She fell silent, thinking. And then: 'Number 137... No, sorry. It rings no bells.'

That seemed a bit odd. I thought the [deleted].

'And 44 Cavendish Road?' I asked. 'And Harrogate and Bracorina and the graveyard at Tongue? Don't these places mean something to you?'

Her frown deepened. 'Not a thing, sorry. I told you – I never went to Scotland with Jon. And Harrogate doesn't mean a thing. Yorkshire, isn't it? N3 – isn't that Hampstead?'

'Finchley,' I said. I felt a sudden bitter [deleted].

And then we'd drunk our coffees, settled the bill, and it was time to go. It was only then that I remembered something. 'Ivan sends his best wishes. Ivan Jensen – dad's great friend. Remember him?'

She did. Though the Ivan she described (long blond hair down to his collar, tight blue velvet trousers with bell-bottoms, a string of bright beads around his neck) was very different – comically different – to the one I'd ever known.

And then [deleted].

I formally shook hands with [deleted] exchange Christmas cards and make promises to visit – promises [deleted].

171

'There is a small house at Grasmere empty which perhaps we may take, and purchase furniture but of this we will speak,' wrote Wordworth to his sister Dorothy.

172

The rest of that weekend I remember as bright and empty. I walked through a crowded Saturday market and turned off through an archway that led to the Quai des Étas-Unis. I went up to the park overlooking Nice and admired the fabulous view across the great curving bay. The Baie des Anges glittered under a cloudless sky. Somewhere behind me, beyond a coppice, children were shouting and laughing. I passed a lawn where three slow, serious men were doing Tai-Chi. I sauntered along a quiet path under the trees and came to a wide, shimmering waterfall. It tumbled thirty or forty feet down a wall of rock into a kidney-shaped pool.

A light breeze lifted the spray and wafted it across the path. I paused, waiting for the chance to dart across the wet patch without being splattered. A voice behind me started talking French. I turned and found myself face to face with [deleted].

I walked on, along a pathway dappled with dancing shadows.

I came out of the park and encountered the gates to a graveyard. It was the city's old Jewish cemetery. At the entrance stood a small stone temple dedicated to Nice's victims of the Holocaust. I deciphered the inscriptions, then slowly followed a gravel path round the white graves.

Some of the tombs had photographs embedded in them. Cypress trees in the distance stood stark against the perfect sky like frozen dark green flame. A plaque on then perimeter wall commemorated a nineteen-year-old, executed by the Germans in 1944. The horror seemed muted, remote. One of the tombs was cracked, with a dark hole at the base as if an animal used it for passage. I walked out of that place and descended a zig-zag road to the harbour.

There, I stared across at yachts and cabin cruisers which seemed to be in a competition for size. Some of them looked as if they'd be more at home in a James Bond movie. Then I made my way back into Nice. I took the advice of my travel guide and walked to the theatre to take a look at the sculpture of the Loch Ness monster. An odd thing to have outside a municipal French theatre... I was disappointed. I was hoping for a big, lifelike plesiosaurus. This creature looked nothing like Nessie at all. With its silver flanks, spiky head and strange surrealistic torso it resembled a jaunty, playful dragon.

By now I was feeling tired. I plunged into the city's old quarter for coffee. I passed a perfume shop and bought a bottle for Blanche.

The next morning was just as sunny, every bit as bright. I checked out of the hotel and took a bus out to the *Le Musée Matisse*. I walked through a square of olive trees to the entrance.

The gallery had just opened and I was one of only a handful of visitors. I strolled the big empty rooms. Some of the paintings were familiar from posters. Other exhibits were a surprise, like the thick, chocolate-coloured bronze bodies with massive buttocks. I bought a book about Matisse and then went to a café in the adjacent park for coffee. After that I went back into the centre of Nice for an early lunch. After that it was time to catch the airport bus along the seafront. After that, after that – this was my life, I [deleted].

deep down I wasn't sure I really liked Matisse all that much. His work seemed too simple, too child-like in its lines and colour. It was charming and sinuous and pleasant, but it lacked the depth and hard-edged complexity of those painters I really liked: Ernst, say. Or de Chirico. Or Peter Doig...

Watching Nice recede through the bus window I felt acutely the hollow in [deleted].

As the Mediterranean slid from sight and the droning throbbing 727 turned north, nosing its way back to Heathrow through a belt of dull grey cirrus, I thought: [deleted].

173

The Dove and Olive Branch was a small inn. Later it became a residential property. When Wordsworth lived in the house it had no name at all. The poet died in 1850. In 1889 an admirer named Stopforde Brooke successfully campaigned to have the property purchased as a literary shrine, open to the public. It was renamed Dove Cottage.

174

At the end of the week I once again headed down to Warblington for another mammoth clear-out. Soon [deleted].

Ivan and Miranda drove down on Saturday morning and [deleted].

Over supper I told them about my meeting with Alexandra Pendleton.

[deleted]

In my heart I knew I was [deleted].

The agent Samuel Hole had [deleted].

I was excited to be working with [deleted]. I'd read his first novel and, like most other people, been blown away by it. *Nowhere* is the story of a man who, lying in the bath one day, notices a brown stain on the ceiling. Mysteriously, it prompts a complete nervous collapse. The man breaks up with his girlfriend and retreats into total isolation in a crumbling hotel on the coast of County Galway. There he reads *Finnegans Wake* and plots to assassinate a notorious royal prince. The twist at the end reveals that he is actually in prison, sentenced to life for murdering his brother, a famous Joyce scholar.

The book [deleted].

I'd been deeply disappointed by his follow-up novel, *Brighton Dome*. Reviews had been polite but tempered by a sense that the promise of *Nowhere* (a truly original and strangely compelling read) had not really been fulfilled. In *Brighton Dome* a university physicist whose student girlfriend is writing a thesis on James Joyce discovers a new method of rocket propulsion. He plans to take her on a trip to the moon. It was supposed to be a comedy, but there were few laughs, and the analogy between experimental physics and Joyce's modernism was, at best, laboured.

The third book, *Zoo Ooze*, features an incestuous time-travelling brother and sister who work at the Vienna Zoo. The book – almost 600 pages long – is a compendium of bizarre adventures threaded around the history of zoos over the past two hundred and fifty years. Sigmund Freud puts in a number of appearances. *Zoo Ooze* features lots of kinky [deleted]. McCartney had the good fortune to have his book labelled 'depraved and disgusting' by the *Daily Express*'s pugnacious columnist, Bryony Flappe. She'd frothed that the book was [deleted].

I found the book disappointing. *Zoo Ooze* tries desperately hard to shock – there are some graphic descriptions of the hero's penis being inserted into a variety of [deleted] and the empurpled prose struck me as being less Joycean [deleted]. I was inclined to agree with the reviewer in the *San Fernando Times* who caustically commented, 'McCartney's tropes are desperate and his slack prose is encrusted with a showy vocabulary drawn not from the mouths of living people but from a desiccated pedant's dictionary. *Zoo Ooze* is not nearly so experimental and daring as it likes to think it is. It is little more than a Victorian novel slickly re-imagined and updated by someone with a literature degree who has their eye firmly fixed on the bestseller lists.'

[deleted]

So it was with some trepidation that [deleted].

I desperately wanted *Impossible State (of Longing)* to be as good as *Nowhere*. The book had the benefit of brevity, and was about the same length as [deleted]. The book was pitched at the American market and was set in an unnamed U.S. city on the edge of a desert. A couple's relationship founders as a strange paralysis afflicts them. The wife stops going to work and spends her days stretched out on a day bed. She gives up on her house and garden and all the chores. The husband struggles to his office each day but finds himself staring at a dead computer screen. In the evenings they send out for takeaways. The town's population thins and starts to disappear. The husband gives up going to work. Their garden becomes overgrown with weeds. Sand starts to seep in through the doors and cracked windows. It rises up around their ankles. Their days become filled with dreams and fantasies. In the end they die, naked, in bed, lapped by soft white sand.

[deleted] had been reading J.G. Ballard. The arid, desolate landscape and the theme of inertia seemed oddly familiar. The writing was more powerful than his previous two books. But what was lacking was human interest and engagement.

[deleted] I met up with him at the London venue of his choice – the vintage bar at the top of Centre Point. It's all leather and chrome and walnut veneer up there. The décor and the strip-lighting make it feel like being in a museum – or a Swinging Sixties movie. [deleted]

I stared out. That day the top of the tower block (tall by West End standards – puny by New York's) was swathed in low, fuzzy cloud. It was like looking out of a dirty train window. The British Museum was a briefly glimpsed dark lump embedded in some blurred netting. Clumps of weed dotted the bed of this murky waste.

[deleted] was plumper than in the publicity photograph used for the dustjacket of *Nowhere*. That shows a slim man, casual but smart, with a lean, intelligent face. With a striped silk scarf draped around his neck and a snappy open neck shirt, he looks like a university lecturer. But then that was what for many years he'd been. Hence all the intimidating jargon he was prone to use in interviews – dissonance, diachronic, dialectical. With his fondness for abstruse words beginning with 'd', he was, aptly, a Derridean. [deleted]

Successful sales had taken their toll. [deleted]

Impossible State (of Longing) was about [deleted] but its theme of human paralysis struck me as being not unconnected to McCartney's own physical state. He must have put on two stones since his first novel. The once handsome face was now a little puffy, with a double chin starting to take shape below the firm jaw. A network of fine but very distinct veins was beginning to manifest in those pink cheeks. And somebody needed to tell Jonathan to trim his [deleted].

He'd let himself go. When his jacket moved I noted a small yellow stain on his [deleted].

175

They shared a voracious and eclectic love of books, a gift for serpentine sentences, and an addiction to opium.

176

[deleted] charm lasted another twenty-four hours. At the reading in Bath he was fluent, amusing, self-deprecating. He toned down the Derrida [deleted]. He spoke of the influence of *Ulysses*, which he described as a patterned narrative, marvellously textured, like embroidery. The implication that he was James Joyce's only true successor was nuanced, discreet, wry. *Impossible State (of Longing)* was an homage to modernism, he asserted. Afterwards

[deleted].

The issue of his probity had again been raised by his claim to have been a student of Jacques Derrida. This [deleted].

I had the strong sense that he'd never again produce something as innovative and compelling as *Nowhere* and I felt that his obvious lust for popularity and commercial success was sapping and dissipating his artistic integrity and talent. But [deleted].

The next evening [deleted].

That explained why Jonathan's socks had been slid over the smoke detector on the ceiling, like condoms.

He [deleted].

As my heart settled like the debris of a sinking ship hitting the ocean bed I could suddenly see the funny side of things. [deleted] I said.

I left him to process the meaning of this remark using his multi-tasking *I'm All Right Jacques* approach to discourse.

177

3 October 1837. News – news I must seek for news. My own thoughts are a wilderness – News then is my resting place – news! News! The Doves behind me at the small window – the laburnum with its naked seed-pods shivers before my window and the pine-trees rock from their base. – More I cannot write so farewell!

178

Back at The Vicarage I [deleted].

inside that uncurling certainty remained a fold of doubt. I was as fastidiously reluctant to acknowledge my heart's tuggings as a Jane Austen heroine. I also lacked [deleted].

I'd started, quite arbitrarily, with her Venice novel and it struck me as entertainingly original – a crime novel without a crime, and a narrative of murderous suspense which fizzles out, mocking the reader's expectation of a violent denouement. Only an accomplished and commercially successful writer could get away with a trick like *that*, I reflected.

Then I read [deleted] for the way it also upset convention. The stalker became the sympathetic object of interest – not his victim. The contrast with one acclaimed contemporary novel about being stalked was marked.

Now I was [deleted] in which a man dreams of murdering his wife. His wife says she needs a break and goes off to Brighton, where she stays under a fake name. There, she is seeing a man, a stranger she barely knows, and quite fancies having a fling with him. Meanwhile her husband's friends and in-laws grow increasingly concerned and suspicious about his wife's disappearance and his very relaxed attitude to her lengthening absence from his life.

I'd bought the old Pan books edition, plucked from the shelves of Judd's in Marchmont Street, the cover of which showed a snub-nosed blonde wrapped in a red tartan blanket, under a wreathe. [deleted]

I woke to the distant repeated soft murmurings of a wood pigeon.

After an early breakfast I [deleted].

dragged an old brown sofa to the end of the garden. It left a scar of broken turf behind it, where a brass castor wheel had gouged the soil. A worm, exposed to sunlight, blindly sought refuge back inside its dark moist ripped-open world.

I dragged the sofa to the circle of ash where other furniture had been burned. I went back to the garage and returned with a can of petrol. I poured the fuel over the seat of the sofa and returned the can. Then, standing back, I tossed a match.

It went out.

Indifferent to my presence, a blackbird appeared nearby. It skipped across the grass and began to take quick sharp stabs at the worm. It was a matter of seconds before the slow, hapless creature was sliced up and swallowed.

I went a little closer. At my fifth [deleted].

This burning, belching mass soon reduced itself to the X-ray of a sofa. Then the structure collapsed, snapping and popping like a breakfast cereal. A nest of black springs lay on the low uneven heap of ash.

I waited until the glowing embers had dulled then walked back to the house.

The Vicarage had gradually been emptied [deleted]. But there was one space I had deliberately left to the end – the loft. Because the ceilings in the vicarage were much higher than in a modern house, it required the taller of his two stepladders to get up into the loft. The hatch itself was a square of wood two feet square, which rested on a frame. To open it all you had to do was push, then slide it to the side as it lifted.

[deleted] What was there was a small mountain of jumble, receding into angular slabs of complete blackness. This loft space was massive. The Victorians built their lofts high, with just a few enormous crossbeams to support the roof joists. [deleted] a single bare bulb which dangled from a crossbeam near the loft hatch. [deleted] From this small, central platform a few narrow walkways of chipboard radiated out into the darkness. Suitcases, boxes, old toys, a sack from which protruded two walking sticks and a striped windbreak, and other miscellaneous clutter could be seen balanced on the joists adjacent to these rudimentary passageways. [deleted]

The air tasted different in that place – very dry. The acoustics were much sharper, too. The noises outside the house pierced the layer of felt and tiles and sounded much louder and nearer. Downstairs, the sound of traffic on the A27 wasn't audible. Up here the unceasing flow of motor vehicles was inescapable – a perpetual distant whine.

A mistle thrush screeching on a tree in the garden sounded as close as if it were with me, somewhere in the surrounding darkness.

I started with the suitcases. There were eight of them. Six belonged to the prehistoric age, when cases didn't have wheels. Some bore old luggage labels; some even had airline baggage tags wrapped around the handles. Geneva, Berlin, Cairo... I recognised my mother's neat handwriting on a tag the colour of sand: *Mr and Mrs J. Tain, The Old Vicarage, Pook Lane, Warblington, Hampshire, England.*

One by one I carried them down. Seven were empty. The eighth, heavier, contained a pair of curtains. I unfolded them and saw that they bore a William Morris pattern – loops of green foliage, exquisitely embroidered stems, crisp lush leaves, oranges which shone with a juicy perfection. I had no [deleted].

The cases I took to the end of the garden and burned.

[deleted] went back up into the loft and took down a heavy cardboard box that just went through the hatch. Opening it downstairs I discovered that it contained some old handbags of my mother's together with ancient copies of *Vogue*. These I also burned.

By now I felt [deleted] David Attenborough was talking about Angolan wildlife during a drought. I watched some footage of cute baby elephants, then catfish thrashing in a pool, then some squabbling eagles. After a while I [deleted].

The clocks. The house was full of clocks, some silent, some ticking loudly, marking off each passing second.

Like as the waves make towards the pebbl'd shore,
So do our minutes hasten to their end.

[deleted]

In retrospect, that afternoon and evening seemed to pass in slow motion – until what happened, happened.

The sun descended behind a yew tree and the shadowed lawn suddenly felt a little chilly. [deleted] and of the agglomerations of cobwebs, hanging down from crossbeams like great lengths of grey, clinging curtain. [deleted]

brought down eight sealed cardboard boxes, my old pink tricycle, a dusty selection of Barbie dolls, a pink carriage and, unexpectedly, an old fishing rod. [deleted] holding up a grey cylindrical container about the same length as the fishing rod. 'I didn't know what it was, even when I opened it. But then I found its companion...'

He held out a box with an open lid. The sticky tape which once sealed it up had dried out and the flaps had popped open. Inside I saw a grey, box-shaped contraption with what looked like a camera lens protruding from one end.

'It's an old eight-millimetre movie projector,' he explained. 'And this is the screen.' He tipped the cylinder so that the screen came slowly out. It was rolled up like a carpet. [deleted]

The technology had collapsed around the time I [deleted].

The day faded out. While [deleted].

179

The literary life. When the poet Charles Lloyd turned up at Dove Cottage he said he was the Devil. Coleridge described him as suffering from *agoniz'd Delirium*. Thomas De Quincey also had Satan on his mind. Never describe Wordsworth as equal in pride to Lucifer, he wrote. No. But if you have occasion to write a life of Lucifer, set down that by possibility, in respect to pride, he might be some type of Wordsworth.

180

'Try not to show you look surprised,' I said as I entered the dining room. 'In fact try to look as normal as possible. The thing is [deleted].

'Now don't forget. Be ready to open the window. And have your phone in your hand.'

He stood and left the room.

[deleted] The passing seconds seemed like hours. A clock in another room was ticking. Its strokes were piercing.

The window was to my left, a rectangle of blackness. The blackness reflected the ghostly outline of the dinner table.

A tongue of wax slowly dribbled down the side of the candle. The candle was now only half its original height.

The clock ticked.

Nothing happened. Nothing was happening. What was [deleted]. The clock ticked.

The convulsion in the garden, when it came, did not [deleted].

My eyes widened in astonishment.

[deleted] jerked round at my warning. He flicked his head back as the pot came rushing down.

[deleted] helped him drag the big heavy black-panelled machine back through the hedge to the road. [deleted] started the bike and rode away.

181

A Methuen Modern Play paperback. Max Frisch, *Andorra*. Translated by Michael Bullock. Inside, handwritten, the date May 26. Handwritten: 'For...' The writer sees his name. After it a hyphen and the words 'on our third day in London'. And then a signature.

182

We [deleted].
    My heart [deleted].
    But we'd [deleted].
    'Oh, [deleted].

I [deleted].
    Later I [deleted].
    a Mozart CD. The Sonata in A Minor, played by Jean-Bernard Pommier. Another [deleted].
    A long winter was [deleted].

We [deleted].
    The mill pond was full of elegant, aloof swans, going somewhere important. On the estuary side the tide had receded.
    [deleted] looked for Albert Finney, who had a home nearby. There was no sign of the actor. But [deleted] knew it was Finney because this was just after *Skyfall* came out, and [deleted].
    [deleted] emptied it of all it contained – boxes, packing cases, a crate filled with dusty glasses, a bag filled with three old kettles and some extension leads, a bucket containing old dark stained teapots, and other miscellaneous bric-a-brac. [deleted]

[deleted] to open half a dozen of the boxes from the loft. I found old books I'd forgotten I'd ever owned (*How To Draw Like An*

Artist – another Road Not Taken). There were more sets of crockery, more collections of maps, even more teapots. An assemblage of the detritus of lives which were over.

[deleted] The ending wasn't at all what I expected it to be. [deleted]

183

'Through the little gate I pressed forward: ten steps beyond it lay the principal door of the house. To this, no longer clearly conscious of my own feelings, I passed on rapidly; I heard a step, a voice, and, like a flash of lightning, I saw the figure emerge of a tallish man, who held out his hand, and saluted me with the most cordial manner, and the warmest expression of friendly welcome, that it is possible to imagine.' Wrote Thomas De Quincey in that posthumously published assemblage entitled, by one editor, *Recollections of the Lakes and the Lake Poets.*

184

'Good news,' Mike [deleted].

'Okay, so she's nuts. So what? People buy her books. In case you'd forgotten, that's what matters in this neck of the woods. Don't call her mad: call her a contrarian. A controversialist. The Woman Who Really Makes People Sit Up and Take Notice.'

'Why don't *you* go?'

'Because she's nuts. And I'm the boss.'

'Bastard.'

'It's possible. You'd have to ask my mother.'

[deleted]

[deleted] the book that Bryony was promoting. *The Subversion of Culture* was [deleted]. Where was today's George Eliot? Where was the modern Tolstoy? Where was the writing which celebrated simple tales of masculine courage in the face of great adversity? Where were the novels which celebrated marriage?

Bryony was especially scandalised by the publication of *Zombie*

Siege at Northanger Abbey, Emma of the Undead and *Vampire Persuasion*. She compared this treatment of Jane Austen to Cromwell's hoodlums smashing up churches and cathedrals. Bryony had also shrewdly spotted a statistical correlation between local sales of novels about vampires and zombies, and violent crime and teenage drunkenness in Birmingham and other Midland towns. The link was *scientific*.

[deleted]

I turned to the biographical section. [deleted] Bryony had been educated at a girls' school in York and then gone on to Somerville College, Oxford. She was married to Judge Solomon Bellow, who I'd never heard of.

[deleted] Bryony had once, briefly, in her early twenties, been a leading member of the Committee for a Workers' Revolution. This was a Trotskyist faction which had split from Workers Revolutionary Liberation (which had originally split from the International Workers Alliance for Revolution). This shed a little light on [deleted].

I wasn't sure what to expect. Her regular newspaper column indicated someone whose every waking hour was a hurricane of dissatisfaction. The pusillanimous government! The lax treatment of criminals! Drunken teenage girls in short skirts vomiting in town centres on Saturday nights! Mothers who crashed into you in the street with their enormous, anti-social double buggies! The rudeness of waiters and shop assistants!

Bryony's furious dissatisfactions were galactic in scope. Her every day was a hell of imperfection and provocation. Probably even her toaster let her down in the morning.

Or was this all just a façade? I'd met one notoriously outspoken [deleted].

Was Bryony the same? I'd soon find out.

185

The writer remembered who Bryony Flappe was based on. This was one part of this old manuscript he was beginning to enjoy. It had drifted far from his essential subject but as back-story and padding it wasn't too bad, he felt.

186

I realised that the Orlando directors were a little scared of Bryony Flappe. She'd dictated terms for her promotional tour of London which they'd instantly accepted. This was surprising since her sales, though reasonable, weren't up there with the top purveyors of the restless undead, serial killers in Devon, tough lonely men battling sinister global conspiracies in exotic locations, or even Updike-influenced tales of sleek adultery in Kensington. Most of the time, most fiction outsold most non-fiction – except biographies, gardening books and the Highway Code.

I had to meet her at a private dining club near Piccadilly Circus on Tuesday morning at ten. This was less than twenty minutes' walk from the Orlando offices in Bloomsbury, but I allowed half an hour. A good job I did, as it took a while to find the place. The front door to this establishment was a small, nondescript one just off Shaftesbury Avenue, up a drab side street. The clue I'd come to the right place was a small bronze plaque bearing, in a copperplate font, the single word: *Gerard's*. I'd never heard of the place. But this, apparently, was where seriously rich people dined.

I pressed the button and after about thirty seconds a stockily built man in a suit and tie opened the door. He looked like a bruiser. The top of my head just about reached his rib cage.

'I'm meeting Bryony Flappe. She's expecting me.'

He nodded and ushered me inside. Without saying a word, he pointed up a flight of stairs.

It didn't seem particularly posh. The stairway was as bleakly functional and as dull in its décor as the one which led up to Edward Blake's office.

All that changed when I pushed open the door at the top. I stepped into a reception area blazing with light. The décor was silver and red. Mirrors were everywhere, giving a sense of space and depth. There was the reception desk, a cloakroom, a long bar, a zone of sofas and armchairs... Beyond all this, the other side of panelled glass doors, were two separate dining areas.

A woman my own age emerged smiling from behind a kind of lectern. She was dressed in a black smock bearing the word *Gerard's* embroidered in silver, a short black skirt, and black stockings. Her long slim legs were supported by shiny black high-heeled shoes. She was clutching a clipboard. Her smile contained two rows of perfect white teeth.

'I have a meeting with Bryony Flappe,' I said. 'My name is Tain.'

She glanced at her clipboard. 'Thees way, pliz,' she beamed.

I was escorted to a table by a window overlooking Shaftesbury Avenue.

'You like some water?'

No, I did not require that liquid.

Since Bryony hadn't arrived yet I pulled out her book-signing schedule from my handbag and laid it on the table. Then I stared down at the traffic and pedestrians moving along the street below. London was as busy as it always was.

The minutes crawled by.

I kept looking at my phone to check I'd got the time right. I glanced round at the others in the room. It was mostly empty. There were a couple of grey-haired women drinking tea, a young smart couple eating a late breakfast, and a middle-aged man whose face seemed familiar. He was sat at a table having an animated discussion with three smartly dressed young people – an Asian male, a white man in a navy-blue blazer with gold buttons, and a chic young black woman. The Asian guy was tapping something into a laptop.

'Jane! How marvellous to meet you! So sorry I'm late. I had a call from Tokyo. I simply *had* to answer it.'

I sprang to my feet and shook Bryony's hand.

Her entrance had created a stir. I was aware of everyone in the room staring. But then Bryony did have something of an in-your-face image. She was incredibly thin, very tall, and her head was shaven. Originally this had been the consequence of chemotherapy and surgery, but she'd declined to grow her hair again after the cancer and had kept it shaven. She famously said she'd done so on behalf of victims everywhere, especially Jews –

and for all women. Her critics called it 'concentration camp chic'. One prominent *Guardian* journalist commented that she obviously thought she was Joan of Arc.

She was dressed in a silver trouser suit which exactly matched the décor at Gerard's.

Her bare skull was accentuated by her spectacles – circular granny glasses with massive thick black frames. It made her look very distinctive or seriously weird, depending on how you regarded Bryony and her very strong opinions.

As she sat down, the middle-aged man looked across at her, waved and said, 'Hi Bryony!'

She graciously acknowledged his presence. 'Charles! How delightful to see you. Are you well?'

Charles said that he was, and I suddenly realised his identity. He was a member of the Cabinet.

Bryony turned away from this pygmy and focused her terrifyingly fierce eyes upon me.

'I see you have the schedule. Please enlighten me.'

I explained the set-up.

'And these bookshops are aware I require security? I have been subjected to death threats, you know.'

'We are aware of that. And there will be security by the signing table. As well as each bookshop manager, members of staff, and of course I shall be with you the whole time.'

Bryony scrutinised me with a fierce expression. 'Have you done any martial arts training?'

'Actually, no.'

'So you won't be much use, then.'

She looked annoyed. Then she looked across the room and bellowed, 'How much longer are we going to be kept waiting?'

A waiter came running to take our order.

'A large black coffee, for me,' Bryony said. She glared across the table at me: 'And you?'

I settled for a small latte.

When the coffees came, Bryony put three teaspoons of sugar in hers. While she tipped it into her china cup my attention focused on her shaven head, where a small blueish vein had started wriggling above her brow. It resembled a tiny fat worm. I gazed fascinated at its regular pulsing.

Bryony Flappe took some gulps of coffee, then tipped her head forwards, confidentially. Her green piercing irises were enlarged by her thick lenses. The fierce, tight, contracted black pupils targeted me like laser beams. Her face was a rigid mask, the mouth twisted into a scowl. 'You *are* with me on this book, aren't you, Jane? I can't promote it effectively if I feel that the person sitting next to me is unsympathetic.'

'Everyone at Orlando is terribly enthusiastic,' I piped. 'Especially me. It's such an honour to be chosen to accompany you around London.'

Mike would have been proud of me, I felt. *Always be their number one fan*, he kept reminding us.

'Good. That's very good.'

Thankfully she left it at that. I had a horrible suspicion she might start interrogating me about her book, or, worse, about opera. Or even vampire mash-ups...

She glanced at her watch, 'Mercy! Is that the time? I must go.'

She ran off, giving a little wave to the Cabinet minister. He bowed, as if he'd just encountered the Queen.

187

Thomas De Quincey had long nervously dreamed of travelling to William Wordsworth's little house and knocking on the door. Now it was done. He later wrote that at this moment he felt stunned almost with the actual accomplishment of a catastrophe so long anticipated and so long postponed. A *catastrophe*? The writer was a little perplexed by De Quincey's definition of this encounter. Dazed, De Quincey mechanically went forward into the house. A little semi-vestibule between two doors prefaced the entrance into what might be considered the principal room of the cottage, he wrote. It was an oblong square, not above eight and a half feet high, sixteen feet long, and twelve broad: very prettily wainscoted from the floor to the ceiling with dark polished oak, slightly embellished with carving.

Next morning at eleven a black cab took me across town from the Orlando offices near the British Museum to the house in Notting Hill where Bryony lived when she wasn't at their mansion in Dorset or the villa in Tuscany.

Her London home was a four-storey terraced house near Powys Square. A manservant opened the door and advised me that Bryony would be down in a moment.

I returned to the taxi and waited for her.

She came down the steps with an angry expression on her face. I opened the door for her.

'You should have waited for me by the front door,' she snapped. 'You really aren't taking my personal security very seriously, are you, Jane? There are people out there who want to *assassinate* me.'

I glanced up and down the almost deserted street. A woman was pushing a pram. An elderly man was walking his bulldog. A postman with a scarlet cart was delivering the mail.

Bryony watched me watching. Her fury intensified. 'I don't mean that there *is*. I mean that there *might be*. You really do need to be more alert, Jane.'

'I'll certainly try to be, Bryony,' I said brightly, forcing myself to smile at the mad old bat.

Apart from that faux pas on my part the first morning, the Wednesday and Thursday went according to plan. Bryony's signings attracted respectable but not spectacular numbers of book-buyers. I noticed that her fans were almost exclusively male – either ardent young fogeys in tweeds, with a penchant for luminous yellow ties, or elderly, angry men with florid cheeks and check shirts, many of whom forcefully told Bryony that she should be put in charge of the country. Bryony beamed in demure agreement; increasingly she felt that too.

189

'One window there was – a perfect and unpretending cottage window, with little diamond panes, embowered, at almost every season of the year, with roses; and, in the summer and autumn, with a profusion of jessamine and other fragrant shrubs. From the exuberant luxuriance of the vegetation around it, and from the dark hue of the wainscoting, this window, though tolerably large, did not furnish a very powerful light to one who entered from the open air.' (De Quincey)

190

It was on the final day, at the last signing, that the trouble happened. This was at Look on the Book Side, a chic new independent bookstore near Charing Cross. Only twenty-five people had turned up to buy a copy of *The Subversion of Culture* and the bookshop manager looked glum. His attention had drifted away from the signing and he loitered some distance away, talking in a low voice to one of the assistants. This meant Bryony had no one to protect her from prospective assassination apart from the security guard and myself.

While Bryony beside me exchanged pleasantries with a gushing fan and signed his book, my attention focused on the last person in the queue. This was a man of about twenty-five, bearded, wearing faded blue jeans and a black T-shirt. He stuck out for two reasons. The most obvious was his scruffiness. Bryony's fans were people who were invariably smartly dressed and were in daily contact with the concept of grooming. When I intensified my scrutiny, my concern grew. The man's eyes flickered restlessly around the bookstore. He seemed very nervous. There were beads of sweat on his brow.

His copy of *The Subversion of Culture* was held in his left hand, up against his chest, like a shield. His right hand clutched a carrier bag which bulged with something heavy. It was one of those large, sturdy Bag for Life sacks which supermarkets sell at the checkout. Whatever was in the bag seemed heavy – the material swelled out at the base and was stretched and under strain below the handles.

No one else seemed to notice. In the background some Mozart was playing softly. Shoppers browsed the long shelves of brightly coloured spines. It was as soporific as a hot afternoon in the Jardin des Tuileries.

The queue shuffled forward. The security guard was an African male in his early twenties. His gaze seemed fixed on the street outside, where a stream of the world's pedestrians flowed past the big plate glass windows.

'I'm just going to have a word with the security guy,' I whispered to Bryony. I'd decided to get him to ask to see what was in the man's bag. There was no harm in taking precautions.

To my surprise Bryony's left hand sprang forward and seized my wrist. Its impact was a little shocking. Her grip – cold, bony, a little reptilian – was surprisingly strong. I remembered her profile had mentioned her daily workouts.

'Don't leave me,' she hissed.

'I just wanted a word with the security guard,' I whispered back. 'There's a guy in the queue – '

She cut me off. 'You will stay here. By my side. That is *your job.*'

The contrarian habit was so deeply ingrained in Bryony that disagreement was her default option in any situation which she wasn't personally controlling. Impressively, Bryony managed this staccato conversation with me while simultaneously smiling and nodding at her current fan, inserting the inscription he'd requested, and strongly agreeing with him that the government was supine and pathetically inadequate in its response to The Problem. (I didn't hear what The Problem was. There were so many...)

The fan – an intense, unsmiling youth with blond hair and flushed cheeks, in a navy-blue blazer – moved away from the table and out through the gap in the little roped-off half circle that kept the customers back from the signing table.

It was then that it happened. The next admirer, a rather stout woman in a floral dress, began to move towards the space between the flimsy knee-high barrier supplied by loops of scarlet rope. She had just passed through it when the scruffy bearded man shouldered her aside. The woman grunted in angry surprise. Beside me, Bryony simply stared, impassive, having no notion of what was about to happen. Her lips had formed the professional smile which she shone on those who'd purchased her book.

She was still smiling as the man brought the bag up level with his stomach, then jerked it forward.

191

In the gloom of the cottage De Quincey saw two women enter the room, from a doorway opening on to a little staircase. A tall young woman advanced and presented her hand. This was Mrs Wordsworth. She furnished a remarkable proof, wrote De Quincey, how possible it is for a woman, neither handsome nor even comely, according to the rigour of criticism – nay, generally pronounced very plain, – to exercise all the practical power and fascination of beauty, through the mere compensatory charms of sweetness all but angelic, of simplicity the most entire, womanly self-respect, and purity of heart speaking through all her looks, acts, and movements. Words, I was going to have added, wrote De Quincey; but her words were few.

192

It contained a tin of paint – two litres of yellow silk emulsion, to be precise. A thick, sloppy tongue of the stuff shot forward and hit Bryony full in the face.

Her face metamorphosed into a dripping shapeless yellow slime.

'That's for asthma,' the man seemed to say.

A baffling remark.

Although Bryony had taken a direct hit, the splatter went everywhere.

The table and the carpet were coated in lurid puddles.

The woman in the floral dress had either fainted or tripped over the rope, and lay on the carpet, streaked with yellow, moaning.

Bryony herself resembled a seal piteously raising its head out of a yellow polluted sea.

She pushed the chair back.

I stood too, and took out my hanky.

I tried to dab at her face but she pushed me away.

'*Don't touch me,*' she shrieked.

She gulped and spat, having swallowed paint.

Instead I handed her a paper tissue.

She snatched it and began mopping at her eyes.

Then other people crowded round and Bryony and the plump woman in the flowery dress were led away to the manager's office.

I looked round.

The security guard was telling people the bookshop was closed, and was ushering the customers out.

He'd just finished when a police car drew up outside.

193

In reality, De Quincey continued, acid dripping from each calculated word, she talked so little that Mr Slave-Trade Clarkson used to say of her that she could only say 'God bless you!' Certainly her intellect was not of an active order... Drip, drip, drip. Mrs Wordsworth was evidently, in De Quincey's opinion, a simple, good-natured dullard. The writer turned to the notes at the back of *Recollections of the Lakes and the Lake Poets*. Thomas Clarkson (1760-1846) was described as an 'anti-slavery agitator'. It was a reminder that the writer had not yet read his copy of Michael Taylor's *The Interest*.

194

In the confusion the attacker had calmly walked away, out of the bookshop, into the street, and away into the afternoon. When the news was broken to Bryony she went berserk. Her yells throbbed through the closed door of the manager's office. She screamed threats to sue the bookshop, the publishers, the security guard. She bellowed that she was married to a judge.

The fine detail of her anger was distinctly audible, even at the back of the store, where I sat in an armchair giving a statement to a young constable. His manner was professional but his eyes flickered with amusement.

'Could you say that again, please?'

I was giving a short statement, and Bryony's rage was distracting us. I repeated my description of the attacker, and what I thought he'd said.

'Asthma?'

'That's what it sounded like. But I'm sure I must have misheard. Maybe he was saying a name.'

The cop frowned. 'A name?'

'You know, like Aslan.'

'Eh?'

'The lion in *The Chronicles of Narnia*.'

'Eh?'

'Or perhaps Astor.' I racked my mind. 'Or even Astra.' I added lamely: 'Or something like that. But it did sound to me like "asthma".'

In the background Bryony was still shouting. The cop closed his notebook. He gravely assured me that they would get in touch with me again. 'If we catch the guy, that is.' He didn't seem particularly excited by the prospect.

Having given my statement, I decided to phone Mike. I described what had happened.

'That's fantastic!' he said. He sounded overjoyed by the news. That's because he was. 'That's brilliant. That's really, really good.'

'Bryony doesn't think so. Listen.' I held the phone up so that he could hear her ranting.

'Did you get a picture?'

'I was being splattered in paint at the time. So incredible as this may seem to you, Mike, photography wasn't uppermost in my mind.'

'Don't worry, I'll check Twitter. With luck someone in the bookshop will have snapped it. But just in case, make sure you get a pic of her right now. You know, with paint on her clothing. This is a terrific story. It will do wonders for her sales.'

'She'll kill me if I try and take her piccy.'

'Do it. I'll pay your funeral costs. And get it to me a.s.a.p. If I move fast we can make the rush-hour issue of the *Standard*.'

He rang off.

The writer puts De Quincey away to return to at a later date. Now he is reading a lengthy essay about a twentieth-century English novelist whose first novel became an instant bestseller. The essayist wrote that although the novelist had denied any autobiographical resemblances, the central character of his book is an obvious projection of his author's aspirations. In the first flush of post-publication notoriety, the novelist stated flamboyantly, 'What I want to do is to drive through Bradford in a Rolls Royce with two naked women on either side of me covered in jewels.'

In the office the manager was on his knees, dabbing at Bryony's skirt with a damp J-Cloth. He was babbling apologies. He looked genuinely tearful. Perhaps he was afraid he'd lose his job.

I tried to be discreet but Bryony twisted her head round unexpectedly and caught me out.

'What are you doing, Jane?'

'I was just taking a picture. This is useful publicity, you know.'

Bryony's face twisted and stretched, as if reflected in a fairground's distorting mirror. She looked so furious I took another quick snap.

Bryony was now quite literally inarticulate with anger. She gurgled. She was speechless. Her mouth chopped at the air, seeking to gulp it down. Her eyes bulged and a layer of froth appeared along her lower lip.

'I'll go and organise a taxi,' I said brightly, and made my escape.

The writer looked at the anthology of English poems, which had been published in 1932. It was subtitled BEING 1150 POEMS AND EXTRACTS BY 300 AUTHORS. On the title page two lines by Cowley:

Poets by death are conquered, but the wit
Of poets triumphs over it.

198

In the street I sent Mike the photos. He liked them. U R AN ANGEL, he texted. Except that in his excitement he wrote ANGLE.

I needed his support at that moment because a few seconds later Bryony emerged and came storming up to where I was standing by the bookshop entrance. The security guard was standing by the locked door. He looked apprehensive.

Bryony treated the man to a steely, eyes-narrowed Flappe glare. 'You, boy, are *toast*,' she snarled. 'You were supposed to be *fucking protecting me*.'

Her language startled me. She'd flipped. She really was unhinged.

Outside a black cab pulled up. I gave the driver a wave.

'Taxi's here, Bryony,' I said sweetly.

She came up to me and positioned her face just inches from my own. Her breath smelled minty.

'The chairman of the board of Orlando is a very good friend of my husband,' she said in a quiet, intense voice. It throbbed with anger. 'I shall see to it that you, Jane, never work in publishing again. What happened today was *entirely your fault*.'

I acted as if I hadn't heard a word she was saying. 'Would you like me to come with you to Notting Hill? You know, in case there are assassins waiting for you there.'

Bryony was not that day attuned to the possibility of sarcasm. Her angry glare became more intense.

'That is a very real possibility, Jane. Which is why I shall not require your presence but that of professionals. My husband is at this moment hiring two men with SAS backgrounds. I believe they may be rather more up to the job than a girl from a publishers. Goodbye, Jane.'

She flounced away and wrenched open the cab door. I heard her shout 'The Hilton Hotel,' at the driver, and then she was gone.

The writer was startled to discover that the anthology was arranged not chronologically or thematically but alphabetically. ADDISON, JOSEPH (1672-1719) to YULE, SIR HENRY (1820-1880), with an appendix: UNKNOWN. Arranged this way you could see just how many poets' surnames began with the letters B, C, D, H, L, M, P, S and W. Only two with I – INGELOW, JEAN (1820-1897) and INGOLDSBY, THOMAS (although after his name was the note '*see* BARHAM' – which took you to BARHAM, RICHARD HARRIS (1788-1845)). No X or Z and only one Q. QUARLES, FRANCIS (1592-1644). The writer glanced at random poems, random lines. So long as I was in your sight I was your heart, your soul, your treasure. Mountains divide us, and the waste of seas. We each day grow older.

I raced back to Orlando H.Q. to report to Mike and [deleted].

He was holding an animated conversation on the phone when I looked in through the glass wall of his office. His head bobbed and nodded like a child's toy. He saw me, grinned, and raised his thumb.

I went off [deleted]. By the time I'd gone back to Mike's office he was off his phone.

'This is just all so *fucking brilliant!*' he said. He was elated. 'The nationals are running with it. The *Standard* is putting it in their late edition. Everybody loves it. Some guy in the bookshop snapped Flappe just after she'd been splattered. With his pics and yours, this story is *quadraphonic.*'

'[deleted].

'Termagant,' he said, acidly. '[deleted] – if this story doesn't shift copy then my name's not Donald Duck.'

[deleted]

'Her parting shot was that [deleted].

'If they want to fire you it will be over my dead body.'

'If your flimsy, putrefying carcase is all that stands between me and penury then I'm doomed.'

[deleted] and hurried off to Waterloo Station.

On the crowded concourse, with departure announcements booming from the speakers overhead, I joined the other homeward-bound commuters snatching up a copy of the *Standard* from the towering piles in the open blue metal containers.

I was expecting to read a small news item about what had happened, fitted in at the last moment in the *Londoner's Diary* on page seventeen or somewhere later in the paper. Instead I was stunned to see the story as the lead item on the front page.

BRYONY FLAPPE ATTACKED IN LONDON BOOKSHOP screamed the headline, which was accompanied by two photographs. One showed Bryony just after the assault. Her shaven head was tipped forwards and she was covered in paint. She looked like a crash-test dummy after a collision, dripping yellow blood. Mercifully the photo had been cropped and enlarged, so that the only portion of me that was on the display was my right hand.

The other photo was the second one I'd snapped in the manager's office. It showed Bryony's face staring upward, her eyes wild, her mouth twisted by rage.

My heart sank. I was sure that Bryony would never, ever forgive anyone involved in this farrago. From her career perspective, this was a PR disaster. These photographs would surely follow her to the grave, and beyond. In the digital galaxy, a photograph is eternal. And these pics made her look both comical and deranged. You could be one hundred per cent certain that they'd be appearing, with ironically captioned bubbles, in *Private Eye*. Bryony's many enemies would use them repeatedly to mock her. In the bookshop manager's office she even *looked* like a crazy woman.

I didn't share Mike's chirpy [deleted] for all it was worth. The story didn't really amount to very much, and the motive and identity of the attacker remained obscure. But Orlando was determined to turn it into a titanic combat between the powers of darkness and light, on a scale roughly equal to the cosmic dimension of *Paradise Lost.*

I read and re-read the story as the train pulled out and began to speed on its way to Woking.

Michael Spark, spokesman for Ms. Flappes's publishers, Orland Books [sic], *said: 'This outrageous attack on a brave and fearless woman is nothing less than an attack on freedom of expression.*

'This cowardly attack underlines Bryony's fear that we are entering a new dark age of intolerance and violence.

'Bryony has never been afraid to speak her mind, and whether or not you agree with her, she has a right to be heard.

'We must stand together against those who want to silence anyone who disagrees with them.

'I would urge everyone to show their support for freedom of expression by buying this exciting and very provocative book. Don't let Bryony be silenced.'

It was odd to see Mike identified by his full name. I grinned at his brazen insincerity. His shamelessness was, well, shameless.

For anyone involved in the trade, the story was all too obviously simply a regurgitated press release. It probably wouldn't have worked if the pictures hadn't been available. And would the publicity help sales of the book? I wasn't sure a title by Bryony Flappe really had that big a market. Time would tell.

I read the story twice more, than put the paper away, turned up the volume on my MP3 player, and closed my eyes. I tuned into Mumford & Sons as far as Guildford. Then I moved on to Dizzee Rascal, who took me as far as the halt just before Havant station.

Here, my heart thumped as the train waited for the red light to change. Don had texted twenty minutes earlier to say he'd arrived at Havant [deleted].

A sparrow fluttered in a tree close to the grimy window. It flew off as the train jerked into motion once again. The trees dropped out of sight as the train rolled across a level crossing with a line of waiting cars.

The platform slid into view and I stood up and joined the other passengers standing expectantly in the aisle.

With a *ping!* the door unlocked. It hissed open and [deleted].

Don [deleted].

'And the guy said it was for asthma?'

'That's what it sounded like.'

'How very odd.'

'Anyway, can we [deleted].

201

SUBJECT INDEX Addison, Ambition, Animals, Art, Autumn, Battles, Beauty, Bees, Birds, Blindness, Books, Boys and boyhood, Browning, Chapman, Charity, Chaucer, Children and childhood, Classical mythology, Content and calm, Country scenes and life, Courage (see Heroism), Creation and the Creator, Cromwell, Cuckoo, Daffodils, Dancing...

202

I'd had the foresight to make a reservation at Restaurant 36 on the Quay – the Emsworth restaurant for serious foodies. Afterwards [deleted].

After breakfast I drove to Waitrose in Havant to buy all the morning papers and to stock up with food and drink.

When I got back Don had brought down more boxes from the loft. He's set himself the task of clearing it before he went back to Scotland.

We read the papers over coffee. There hadn't been much happening in the world in the previous twenty-four hours – no outbreaks of war or revolution, no births or deaths among the famous, no disasters involving major loss of life. Not even a beached baby whale to tug at the reader's emotions. So the industry was hungry for an episode like the one involving Bryony. It was sexy. It had pictures. They needed to fill up that space between their major source of revenue – not paper sales but advertising.

The *Sun* gave it a page, with both pics and a one-word headline:

SPLAT!

The *Mail* went for MYSTERY MANIAC POURS PAINT OVER BRAVE BRYONY.

And a wacky, imaginative sub-editor at *The Guardian* came up with PAINT THROWN AT BRYONY FLAPPE IN BOOKSHOP.

Mike would be pleased, I thought. I sent him a text of congratulation.

After a morning of [deleted].

went through into the departure lounge and was gone.

The week which lay ahead of me was ostensibly a quiet one. The crime writer Lillian Joyce had another upcoming title in her popular Douglas Jackson series. *I Came upon a Worm* was due out in a fortnight and I was tasked with organising Lillian's interview schedule and her book launch as well as chasing up potential reviews in the nationals.

When I arrived back at the office on Monday morning, the mood was ebullient. The Bryony Flappe story was still running – SAS MEN GUARD BRYONY screamed the *Express*. This was another Mike Spark concoction, based on nothing more than Bryony's final words to me before the taxi whisked her away to the Hilton. The *Express* had found an unnamed source (in a bar, presumably) who intimated that Al-Qaeda might have been involved in planning the attack.

No arrests had been made. COPS SEEK MYSTERY ATTACKER contributed the *Mail*, which rehashed its Saturday story, with added comments by a couple of Conservative MPs, chums of Bryony, who spoke of their outrage. The MPs thundered that assaults like this deserved long prison sentences.

Once I'd told my story to everyone in the office who wanted a first-hand account, I got on with my work. I speed-read *I Came upon a Worm*, which wasn't really my cup of tea but which was perfectly competent and readable. Lillian wrote to a formula and it was a formula which sold – that was what counted. She also liked to think of herself as a stylist, and a bit 'literary'. The title of her new thriller came straight out of a troublingly dark dream poem by Emily Dickinson.

I was sure the fans would love this latest saga involving Douglas Jackson. Douglas was a woman who ran a private detective agency in Padstow. Douglas was gay, as was her ebullient sixteen stone creator. Lil made no secret of her sexuality, and went through a string of lovers. She was a hurricane of a woman, loud in every sense. The first time I met her at a book launch she jovially invited me to discover the joy of [deleted]. She exploded with laughter at my retort, as if I'd said the funniest thing imaginable. Her vast frame shook; her many chins wobbled like the walls of a bouncy castle. Lil bore no grudges. She enjoyed life to the full. Everyone loved her, if not always in the way she'd have preferred.

Lil came from Cornwall and her crime series never went outside that county. In this latest instalment the police are unable to solve the mystery of a murdered teenage girl, so her grieving father hires Douglas to find out who the murderer is. Douglas duly uncovers a powerful crime family who ship cocaine and heroin into lonely Cornish coves at night. The girl had stumbled upon the drug running and was silenced. It was all tied in with back stories involving the blackmail of a gay vicar, embezzlement at a bank, and a police superintendent who had fallen for an expensive call girl. Everything was wrapped up at the end, and truth and justice emerged as the winners. The pacing was ideal and the cover design was snappy. Lil had come up with another cracker.

I made my phone calls. The day passed.

The next day was more sombre. Mike was called to a meeting and came back looking grim. 'That Flappe fucker is stirring shit,' he said to me when no one else was around. 'She wants blood. I'm gonna see she ain't gonna get it.' He winked.

The next day the word was all around the office. Bryony Flappe wanted me fired. Mike had been in meetings with the MD. The MD was inclined to dump me (thanks, Charles). Mike told him not to make any hasty decisions. The mood was dark. Mike spent all day in his office, making phone calls. He kept his door closed, which was out of character. When people tried to get in to see him he barked at them to go away.

The next day was the same. Mike kept himself hidden away.

People started being extra nice to me, as if my days at Orlando were numbered and the number was a very, very small one.

It wasn't until the last day of that week that the matter was resolved. Mike produced several bottles of fizz and we all toasted my continuing future with the publicity department. He explained how he'd won. He'd rung around all the authors I'd had dealings with, and bluntly told them that Orlando wanted to dump me, and why. They'd all, to a man and woman (bless them) rallied round and given me their support. Mike was then able to go and see the chairman of the board and have a frank exchange of views. It boiled down to either humouring Bryony Flappe's sense of self-importance, or losing a string of very profitable authors. Because the genre gang, and even the lit fic lot, had said that if I went, they'd follow. They'd dump Orlando. It would be a big publishing story and Orlando would come out of it very badly for bullying *a mere slip of a girl*. More to the point, the financial consequences would be considerable, seriously so. To lose one best-selling author is a misfortune. To lose a crowd of them is a disaster. The shareholders would not be happy. Hard questions would be asked at the AGM.

The chairman crumpled and capitulated.

I didn't envy whoever had to break the news to Bryony.

203

Death (Miscellaneous)
  - death-bed and burial
  - desire of
  - fear or fearlessness of
  - for country's sake
  - inevitableness of
  - mystery of the hereafter
  - of children
  - orations
  - prospect of
  - victory over
    - *See* Elegies and Dirges, Epitaphs &c, Love, Murder and Suicide

As it happens there was one good piece of news for Ms Flappe. Her attacker was identified.

Joe Herdman was twenty-four, unemployed and lived on an estate in Canning Town. He also wasn't very bright, because he'd boasted of what he'd done on Facebook. One of his mates had grassed on him.

Joe Herdman's motive was less political than aesthetic. I *had* heard him correctly. 'This is for asthma,' was exactly what he'd said as he threw the paint.

He meant Asthma, the band. A group I'd never heard of. But Bryony had. If I'd actually bothered to read her book from cover to cover I would have come across her brief mention of this bunch of musicians who, she asserted, represented 'the complete depravity and degradation of our society'. They were 'brutal, insensitive, fascist in essence'. Their recording contract signified 'the debasement of all sound judgement and the complete collapse of decency'.

In short, Asthma was a heavy metal band from Braintree. Their lyrics were disagreeable. They were obviously little publicity sharks desperately seeking to supply offence of the sort which would be noticed, which would produce a response, and which would give them huge street-cred with their fans and, most of all, record sales.

They'd achieved minor notoriety with a song celebrating a man's violence against a woman:

You gimme a fistful of barbed wire
You said it was a rose
You broke my heart you bitch so now
I'm gonna break your nose

The band had a gift for melody, if not for lyrical nuance. But this latter lack didn't seem to matter. Asthma's fans (who tended to be adepts of tonsure) were not the sort of people who read books, let alone one as lacking in narrative drive as *The Subversion of*

Culture. But someone close to the band had heard of Bryony. They'd read a slighting remark about Asthma she'd made in an interview, and had somehow wangled an advance copy of her book. The band's website had tipped off their fans about their detractor. An Asthma fan had tweeted about Bryony's forthcoming signing, and Joe Herdman had seen it as his fan's duty to even up the score.

The reason he'd chosen yellow paint became obvious. It was in tribute to Asthma's song 'Vomit':

This whole countree is full of shee-it,
Kinda makes you wanna vom-eet.
Yeah, vom-eet, vom-eet,
Puke it out, baby,
Puke it out,
Empty yer guts
And the snot from yer snout.

It wasn't really a surprise when, months later, it emerged that the band wasn't really from Essex at all. They'd been fabricated by an entrepreneur with all the shrewd commercial sense of a Simon Cowell. Far from being raised by single mothers in poky social housing riddled with mildew and cockroaches, the band members were all nice Home Counties boys who'd met at Wellington College. But by the time the truth came out it didn't matter. The music had sold in profitable quantities, the Glastonbury performance had been secured, the fibs were airbrushed.

Everyone was a winner. Bryony's book topped the non-fiction bestseller lists for three weeks and Orlando turned in a reasonable profit.

The paperback edition later also made the charts.

Yes, everyone was a winner except poor, foolish Joe Herdman. The press and the politicians screamed that this yob should be made an example of, and the judge duly obliged. Herdman was sentenced to three years in prison. A bit harsh for a paint job, I felt.

But I wasn't going to sign any protest petitions. I had [deleted].

205

The man in the moon
Came tumbling down,
And asked the way to Norwich;
He went by the south,
And burnt his mouth
With eating cold pease-porridge.

206

The first was [deleted].
　'Yes, I do,' I said coolly.
　'What colour was his motorbike?'
　'Red.' I still vividly remembered that moment. It was disturbing
and threatening. And [deleted].
　what all this meant. It wasn't long before I learned – but not
just yet.

　[deleted] apart from Blanche, and I hadn't seen her for quite a
while. She told me she was very busy at work, and [deleted].
　Each evening I sorted through more of the boxes I'd [deleted]
boxes of old knitting patterns, a stamp catalogue, postcards sent
by friends from the era when to travel abroad was an exotic
experience. I came across toys, coloured pencils, knitting needles,
a wooden darning toadstool, a model centurion, a ban-the-bomb
badge, a Polaroid camera with a battery compartment filled with
dust. There were packets of anodyne letters I'd written my parents
from university ('I am having a very nice time in York, and
working hard'). There was a moth-eaten bobble hat wrapped
around a guide to playing the banjo. There were boxes of dusty
hardback books, including such marvels as *Paris to New York by
Land*, *The Burden of the Balkans*, *Famous Modern Battles*, and
(how Mike Spark would snigger when I showed him!) Dr John
Kerr's long-forgotten *Memories Grave and Gay*.
　There were [deleted]. Let the winds of life sweep the past away!
　And then I came to a box which I'd set aside because of how

well it was sealed. There was band after band of parcel tape wrapped around it – horrid brown sticky stuff that wrapped itself to the scissor arms when you tried to cut it, and which left a smear of adhesive along the silver blade. I turned it over, working out which side of the cube was the top. Its dimensions were about two feet square on each side. On what I finally decided was the top, and the best place to start cutting it open, I noticed at the centre a small sellotaped 'M'. It meant nothing. I proceeded to slice at the tape, growing increasingly irritated by the way it clung like weed to the scissors. When I tried to detach it from the scissors it attached itself to my fingers instead.

It was a Friday night, about nine. It must have taken me a good fifteen minutes to hack the box open. Inside, incredibly, was more wrapping – a black plastic rubbish sack inside a second sack, also sealed with band after band of parcel tape. Whatever was inside was well waterproofed.

None of the numerous other boxes I'd opened had been sealed up like this. What was inside, I wondered? Financial documents? Share certificates? Unlikely – my father had kept stuff like that tidily organised in labelled files in the filing cabinet in his study.

I ripped through the last dark membrane of plastic and found it enclosed a bunch of bulging foolscap-size brown envelopes, each one tied with string. Each envelope was numbered, so it seemed logical to begin with number one. It was top of the pile, in any case: the first one in the pile.

I tore it open.

207

The writer dimly remembered that there had once been a popular novel called *The Pumpkin Eater*. Was it by Penelope Mortimer? And wasn't there a film? He'd never read the book, nor had he seen the movie. Memories stirred by a nursery rhyme he'd never come across before. Plainly, as a child, his knowledge of this genre had been seriously deficient. Nor, for that matter, had he ever read *The Wind in the Willows* – a text he associated only with early Pink Floyd. The works of Beatrix Potter formed no part of his early reading. His early childhood had been a working-class one. He didn't become lower middle-class until his teens. There were few books in the family home. Now, for the first time, looking through the anthology of nursery rhymes, he read these words:

Peter, Peter, pumpkin-eater,
Had a wife and couldn't keep her;
He put her in a pumpkin shell,
And there he kept her very well.

208

It contained letters – sheet after sheet of handwriting, on flimsy blue airmail paper. But first, attached to the letters by a rubber band, was a newspaper cutting.

Obituary: Militká [deleted].

Militká [deleted] was born in Prague in [deleted]. Her father, Gustav [deleted], was Jewish and spent the war years incarcerated in Terezín (Theresienstadt). He died shortly after arriving in Canada. Her mother, Ulla Lazarová, was a noted Czech opera singer, who briefly found employment in Toronto's theatre world.

Militká [deleted] graduated from the State University of New York with an English degree in [deleted]. She subsequently studied at the University of British Columbia, completing a Ph.D. on the Jacobean stage in [deleted]. Lazarová joined the Faculty of English at U.B.C. in [deleted] and married her Russian colleague Boris [deleted] in [deleted]. She was promoted to Professor and Head of Faculty in [deleted]. Militká [deleted] was widely acknowledged as an authority on the Jacobean stage and the plays of John Webster. Her editions of *The White Devil* and *The Duchess of Malfi* are still regarded as definitive. She died at her home in Vancouver on [deleted]

I set this obituary to one side – the name meant nothing to me – and began reading the first letter.

209

The writer never forgot the impact which *Carve Her Name With Pride* had made upon him when he first saw the movie as a child. In particular, three things. That haunting incantatory unforgettable poem. The shocking sudden brutal execution. At the end, the child running out into the empty London street. Decades later the writer read a book which informed him that the poem was written by Leo Marks, who was the Special Operations Executive code master. Agents were taught to code messages using a poem. At first, in training, Violette Szabo tried using an old French nursery rhyme. But though she knew it off by heart she couldn't remember how to spell all the words correctly, which made it useless for coding purposes. It so happened that Leo Marks's lover was a young woman called Ruth. He was passionately in love with her and wished to marry her. In December 1943 she went to Canada, where she was training at an air-ambulance base. On Christmas Eve Marks heard from Ruth's father. She had died in Canada, in a plane crash. *Not knowing what to do and wishing he had told her things that would now remain forever unsaid, he went up to the roof of Norgeby House, another of SOE's premises in Baker Street, and wrote a poem for her.*

210

August 26, 1 p.m. – In flight

Here I sit reading imagining that your eyes will rest on the same pages. I am drinking gin and tonic and my Love, my Love, my Love, I am so full of your presence that my eyes keep brimming over and I hear your voice in my ears and feel your hands on my body and all the words I say express only a minute fraction of what I feel.

I have thought a thousand times that I am the luckiest woman under the sun because you love me.

I once told you that I always waited for something during these past years and at the same time I thought and said to myself: 'Don't be stupid, life consists of irrational feelings and expectations and you are an unrealistic fool or a child or a naïve woman outstaring life and its relentless earthy laws.' And then *you* stepped into my life and when an unknown power made me touch your face, my fingers felt as if they had touched an inexplicable region to which I was drawn. When I left you that day I held my hand to my own face (I never told you that) and I am down the library stairs with my heart beating in my ears.

My thoughts whirl through my head. One thing I know: that my love for you is rooted in my heart for as long as I breathe. I have lived so long (relatively speaking) but I have such a feeling as if I realized only now the nature of love or life – God knows I cover my eyes in the palm of my hand – and I feel you inside me and I feel the sweetness of your skin under my fingertips. – My Love, once when you are in the mood, will you tell me *why* you think we love each other so? The three levels we talked about (intellect, emotion and Eros) are OK.

Where are you now, my Love? Walking along a street? I followed you with my eyes when you walked away through the crowd and I wanted to run after you and then people pushed me on... All I could think of then was the moment when I will see you emerging from a door or a crowd. My Love, I am disjointed and my thoughts whirl through my head. One thing I know – that my love for you is rooted in my heart for as long as I breathe. I have such a feeling as I realized only now the nature of love or life – God knows. I cover my eyes in the palm of my hand – and I see you before me – and I feel you inside me and I feel the sweetness of your skin under my fingertips. –

My Love, once when you are in the mood, will *you* tell me why you think we love each other so? The three levels we talked about (intellect, emotion and Eros) are OK but I want to know more! If you like, I will tell you too but my words would be so awkward and grotesque messengers of my feelings. But *you* tell me! And, since we both love irony and basically grin at emotional wallowing, tell me ironically, with salt on your words and a bright searching spotlight on your feelings (excuse mixed image). I am so thirsty for all that concerns you and us! The present is ours – yours and mine – and *no one* can match that, but I wonder and think so much about you that I feel I must tell you the truth about wanting to know about you. I have such a serene feeling about our love. I did not even thank you for our final glorious week. I was so confused and dazed and lightheaded this morning that I hardly know what I was saying and doing. – We will both work now like fury. I hope, my Love, you have the strength to make it. I wish I could be with you all the time. – We will see. – Life is such a mystery. – Is our love-making also such a glorious miracle, or miraculous glory to you? If so, tell me about it.

Militká XXX

211

What are the ethics of using in a book intimate private letters from a still living person? It depends on the impact which publication will have on that person, the writer supposed. Less of a problem once that person dies. Especially if they have no children or other surviving family. Especially if their spouse is now dead.

212

There were many, many more letters written on the same thin blue paper, in the same hand and in the same vein. Love letters. Love letters from Militká [deleted] to my father, Jon Tain. They were written over the period [deleted]. And then they stopped.

I flipped through them with increasing amazement. They were all written with the same white-hot intensity.

I looked again at her obituary and realised something else. The age indifference! She was twenty-one years older than my father. And a married woman, too. Their affair had occurred when he was a postgraduate student. He was twenty-six years old and she was forty-seven.

Forty-seven, I thought. How *incredibly old*. I couldn't imagine having a fling with a man twenty years older than me. I winced at the thought of it. At that age men were *wrinkled*.

That night I didn't read all the letters. There were so many of them – hundreds of tiny pages, every one handwritten.

I found myself shaking. My father had held this secret deep inside him and never hinted at it, not even [deleted].

Those emotions expressed by this woman called Militká. They were overwrought, tipped with a passionate intensity. They were written out of a kind of emotional extremity I found it hard to relate to.

No lover had ever addressed me in such extreme flowery language. Nor could I ever conceive of myself writing such sentiments. My generation was the text-message generation. Brevity and abbreviation cut through all the murk and rolling fogs of the human heart.

Militká [deleted] was a woman on the edge. Reading her letters was like staring into the bubbling golden cauldron of a volcano on the brink of a last, cataclysmic eruption.

213

Reading her letters was like staring into the bubbling golden cauldron of a volcano on the brink of a last, cataclysmic eruption. Distinctly over-wrought prose. The kind that used to be called purple. Guilty of hyperbole. The verdict of the people's court is unanimous. Liquidate! This is the type of prose that makes any sensible person reach out to their nearest bookshelf, where they keep their most important instructional manuals. Select that grey-jacketed little volume – V. I. Lenin's *On Literature and Art*. The writer reflected dolefully that truly bracing criticism is sadly lacking today. The writer then opened the page at Lenin's views about Mayakovsky's *150,000,000* and Lunacharsky. The poet's work is penetratingly dismissed by the great revolutionary as 'nonsense, stupidity, double-dyed stupidity and affectation'. But, a liberal and humane man with a warm, generous spirit, Lenin saw no reason to block publication. Simply limit the print run to 1,500 copies, he suggested, 'for libraries and cranks'. Adding, 'As for Lunacharsky, he should be flogged for his futurism.' (A joke, comrades; just a joke.)

214

I put the letters to one side and ripped open all the other bulging foolscap envelopes.

One contained a green notebook on which was written in my father's hand SCOTLAND TRIP.

It was an impromptu diary. And it told me everything. It detailed the drive to Scotland which he and Militká had taken in June of that year. There were addresses, diary entries, even, bizarrely – reminding me that at heart my father had always been a scientist, obsessed by the unambiguously factual – mileage readings.

Everything was in that cardboard box marked with a little 'M'.

That night I was too shaky, too shocked, to fit all the pieces together. A complete understanding only came later – in so far as you can ever have an understanding of the love between two other people. But even that night I was able to grasp the basic outline of what happened.

There were more notebooks, all kinds of miscellanea, and an envelope filled with photographs.

I tipped the photos out and hungrily scanned them.

215

The life that I have is all that I have and the life that I have is yours, the love that I have of the life that I have is yours and yours and yours. A sleep I shall have, a rest I shall have, yet death will be but a pause, for the peace of my years in the long green grass will be yours and yours and yours.

The first thing that struck me was their format. They were the same size as the funny little square snapshots which I'd seen of my father standing in a Norwich street [deleted].

At first I barely recognised my father. He was younger than I am now. His youthful face was framed by a huge shock of dark hair. [deleted] In the foreground of the snapshot can be seen the rear of a blue car with its boot wide open, packed high, with the curl of a brown sleeping roll visible. My father is walking towards the camera holding a blue suitcase. He's wearing a navy-blue shirt, a denim blue jacket and white trousers. His hair billows out like sails.

Militká was smaller than my father. Two of the snaps showed them together. She was slim, pretty, with dark hair that was sometimes tied up in a bob, sometimes in girlish ponytails. She was holding on to my father tightly, as if reluctant to let him go. Militká didn't look her age.

I opened the last of the envelopes. They contained nothing but a few cheap paperbacks – a copy of John le Carré's spy thriller *Tinker, Tailor, Soldier, Spy*, an old, crumbling broken-spined copy of *Four Quartets*, a small cheap edition of *The Rubáiyát of Omar Khayyám*, and an edition of *The Observer's Book of Trees* not much bigger than a smart phone.

[deleted]

I surveyed the strewn contents of the box. They included an old one-inch Ordnance Survey map of Cape Wrath and a blue five-dollar Bank of Canada banknote (probably defunct, I guessed).

Out of this network of old chronologies there was one distressingly obvious fact.

When [deleted].

The subtitle was what made him finally decide to read this remaindered hardback biography, with the circular scarlet sticker on the cover obscuring much of the poet's right cheek, sideburns

and most of the ear. REDUCED TO £4.99 THIS LABEL PEELS
OFF. Remaindered perhaps because there was not much of a
market for Browning biographies. *Robert Browning: A Life After
Death*. 'After' with a capital 'A'. Would the poet have objected to
this lamentable flouting of convention?

218

[deleted]

I remember being woken by the sound of shouting in the street,
then I drifted off again. I was woken a second time, this time by
the metallic droning of the police helicopter. It sounded as if it
was just a few inches above my roof. The window frame shook. I
drifted off again, and when I woke the room was filled with grey
light. It was 5 a.m.

I made a mug of black coffee, tipped in two indulgent spoonfuls
of sugar, and took another look at [deleted].

Obituary: Professor Boris [deleted].

Boris [deleted] was born [deleted].

an expert in modern Russian history and the author of nineteen
books, including *Lenin's Legacy* and *The Cold War Reconsidered*.
Professor [deleted] lectured at universities around the world and
much of his writing has been translated into other languages.
Married to Militká [deleted] he died in Vancouver General
Hospital on [deleted].

I put the name into Google and it threw up just one photograph.
The professor stared out from a pair of spectacles with thick black
rims and arms, his thin lips pulled back, forming a curiously
ambiguous half smile. The crown of his round, bald scalp
displayed a low, receding wave of combed-back silver hair. There
was no happiness in the eyes, one of which was barely visible
under a drooping lid. His skin was dappled with the marks of age.
The sagging flesh beneath his jaw was fissured and soft. He
looked like an old man who has just had all his teeth extracted.

I quickly calculated that [deleted] was fifty-five when his wife Militká began her affair with my father. But the image plainly belonged to a much older man. The affair had ended, and Militká spent the rest of her life with her husband. Judging by the subdued misery embedded in that old face the knowledge of [deleted].

My immediate instinct after scrutinising the [deleted].

I wanted to talk. I needed to talk. I wanted at once to tell [deleted].

By now it was just after six in the morning. Dawn was leaking a silver light among the rooftops and the trees. The birds were burbling the joys of a new day.

I decided to [deleted].

No answer.

Maybe he [deleted].

That left only one person to tell all this to.

Blanche.

If I left soon I could be in Camden inside an hour. I decided then and there to go for it. I'd buy fresh croissants from one of the bijou local patisseries and turn up on her doorstep with breakfast for her and Thomas. *Smiley-face! Surprise!*

I gathered up my father's Scottish journey notebook to read on the tube. I also took Militká's first, amazing letter. Then I [deleted].

Dear, dear Blanche. When I [deleted]. A fact is a cold, hard thing. Facts lack emotions. Facts can be rearranged in misleading ways, misused and abused. But facts cannot be refused. What happened, happened, no matter what interpretation we later put upon it.

Later. There is always a later...

Later, my record of the days began to congeal into questions addressed to [deleted].

darling Blanche. My oldest, deepest [deleted] the oddity that all the time I was writing this for your sympathetic eyes I was unaware that by the end I would not wish you ever to read it.

And so it came to pass (as they used to say) that early on that Saturday morning I took a mostly empty Victoria line tube train to Kings Cross station. There, I switched to the grubby old

Northern Line. In Camden I soon found the kind of establishment I was looking for and bought three freshly baked almond croissants. For good measure I threw in an artisan stone-ground loaf. I remembered that [deleted].

The street was very quiet. A man was walking his terrier towards the Primrose Hill end. Apart from him, no one. The parked cars stood in motionless silence like a row of tombs.

I pressed the white china-capped doorbell and heard a muffled sequence of chimes deep within the house.

I waited for a couple of minutes, then pressed it again.

Blanche was a long time coming to the door.

I was about to press the button a third time when there was movement in the frosted glass panels of the door. A pale shape appeared amid the mosaic of fractured shadow and light, solidifying into a white pillar as the door opened.

It was Blanche, wearing a loosely tied white bath robe. She was obviously naked underneath it: I could almost see her nipples.

Her hair was dishevelled, her cheeks flushed. She looked tired. She rubbed her eyes and frowned.

'What *the fuck* are you doing here?' she said. She didn't seem overjoyed to see me.

'Blanche, [deleted].

'Oh,' she said. She seemed distracted; nervous almost.

'How is Thomas? Well, I hope?'

'Thomas is in Tokyo. And I was in bed.'

'Look [deleted].

'I can't talk now, Jane. I'm sorry, I really can't.' As if aware of how loose her bathrobe was, she pulled it closer over her breast.

She said: 'Look, can't this wait? I could meet up with you on Monday. Today's really not a good day. And neither is tomorrow. But Monday would be great. Shall we say Covent Garden on Monday? The usual place, the usual time?'

I felt a huge pang of disappointment. My oldest friend was giving me the brush-off, just at the very moment when [deleted] the door halfway; now she was slowly closing it. The signal she was sending me was rudely obvious. She didn't want my company.

'Look, I'm really sorry if [deleted].

I didn't understand what had put her into this mood. It really wasn't like Blanche to be so rude, least of all to me. She could be impulsive and hot-tempered at times but never calculatingly insolent.

Another thirty seconds and the door would have closed, I'd have gone back down the steps, and maybe I'd never have known. But that didn't happen. As Blanche stared at me, plainly desperate to get rid of me, a voice called down the stairs.

'Baby,' the voice. 'Is everything okay down there? Come back to bed. Mr Richards is ready to say hello again.'

The voice was unmistakeable. It was like someone had plunged a serrated knife inside my breast and twisted it. An explosion of pain burst inside me. I felt sick.

219

The writer had read too many bad commercial novels and seen too much television. It had rotted his prose and his plotting. It would have to go, all of it, even the satirical Bryony Flappe sections. This manuscript was like a house in a condition that made renovation impossible. The only option was complete demolition. Build something new on the rubble.

220

Blanche's face was a mask of horror.

221

You can't really blame Blanche, finding herself stranded in prose like this. Desperately dreaming of a return to a folder in a filing cabinet. The long hibernation of deformed characters, mute inside a desert of unpublished words. Like the crew of the *Nostromo* before the lights go on and they are prodded into a worse horror. A facetious reflection indicating a return to a condition where the writer can begin to bear – and bare – the passage of time. As for the dialogue!

'Listen, Jane, sweety, I was going to – '

'It doesn't matter,' I said thickly. My eyes were suddenly brimming with hot bitter tears. 'I must go.'

As I went away from her door, Blanche cried out imploringly, 'Don't tell Thomas. Please don't do that.'

I didn't answer. I just wanted to run. It was incredible. It was [deleted] and a throbbing sense of incredulity. I ran past the blue plaque to Yeats in a blur of tears. I turned left, into a square, still clutching the bag from the bakery. I shook it empty onto the grass.

At once a convulsion of birds came from nowhere, shooting low over my head, screaming, circling. The braver ones swooped and tore at the curls of pastry. One of them was a huge yellow-beaked gull, for Christ's sake. What in hell was a seagull doing here in Camden Town?

Wings outstretched, flapping wildly, the gull stabbed its beak into the ribs of the stoneground loaf, showering crumbs and provoking a fresh frenzy of feathered hysteria.

I ran on and didn't stop running until [deleted].

223

Terrible – except possibly 'a convulsion of birds'.

224

It was a bitter irony that I had [deleted].

'That's right. I got back on Monday. Tokyo was great. It's so clean out there. Quite a change from London. And people actually wait politely to get on the tube. Nobody pushes in. Amazing.'

'So you're fine.'

'Never better.'

'That's [deleted].

The next day I received an email from her.

My dear Jane,

I know how angry and upset you must [deleted]

Forgive me,

Blanche XX

P.S. [deleted]

Let's talk soon. B.

I was [deleted].

These angry suspicious thoughts ran around the corridors of my mind like homunculi. They were raucous, furious, demented. And they never slept.

I had the Militká material to wade through. I'd quickly deciphered the outline of that relationship, which stretched over a period of [deleted] who he referred to as 'that boy'. The Professor had had a complete nervous collapse and had begged Militká not to leave him. The poor woman was then torn between the importunings of a man she'd lived with for almost twenty years, or the Anna Karenina option of casting everything aside and following the devastating gravitational pull of her heart.

In the end she'd [deleted] and in the end destroyed him.

I looked again at the two books found in his car parked at the graveyard. One I'd written off as an obscure work of science which it was characteristic of my father to be interested in. But in context Darwin's *The Formation of Vegetable Mould Through the Action of Worms, With Observations on Their Habits* was like another wry signal on his part. He knew he was going to [deleted].

I'd gone through the other book, the little paperback of *Romeo and Juliet*, looking for clues. But there were no underlinings, even though the book appeared crumpled and well read. But then again it might have been bought second hand. What I'd missed, and what I now saw the significance of, was the name of the academic who'd edited the volume and supplied a critical introduction. It was, of course, Militká. The edition had been published the year before she [deleted].

There was a little blue notebook which consisted of nothing but short quotations copied from novels my father had read. The focus of their meaning was all too plain. A random sample – there were hundreds – is this one:

You felt that nothing you could say would reach the seat of the still and benumbing pain.
(Joseph Conrad)

[deleted]
Thankfully, most of all I [deleted].

225

The writer listens to Taylor Swift's old album. His favourite tracks are 'Soon You'll Get Better' and 'Cornelia Street'.

226

If you walk south of the [deleted] you pass the famous [deleted] and the little cliff with the stub of white lighthouse protruding from behind the houses. Keep going and you pass [deleted] and the strange little octagonal building called [deleted]. After that the town drops away and [deleted].

It was here, sitting on a [deleted].

The case had been wrapped up much quicker than anyone had hoped or expected (under the pressure of repeated questioning the killer had cracked and confessed). That meant Don was able to [deleted].

We had three things to talk about that weekend. But [deleted] he said he understood [deleted].

After breakfast we [deleted] its slate surface empty apart from a tiny white yacht on the horizon. [deleted]

'I began to think the mystery motorcyclist might have something to do with the collision. I dug a little deeper and found out two interesting things. [deleted]

Don teased: 'You ought to be a cop. You're wasted in publishing.'

'Bryony Flappe certainly thinks so. The last bit, I mean.'

'How is Bryony now? Have you had an update?'

'She's apparently calmer. In so far as as a human catherine wheel like Bryony Flappe can ever be calm.'

'She should take up Buddhism. [deleted]

'Your colleague Jack MacLean is a Buddhist?' I said, incredulous.

227

As well might be the reader, the writer thought, a grim expression forming upon his face. (No, not really.)

228

Don wasn't smiling. 'He is, yes,' he said gravely. He added: 'You mustn't [deleted].

'What happened next?'

'I talked to [deleted].

'To cut a long story short, in the end he admitted everything. His wife was [deleted].

'What sentence will he get?'

229

In prose like this: a commonplace one...

230

[deleted] at least, I imagine. The judiciary takes a very dim view of murders involving that level of calculation and cold-blooded planning.

A thought occurred to me. 'Am I [deleted].

Don shook his head.

231

People used to put plastic dogs on the back shelf of their cars. While the car was in motion the dog's head nodded ceaselessly. You don't see these dogs anymore. But in modern fiction the characters continued to shrug, nod or shake their head, with great regularity. It is expected of them. Narrative momentum could not occur without these comforting familiar spasms.

232

'Not necessary. The guy's confessed. End of.'
   He took my hand and [deleted].

Most of that weekend I spent talking about what I'd uncovered about my father and Militká [deleted]. I'd taken along some of the letters, photographs and other mementoes to [deleted].
   'Remember what you said once? Find the unhappiness. Well in the end I did.'
   I [deleted].
   Don looked grim.

233

You can't blame him. He's a fossil stuck in a layer of inert matter. This narrative moment makes the writer think of Lenin's remark that a mirror which does not reflect things correctly can hardly be called a mirror.

234

'You witheld evidence,' he said. 'That's serious.'
   'Are you going to arrest me, then? What difference does it make now?'
   He looked grave and fell silent.

But he did not fall silent for long. Almost at once he whirred into action again. More dialogue was squeezed out of him, as predictable as the contents of a tube of toothpaste.

236

'I suppose you're [deleted].
    'Wet-what?'
'Wetumpka. It's where the remains of the crater are. You know, the one that [deleted].
    'Remind me again where Wetumpka is.'

237

Here it comes. The information dumping...

238

I smiled. 'You must remember [deleted]. He had nowhere to live so he rented a room in London. Guess where.'
    [deleted] 44 Cavendish Avenue. Militká told her husband she had to go to a Shakespeare conference in London and [deleted] and they went to Scotland, via Norwich and Harrogate. Apparently she wanted to see [deleted].
    I passed Don a photograph of Militká [deleted].
    'She looks like a gypsy,' he said.
    [deleted]
    She had a slightly wild appearance – jet-black hair which rippled out in waves, dark intense eyes, a rather fierce passionate face. It figured – her family origins were that part of Czechoslovakia which had formerly been the ancient kingdom of Bohemia. A place of gypsies and poets, wandering violinists and theatre troupes... Central Europe's hot, throbbing artistic heart. And somehow this had been grafted onto a young girl with a Jewish father who'd survived the Nazis and fled to Canada in that

brief space before the heavy, iron doors of Stalin's [deleted].

'The house on the Earlham Road was [deleted]. Militká pulled up the sash window in the middle of the night and climbed out and pissed on the lawn.'

We wandered on, past the [deleted].

Don nodded, and handed the publication back to me. 'I get the picture. He was dull, uninspiring and dogmatic, she was lively, enthusiastic and [deleted].

'Something like that. Even their photographs signal the difference. The Professor was fat, double-chinned and humourless, and she's slim and vivacious and always smiling.'

[deleted]

239

For Robert Browning, wrote the biographer, any too-close association with his life with Elizabeth in Italy was painful to him. At first, the pain had come with the recollection of all that he had lost; then, increasingly, with the discovery of what he had never had.

240

[deleted]

My Love, your letter of Sept 22 is so beautiful. I cry when I read it. You are such a miracle as a man and a human being. Despite the incredible joy of our love I ache at times with indescribable pain, and then I must go and teach the third act of *Hamlet* or the subjunctive, or sit at a meeting, the reality of these things just draws me out of myself. That is what you don't have now. You were for the last weeks thrown totally back on yourself and I hardly ever stop thinking about it, even if I don't talk about it much.

My Day: I get up about 7.30 and dress and prepare some breakfast and Boris comes usually later into the living room and has his breakfast while I still have coffee or so. I leave rather quickly about 8.15 and walk to UBC. I have office hours from 9-930 [*sic*] and then again for an hour at 11.30. Then there are always incredibly many things, reading lists, course problems, petty administrative things which I do not like but they must be done. Three days a week I try to come to the carrel and work here in the afternoon. This week it hasn't worked so well because I had three meetings, always at 3 or 3.30. There is some promotion discussion in the department which has taken on too large dimensions. There is disagreement of opinion and so a lot of time is wasted going over ground covered before. But I don't want to talk about that, my Sweetest Love, I want to talk about you and you and me. In the evening I mostly walk around for a while and then I go back to the apartment and work. Boris works in his study. Everything seems to be peaceful now, but of course only on the surface. You write you can't imagine very well how this can work. I couldn't either, if I did not experience it now. It seems terribly strange to me too and at times I go to the bathroom and take a bath just to lie in the hot water and feel my blood flow a little more quietly and become conscious of the reality of my body which I sometimes lose now.

[deleted] I will write you more about my thoughts xxxxxxxxxxxxxxxxxxxxxxxxxxx [passage deleted in original] but my love is around you constantly. I will broach the subject again whenever I think it is the right moment.

Please do not phone me at home. It would be better not to phone at this point. I must do everything on my own and such a call would greatly upset Boris so that he couldn't listen to me afterwards. Perhaps you had no intention to do it but I am just telling you because you had said you might. Your love, my Love, gives me strength and I look at the sky and say 'God, you see how I love this man!'

Sometimes I am very upset at everything and restless and my moods go up and down. But I am walking on through that fire with your love in my heart.

I also mail this. Another rotten meeting this afternoon. Shere [*sic*] waste of time.

I wish I could write poetry for you and I wish I could express to you my feelings when I feel your warmth inside me... There are no words for that.... Your hands are so real for me, I see them before me. They are so finely wrought – like extensions of your spirit, my Love, xxx Your Militká xx

And here's another shorter one.

October 24

My Love,

It is Sunday evening. I just finished correcting a stack of mid term tests.

Will you [deleted]? The monsters of incertainty [*sic*] twist my thoughts. I feel as if my mind were full of gargoyles turning in all directions.

It is very late. I'll mail this on the way to my cello lesson first thing in the morning.

I think of you returned to [deleted]. I hold you, I kiss you, I hope – I am so hurting inside but my love blazes despite everything, Your [deleted].
    But then [deleted].
    The other letters [deleted].
    Militká [deleted] died in her sleep, alone in her apartment, of cardiac arrest.

241

Two imagined deaths; this one and the other one. In time curiously prescient. The writer abandons the laptop screen and goes into the kitchen. He switches on the kettle and returns to *What's It Gonna Take?* It's not Van Morrison's finest work but it has a jaunty, upbeat sound. The writer likes it. Later he looks at online reviews and smiles at the hostility. After the fantastic opener *Dangerous*, which pokes fun at Morrison's status as the pot-stirring, sneering cynic, the rest of the album's lyrics are obsessed with lying politicians and a brainwashed nation, said *Buzz*. On another site Malachi Lui furiously dismissed the album as a failure in every way, and a depressing one at that. 'Fodder For The Masses', wrote Lui, complains about how the media '[lies] to you continuously' and only serves to 'fill you up with fake news for their masters'. Unlike Lui, the writer had no objection to lyrics like that. Lui concluded: All he does is whine and complain nonstop for the length of an entire CD. Thinking of *Twenty-Twenty*, the writer was unmoved by a critical angle like that.

242

'And that's it?' Don said. We were standing at [deleted]. In the hazy distance, a mile or so inland, a couple of grey giant wind turbines slowly turned.

'Pretty much. I've put all the pieces together – all except one. I still haven't worked out what the significance of the graveyard is. But everything else – yes. No loose endings. The Harrogate address was where [deleted].

'So it's over.'

'Yes, over. Done and dusted. No more trips to Nice or wherever. No more questions that need answering.'

Don gestured [deleted].

Fifteen minutes later we'd left the last of the [deleted].

We hadn't walked for long before we came to a pair of semi-detached houses on the very edge of the cliff. Their windows were bare. They looked as if they'd been abandoned. The sea had eaten away the gardens. High up on the yellow cliff face protruded a broken knob of concrete and several lengths of blue pipe.

At the edge of the sea the remains of a substantial concrete structure could be seen breaking the surface. It wasn't obvious whether or not it [deleted].

Nothing stayed the same here. Impermanence was part of the fabric of each day. We'd both [deleted].

We walked on as far as the headland in the distance. When we reached it we saw that there was a half-promontory here, covered in pine trees. Many of the pines were bent over, leaning at a doomed angle, evidently battered by wind and spray. They had a bleached, desolate appearance, and those closest to the sea had died. The beach here was littered with dead tree trunks.

It was [deleted].

'Let's go back now, shall we?' I said.

'[deleted].

There was a continuing silence, broken by the scream of a distant gull. [deleted] a huge emptiness, devoid of shipping. The wind rattled the pines and gusted through the marshland beside it.

[deleted]

Money wasn't an issue. [deleted]

It's at moments like this – I really should have known this from all the novels I'd read – that you can guarantee that the unexpected will happen.

243

The twist! Every narrative cries out for one. Let's twist again, like we did last summer...

244

After Don and Blanche the person I most needed to tell about my father and Militká [deleted] was Ivan Jensen.

When I phoned him and told him I'd identified the mystery woman in my father's past, and what the trip to Scotland had been about, he sounded astonished.

'Who was she?' [deleted]

'Wednesday will be fine.'

[deleted] with views of St Paul's and the Shard. The Thames was a thin ribbon of blue threaded between distant hazy anonymous blocks of grey and biscuit and the dense whiteness of polystyrene.

Inside the restaurant it was all slices of mirror and shiny teak panels and a multiplicity of discreet lighting. Not to mention waitpersons dressed in chic Goth black who dropped by every seven seconds just to check that everything was completely and totally wonderful. The insincerity of their polished curiosity was palpable. But the food was – to my amateur palate – brilliant. I had [deleted].

I pushed a photograph across the table. 'That's her.'

He picked up the little square snapshot.

What Ivan said next totally stunned me. 'Ah, yes,' he said. 'I remember. A very lively lady. Spoke with a heavy central European accent.'

I felt a rush of indignation. 'You *knew* her?' I said hotly: 'You didn't tell me. You never mentioned her name. Not once!' I felt furious. All the time I'd spent tracking down Mystery Woman and all the time Ivan knew who she was!

'Calm down, Jane.' He put out his hand and rested it on my arm. 'I can see you're upset. Let me explain.'

He took a sip of wine. 'It was an odd year, all told. I was in Athens, Jon was in Vancouver. The company sent me out there on a project. My office in Athens came with a secretary named Eleni. She [deleted].

'So it was a weird coincidence when Jon also started an affair with a married woman in Canada. You have to remember that all this was before mobile phones and the internet. We communicated almost entirely by letter.

'To cut a long story short, I had to return to London once during my Greek project. That was the same time that Militká followed your father across the Atlantic. So I saw her just once. I remember it well. We met up at the Lamb and Flag in Covent Garden. I got there early and grabbed a table for three, then spent an hour telling people the other two seats were taken. Your father and Militká were late. There were delays on the Northern Line – some things never change, do they? – and then they walked around Covent Garden trying to find the pub. The Lamb and Flag isn't easy to find because it's tucked away out of sight up an alley. Anyway, they made it there eventually and we had a few drinks.

'I remember I [deleted]. She was incredibly bubbly. Like she had cocaine in her blood.' He added hastily: '*Naturally*, I mean.

'And that was it. We went off for a meal together.' He smiled and said dryly, 'A Greek restaurant.'

He put his wine glass down and stared reflectively across the hazy rooftops of the city. 'And that was that. I [deleted].

Now it was Ivan's turn to look astonished.

We ordered coffee and I gave him an abbreviated version of the story of Jane Tain and Inspector Don Boston.

This was the week that Mike decided I was fit to be released back into the wild (as he put it). It was largely because Bryony Flappe had, like the position of her book in the hardback non-fiction charts, dropped out of sight. So I was the lucky person to accompany him to the launch of the rock memoirs of Jimmy Josh, the singer in the once mega-selling seventies band Del Rivo. It was a broads, bands, Bushmills and bufotenin book (bufotenin being the name of Jimmy's favourite hallucinogen).

Mike was very excited, as he was a big fan of Del Rivo's classic albums. The band had disintegrated in the eighties but a couple of years ago managed to reunite. They put out a new album which was well received. Next they did a Pension Fund and Alimony tour, which began and ended at the O2 arena. Since then Jimmy Josh had been a regular in the gossip columns, tumbling out of night clubs at four in the morning, drunk, and dating the daughters of the aristocracy. His current squeeze was Lady Henrietta Jane Plunkett-Smythe, who was, according to the columnists, a scion of the Berkeley banking family.

Orlando weren't publishing Jimmy's memoir (which was being marketed under the brilliant title *Jimmy*) but two precious tickets for the launch had been forwarded to Mike. He decided I merited the treat most 'in view of all the shit you've had to put up with lately'. I wasn't a particular fan of Del Rivo but in view of Jimmy Josh's wild-man reputation I thought it might be a laugh to see him in action.

The launch was being held in a trendy dive near Marble Arch. I met up with Mike outside the tube station and we walked the short distance to the venue.

It was the first book launch I'd been to where the paparazzi were waiting outside with their fold-up aluminium stepladders and cameras with lenses the size of bollards. There were about twenty of them.

A red carpet had been laid from the kerb to the door of Ritzy's and half a dozen bouncers in suits loomed menacingly around it, scowling at the world from narrowed eyes set in big flesh-heavy faces.

Luckily we arrived in a gap between the stretch limos. Clutching our passes we showed them to the man holding a clipboard who was standing across the doorway. He checked our names on his list, took another look at our invitations, and grudgingly allowed us in.

While all this was going on I was aware of camera shutters clicking unendingly, like the sound of a sudden shower of hailstones on a glass roof.

Mike grinned delightedly: 'They don't know who we are. They think we might be celebrities.'

'Richard's invited me to Necker,' I said loudly. 'He says Harry will be joining the party. Do you fancy coming?'

The camera shutters went berserk. Mike turned to me, looking at me as if I'd gone mad. Then he realised it was a joke.

'Damn you, Tain,' he hissed. (It wasn't often I caught him off guard. I interpreted it as a sign that he was secretly quite nervous.)

Inside he said: 'Where did you learn about crap like that?'

'I did a bit of research on Jimmy. Just in case I was introduced to him. Then I looked at some of the gossip column links. The *Daily Mail* sidebar is strangely addictive. Almost as good as bufotenin, I suspect.' I had to shout, as music began thumping, headache-loud, from concealed speakers.

'Hey! Who's the pretty lady talking 'bout my favourite side dish?'

We'd gone down some steps and entered a subterranean zone of darkness, filled with shapes, clinking glasses, and a distant vista of a brightly lit bar. Mirror balls threw splashes of light around the room. On a distant square of ceiling, film of Del Rivo in performance was being projected. There was a low roar of conversation. As my eyes adjusted to the darkness I saw that the space was filled with knots of people grouped in sixes and sevens. But the biggest group had assembled around the figure who now loomed in front of me.

Two things struck me about Jimmy Josh, who lurched closer still, until he was only inches from me. The first was how unexpectedly *small* he was. I'd sort of assumed he was normal size but actually he was only an inch or so above five feet tall. Small but perfectly formed. He had skinny arms, skinny legs, and a face which was stretched tight over the skull beneath. His slender torso was immaculately dressed in a suit that screamed Savile Row.

My other instinct was to want to give him *a good ironing*. His face was a network of lines, wrinkles, droops, flaps and irregular fissures. Some of the lines ran at right angles, giving his face the impression of the layout of a crossword puzzle. In a wrinkles competition I'd bet on Jimmy rather than Mick Jagger, Samuel Beckett or even W. H. Auden.

'Excuse me?' I said.

'Bufotenin,' he said. 'I definitely heard you say that word. That sweet, sweet word.'

'I read the publicity pack. Apparently you mention it in your book. Or your ghost writer did.'

Jimmy's decayed face rearranged its patterns of collapse. 'Did you hear that, people?' he wheezed. He was laughing, apparently. 'This babe is kew-ute.'

'People' was Jimmy's entourage. This seemed to consist of Lady Henrietta, who was anchored to his right arm and whose glaring eyes shone a KEEP OFF THE GRASS sign at me. She looked exquisite and sparkled with precious stones. One emerged from the bridge of her pale nose. The size of her nostrils indicated her secret vice.

Add to that Dave, Jimmy's P.A., a rat-like estuary-accented little jerk in a flashy suit. Plus Alfie, his personal bodyguard (big, beefy, bovine, shaven-headed, strangely docile). Plus pudgy Julian

James, M.D. of the company which was publishing the memoirs. Plus gorgeous big-breasted Annette Swift, Julian's P.A. Plus sleek slender Viv White, Mike's opposite number at said publishers. Plus Viv's assistant, Ronaldo, a heavily deodorised young man of twenty who purported to be of Italian extraction. Rumour had it he was shagging Viv, even though she was fifty, white-haired, and married to the theatre director David Blair.

Correction. Rumour had it Viv was shagging *him*. Viv did have something of a reputation where young men in their early twenties were concerned.

'So how you here, pretty lady?' grinned the superstar. His breath smelled of whisky and his teeth were surprisingly and uniformly yellow.

'The lady is in publishing,' I replied. 'I work for Orlando Publishing.'

'Pretty lady should come work for Jimmy,' said Jimmy, whose articulation of the English language may have been influenced by texting, Bushmills, bufotenin, or all three mixed together.

'Pretty lady no fancy work in rock biz,' I said. 'Pretty lady she like novels more than songpops.'

[deleted]

Jimmy's eyes bulged, which I'd like to think was a response to my devastating repartee rather than a physiological reaction to something he'd ingested on his way to the launch. Then he gargled, which was possibly another of Jimmy's version of laughter. His mouth stretched open. A needle of shining saliva stretched from an incisor in his upper jaw to its cousin in the lower jaw.

'This babe is kew-ute.'

Lady Henrietta decided things had gone far enough. 'Jimmy, look! Rod and Penny have arrived. We must say hello.' Her beautifully manicured claws fastened around the big soft vein that looped his wrist. She dragged him away and the surrounding crowd moved with them, as if everyone was handcuffed together.

A solitary piece of jetsam was left bobbing in the wake. It was Dave, Jimmy's fragrant factotum. He pushed a business card at me.

'Jimmy likes you. You should phone him. But not tonight. Tomorrow.' He dipped his head closer to mine and whispered in my ear: 'That Lady Henrietta bitch is toast.'

He winked, and disappeared into the darkness.

'Jesus,' breathed Mike, who'd heard everything. He looked faintly bewildered, like someone suffering from a mild concussion.

And then my phone vibrated and began piping for attention.

245

More Iain Banks imitation-prose. Not *entirely* without its merits, the writer felt. He had attended a number of book launches in his time, so he was drawing on experience for some of these scenes. Once he had even brushed shoulders with Terry Pratchett, although at the time he did not recognise him. He had never read any prose by one of Britain's most commercially successful fiction writers. The writer continued on to the next chapter, which he hoped would be the last one. This text had gone on too long. He wanted it to be over. He had a stack of books to read. Plus he was looking forward to Christmas, when he hoped to view *The Lost King*, *Fall*, *Nope* and *The Image Book*.

246

In a weird way I expected it to be Jimmy. I was expecting more infantile dialogue of the pretty-lady cute-baby kind. But it wasn't Jimmy Josh at all. It was Blanche.

I struggled to hear what she was saying against the low roar of a hundred overlapping conversations and the steady thump of the last Del Rivo album. She sounded excited and seemed to be shouting.

'Hang on,' I said. 'Too noisy here. I'm going out into the street.'

I made my way up the stairs and back through the wall of bouncers. There was a noticeable slackening of tension out there. The paparazzi were relaxed and chatting among themselves. Evidently all the celebrities had arrived. There was now nothing to do until somebody famous took a tumble on the ground, or someone in a short skirt made a point of getting into a limo at an angle that revealed her lack of knickers. Some of the photographers looked up as I emerged onto the street, then lost interest. I was alone. No celebrity is ever alone.

'Say that again,' I said. Blanche wasn't making any sense. She seemed to be crying.

'You must come! Come at once! It's Alec and Thomas! They're fighting! *Someone is going to get killed!* Please come, Jane. I beg you.' She started sobbing again. In the background I heard what sounded like a piece of furniture crashing over. A man's voice shouted something inaudible. 'Blizzard', was it? I pressed the phone closer to my ear. More incoherent yelling and then the sharp splintery sound of something that was either chinaware or glassware, shattering.

No, not 'blizzard'. The word was 'bastard'. But the voice that was shouting was so distorted by rage I couldn't tell which of the two men it was.

[deleted] 'I'm on my way,' I said.

A black cab happened to be cruising down the street. I waved the driver down and told him the address. 'I'm in a hurry,' I said.

'Okay, lady.'

The driver rat-runned through Lisson Grove and then sped down Prince Albert Road, skirting Regent's Park. The entrance to the zoo flashed past. A moment later we turned off into the road alongside Primrose Hill. The lamp posts along the footpaths perforated the dark hillside with lines of bright dots.

Trafiic was at a standstill when we reached the junction with Regent's Park Road, so I paid the driver and jumped out. [deleted] I ran.

Fitzroy Road was quiet after all the cars on the main road. Quiet at my end, anyway. But not at the other. Down there, towards the Chalcot Road end, a woman's voice rang out across the night. She sounded hysterical. She was screaming.

It was Blanche. She sounded utterly distraught.

A dark shape moved across the road down there. Blanche followed. Some words were spoken. Then the figure pushed her away, and with a sharp cry she fell down in the road.

Moments later I heard the sound of a motorbike starting up. Its low powerful roar seemed to swell in intensity until it filled up the space between the dark terraces. Something nearby me rattled, vibrating in response to the waves of sound. Then a headlight came on, jerked sideways, and the biker emerged from behind a car and sped towards me.

I knew it was [deleted] he braked hard at the end of the road, then shot out into Regent's Park Road. He turned north. A car horn blared angrily.

[deleted]

And then there was a single terrific noise like a small explosion. It ripped through the night, penetrating all the lesser noises of a city street.

And then the screaming and the shouting started.

'Jesus, no,' Blanche said thickly. She tore herself from me and ran off, heading [deleted].

a dark shape half hidden under the huge rear wheels of a tipper truck. Someone who had been kneeling over him stood up and shook their head.

In the silence the first siren was already sounding, faraway but slowly getting nearer.

[deleted]

She seemed completely broken. All the energy had gone from her. She [deleted].

When we got there we found Thomas sitting in the kitchen. He was drinking whisky. A pack of Paracetamol lay beside the bottle. His shirt was missing several buttons and a huge bruise had swelled up under his right eye.

[deleted]

I turned to Thomas.

'So,' I said. 'What happened?'

247

A twist after the twist! Just how it should be. The writer reflected that it was strange how he'd forgotten these characters and vast swathes of the plot. Forgettable fiction. He went back to the text. The end was very close.

248

We sat in a food court at Atlanta airport waiting for [deleted].
  'It all seems so long ago now,' I said.
  Don put down his coffee. 'That's how [deleted].

It seemed like a long time ago but it was only a year. And so much had happened in that time.
  I went to Alec's funeral, which was held in Ireland. His [deleted]. But Don came to lend support. Good old reliable Don. My rock. And I never needed him more than on that cold wet day in Galway, with the wind howling in from the Atlantic and a horde of Alec's relatives bombarding me with their condolences. In this theatrical event I was cast as The Grieving Girlfriend. Don got a few odd looks but everyone had to make do with the explanation that he was A Close Friend Lending Me His Support at this Very Difficult Time.
  [deleted]

In the kitchen, knocking back yet more whisky and gingerly touching the throbbing lump under his eye, Thomas filled me in on what had happened that night. As he talked we could hear [deleted] pushed over a side table with a vase of flowers. Then the two men had started fighting. This was when Blanche had phoned me at the Jimmy Josh book launch. While I was hurrying there by taxi, the two men were wrestling in the living room, in a ragged, amateur kind of way. Thomas threw a dictionary at Alec and missed, smashing the flatscreen TV. Alec swung a fist at his jaw and missed. Blanche shrieked at them both to stop. Thomas hurled the cordless phone and struck Alec on the cheek. Alec swore and punched Thomas in the eye. Blanche [deleted].
  The rest I knew.

Our flight number appeared on the screen, and we headed for the

departure lounge.
  Later, as [deleted].

And this, printed out on a fine sheet of A4 size watermarked vellum:

[deleted]

Lyle Lovett, 'Highway Kind'
Waylon Jennings, 'Dreaming My Dreams'
Nico, 'You Forget To Answer'
Bob Dylan, 'Shooting Star'
Johnny Cash, 'Hurt'
[deleted]

The last song [deleted] was familiar and after a while I remembered why.

249

[deleted]
  That scepticism ended when the first shocked quartz samples were found in core samples from deep drilling. Other mineral deposits pointed unambiguously to meteor impact as the cause of the twisted, chaotically mixed rock layers in the region. [deleted]

[deleted]

Wetumpka is south of Birmingham, some forty minutes' drive. You head down Interstate 65 and then peel off. [deleted]
  The Wetumpka Impact Crater Visitor Center had been built on the rim of crystalline rock, not far from the highest point. The architect had designed it to have a slight curve, to mimic the crater wall.
  [deleted]
  drove us around the crater, pointing out the various significant landmarks, including the rebound peak at its heart.

The shock of the asteroid's impact was immense – an explosion equal to fifteen hundred million tons of TNT. It blew open a crater four miles in diameter. It pulverized rock to a depth of over seven hundred feet. An unbelievable turbulence.

And now it was a zone of tranquility, like a love affair long after it's over.

But not entirely. The floor of the crater is eroded by many trickling streams, some of them splashing noisily as they force their way through levels of hard, resistant rock.

Bob gestured with his arm out of the car window. 'The Creek people, who lived here before the white man came, called this place Wetumpka, which means the place of roaring water.'

As we drove out of the great depression I noticed the name of the road which cuts across the floor of the crater. Harrogate Springs Road.

Another tiny coincidence.

250

Do you know, wrote Robert Browning towards the end of 1881, that our London November has been warm and May-like beyond example? In such a mood, wrote Pamela Neville-Sington, one can imagine Browning strolling up and down the newly gravelled path in his garden that November 1881, enjoying the clement, May-like weather, and thinking and dreaming of Katharine Bronson. What was he thinking, she wrote? Katharine Bronson was a married woman, after all.

251

On our last trip to Warblington, Don managed to get my father's old Eumig projector working. He set up the screen, carefully threaded the reel of 8mm film from the Militká box through the projector gate, and flicked the 'on' lever.

A rectangle of blazing whiteness filled the larger white rectangle of the screen, then turned into a sudden whirl of fiery orange shapes. Out of this miasma emerged a blue car, with a woman in white shorts sitting beside it. She had on a striped sweater and was smoking a cigarette. Her head turned and she laughed at the camera.

There was no sound apart from the roar of the projector's engine and the film rattling and jerking through the projector.

Abruptly the movie cut to Norwich. I recognised Elm Hill. Militká was wearing a black and white check shirt and red jeans. She walked towards the camera, again laughing. Her jet-black hair was tied into pigtails.

Then, abruptly, there was what looked like a highland landscape. Militká was now wearing a red jumper, and the same red jeans. The camera followed her as she ran down from what looked like a lay-by to a small sandy bay. She ran across the sand, holding out her arms like a child pretending to be a plane.

In the next shot she returned, but the screen was dense with black shadow and her face was a mask.

The next shot was filmed from a moving car. It might have been almost anywhere in the highlands: a waste of heather, a slope, a dark louring hillside, a rocky ridge.

'Jesus,' I said, when the next shot started. 'Fuck. I don't believe it.'

Don was frozen into silence, staring numbly at the screen. But [deleted].

'This I do not fucking believe,' I said.

Don [deleted].

The scene being filmed was unmistakable. It was a slow panning shot of the graveyard at Tongue. In the foreground were the distinctive tombs like tables, and in the background could be seen the causeway bridge and the distant ragged outline of the mountains.

Cut to my father, his long hair blown by the wind, washing around his shoulders. He was wearing pale bell-bottom trousers and a leather coat that came down to his thighs. He was wandering among the graves, staring down at them. He was obviously reading the inscriptions.

[deleted] on the pedestal of the gravestone where my father had died of exposure. The camera zoomed in on her. She met the lens

full on. At first she smiled, then the smile grew bigger. She looked the picture of happiness and joy. Then she shook her head and flashed her eyes and waved an arm reprovingly, signalling for my father to stop filming.

He did as she requested.

Then the strip of celluloid flung itself free of the projector's teeth, the screen turned into a sheet of blazing whiteness again, and the spool began spinning wildly around its axle.

It was over.

One of the notebooks in the Militká box supplied the final piece of the jigsaw.

My father and the professor's wife had gone as far north as they ever would on that trip to Scotland. Militká's [deleted] and his geologist's solitary researches at Loch Morar.

Beyond Morar it was purely pleasure – a quick tour of the highlands, a place she'd never been. But the graveyard was the last place they ever went to together before [deleted].

No, she did not regret.

She had to live this love.

[deleted]

Trembling, her face the colour of chalk, Militká put down the phone. She [deleted] and was violently sick.

And that, in essence, was the end of everything.

Militká loved my father but [deleted].

I took Militká's letters and scattered them across the blackened circle of ground at the end of the garden. Then I piled on all the other mementoes – the hotel receipts, the snapshots, the journals and diaries. I let the 8mm film reel unspool and scattered the dark perforated strip on top, like spaghetti. I struck a match and lit the first of the crisp blue airmail sheets. The flames spread quickly and soon there was a roaring mass of golden fire.

Before long it collapsed in on itself and the fire died, leaving a hub of glowing, ticking ash. I waited a little longer, stirring the ashes until the last scrap had flared up into nothingness. Then I went back indoors.

[deleted]

We landed in the early evening and went straight to our hotel.

Next morning we took a cab to [deleted].

The apartment block was a dull, functional three-storey building on the outskirts of [deleted].

I pressed the buzzer and waited. Ironically, the woman who came to the door was East European. She was young, in her early twenties, and she held a howling, red-faced baby.

Her English was poor.

I wanted to know what had happened to Mrs [deleted]. Where was she buried?

The woman looked apprehensive. She muttered something about her husband, and closed the door on me.

'You'll get nothing out of her,' a woman's voice said. 'She's Lithuanian.'

I turned. An old woman with a very lined, sun-browned face was leaning out of her doorway. She had a cigarette drooping from her mouth. 'Waddaya wanna know?' she demanded.

'I was looking for some information about Mrs [deleted].'

The woman's eyes narrowed. 'Information? The basic information is she's dead. Died a while back.'

'I know. I wondered if [deleted].

'She lived alone. She was a nice old lady. Very friendly. She did my shopping for me when I broke my ankle.' She exhaled a cloud of thin blue smoke. 'Why you asking, lady?'

'My father was a friend of hers. I'm doing this for him.'

'English, ain't you?'

'That's right.'

'I like English people. Very polite.'

'I wanted to pay my respects to Mrs [deleted]'s grave. If there is one...'

The woman wheezed and jerked her thumb over her shoulder.

'Mountain View. That's where you'll find her.'

She inhaled, then explained.

No, there was nothing to be done with this unpublished text. It would have to be destroyed. Unless the writer sliced it up, deleted whole sections, and interspersed the dead prose with commentary. That might make a book, of sorts...

It was twenty minutes' ride there by taxi. Mountain View cemetery lies west of Fraser Street and extends for twelve blocks. [deleted]. Locating the grave wasn't too difficult. There was an initial difficulty over the name, but once that matter was sorted it was easy.

[deleted]. It consisted of a simple rectangular stone set flat into the surrounding grass. Her name and the year of birth, the year of death; nothing more.

The oddity which had caused the difficulty in the superintendent's office was that she'd dropped her hyphenated married name. In death she'd reverted to being Militká [deleted].

'She finally freed herself from her husband, then,' I [deleted].

'Or somebody made a mistake.'

We lingered there a while, saying nothing more. Ahead of us, to the north, a line of powder-blue mountains reminded me of the highlands. Tall buildings rose out of the haze of the downtown area.

High above us a silver jet turned slowly in the huge sky. Life went on, leaving the dead behind. And [deleted] explaining that the Professor lay some distance from Militká [deleted]. That seemed apt. Not that it mattered, now. These little lives and all their passions were spent; extinguished. These perturbed spirits were at rest. And [deleted]. A story ends; another one begins.

[deleted]

Not long after getting back from [deleted].

It was a memorable few days. One afternoon we ended up exploring Trotternish, the northern peninsula of the island. It was overcast and chilly, and clouds massing to the east held the promise of thunder and rain. When we pulled up at the ruins of Duntulm Castle we had the place to ourselves. But then, apart from the inclement weather, there wasn't much to see – a fenced-off crumbling archway and crumbling walls, some of which might once have been part of a great hall. There were briars and thistles and nettles everywhere. The whole site, perched on a barren rocky headland, was neglected and wildly overgrown.

From a bunch of nettles protruded a wooden sign in poor condition. On it was written, in faded and barely decipherable letters:

Thig crioch air an tl saoghal
ach máiridh gaol is cèol.

[deleted] the only birds I could see in the grey sky above were swifts, a whole flock of them, high in the sky, swooping and circling. Maybe they nested here.

A pair of brown moths fluttered past and settled on the face of the sign. They clung there, completely motionless. I waited for them to fly away but it looked like they had plans to stay.

I started to feel cold. I [deleted].

'I think it's time to go home,' I said.

THE END

254

Over at last. Done. The writer feels a great sense of relief. He can move on.

255

The writer listens to Van Morrison singing 'Stage Name' and smiles. Georgie Fame! The writer had always been a little dismissive of that two-hit-wonder. But when friends had drawn him in to attending a concert by the elderly musician, who appeared onstage with his battered Hammond organ and a backing band consisting of his two sons, the writer had been enormously impressed by the performance.

Books the writer has in abundance. Time to re-read *The Pound Era* and *some thing black* and *Crossing the Water*. Time to read *Malina* and *L'Amour* and *Man in the Holocene*. And Annie Ernaux and other Fitzcarraldo editions. Plus the consolation of music. *Ring Them Bells* and Baez singing 'Love Song to a Stranger'. *The Very Best of Dolly Parton* and 'I Will Always Love You'. *Supertramp live, 1997* singing 'Breakfast in America'. *You're Driving Me Crazy* and Van Morrison singing 'The Way Young Lovers Do'. *Lindeville* and Ashley McBryde singing 'Brenda Put Your Bra On'. And shelves of DVDs. And Netflix. The writer wants to watch *All Quiet on the Western Front* and the latest adaptation of *Lady Chatterley's Lover*. He'll get by. Time can be filled in so many satisfying ways. And there was Van Morrison's next album to look forward to: *Moving on Skiffle*. The song titles were mouth-watering. 'In the Evening When the Sun Goes Down'. 'Worried Man Blues'. 'I'm Movin' On'...

257

Yes, this story is long over. The story beneath the story underneath the text. On the way back to London, after Tongue, the lovers stayed in the Lake District and visited Dove Cottage. That was left out, as so much was left out. And in any case there was a narrative form that seemed to work better and which, years later, the writer used. Yes, this story is over. The story behind this first attempt and then the later, truer one. And even that one missed out so much. Including things forgotten and only remembered later. The walk to the Ahornhütte in Mayrhofen, for example.

258

Now there is only one of them left. There is now no possibility at all of a heart-warming or unbearably poignant last chapter. There will be no reunion; no meeting face to face; no embrace; no final conversation. That last conversation is now fixed. It occurred long ago. And in 'real life' this story could have come to its inevitable termination in any month. That it's a wet, dark November seems apt. A line from a Ted Hughes poem floats into his mind. He goes off to look it up in his copy of the *Selected Poems*.

259

An enduring desolation; an enduring emptiness. The writer believes he has reached the point where he has nothing more to say about this matter. So he will continue, on through that nothingness.

260

The first day of the new month. Labour pains. Night roads, the headlight beams cutting across hedgerows. Christmas trees twinkling in distant windows. A wind-rocked inflatable snowman tethered beside two other festive inflatables. Later, the bright city. A long night. A child is born. And later, not yet two days old, that small face, the narrowed eyes, black eyes, absorbing the world with a stare that seems to combine curiosity with bewilderment. Her wrinkled baby fingers reaching out, touching the writer's little finger. Then folding a tiny fist around it. The grip surprisingly strong.

AN END

www.ingramcontent.com/pod-product-compliance
Lightning Source LLC
Chambersburg PA
CBHW031334170626
46807CB00002B/688